ODD HOURS

Dean Koontz was born and raised in Pennsylvania.
He is the author of many number one bestsellers.
He lives with his wife Gerda, their dog Anna, and
the enduring spirit of their dog Trixie in southern
California.

Also by Dean Koontz

DEAN KOONTZ

Odd Hours

HARPER

This novel is entirely a work of fiction.
The names, characters and incidents portrayed in it are
the work of the author's imagination. Any resemblance to
actual persons, living or dead, events or localities is
entirely coincidental.

Harper
An imprint of HarperCollins*Publishers*
77–85 Fulham Palace Road,
Hammersmith, London W6 8JB

www.harpercollins.co.uk

This paperback edition 2009
1

First published in Great Britain by
HarperCollins*Publishers* 2008

Copyright © Dean Koontz 2008

The Author asserts the moral right to
be identified as the author of this work

A catalogue record for this book is
available from the British Library

ISBN 978-0-00-788407-0

Typeset in Meridien by Palimpsest Book Production Limited,
Grangemouth, Stirlingshire

Printed and bound in Great Britain by
Clays Ltd, St Ives plc

All rights reserved. No part of this publication may be
reproduced, stored in a retrieval system, or transmitted,
in any form or by any means, electronic, mechanical,
photocopying, recording or otherwise, without the prior
permission of the publishers.

Mixed Sources

Product group from well-managed
forests and other controlled sources
www.fsc.org Cert no. SW-COC-001806
© 1996 Forest Stewardship Council

FSC

FSC is a non-profit international organisation established to promote the
responsible management of the world's forests. Products carrying the FSC
label are independently certified to assure consumers that they come
from forests that are managed to meet the social, economic and
ecological needs of present and future generations.

Find out more about HarperCollins and the environment at
www.harpercollins.co.uk/green

*This fourth Odd adventure is dedicated to Bruce, Carolyn,
and Michael Rouleau.*

To Michael because he makes his parents proud.

To Carolyn because she makes Bruce happy.

*To Bruce because he has been so reliable all these years,
and because he truly knows what
it means to love a good dog.*

I feel my fate in what I cannot fear.
I learn by going where I have to go.

     —*Theodore Roethke*, "The Waking"

CHAPTER 1

It's only life. We all get through it.

Not all of us complete the journey in the same condition. Along the way, some lose their legs or eyes in accidents or altercations, while others skate through the years with nothing worse to worry about than an occasional bad-hair day.

I still possessed both legs and both eyes, and even my hair looked all right when I rose that Wednesday morning in late January. If I returned to bed sixteen hours later, having lost all of my hair but nothing else, I would consider the day a triumph. Even minus a few teeth, I'd call it a triumph.

When I raised the window shades in my bedroom, the cocooned sky was gray and swollen, windless and still, but pregnant with a promise of change.

Overnight, according to the radio, an airliner had crashed in Ohio. Hundreds perished. The sole survivor, a ten-month-old child, had been found upright and unscathed in a battered seat that stood in a field of scorched and twisted debris.

Throughout the morning, under the expectant sky, low sluggish waves exhausted themselves on the shore. The Pacific was gray and awash with inky shadows, as if sinuous sea beasts of fantastical form swam just below the surface.

During the night, I had twice awakened from a dream in which the tide flowed red and the sea throbbed with a terrible light.

As nightmares go, I'm sure you've had worse. The problem is that a few of my dreams have come true, and people have died.

While I prepared breakfast for my employer, the kitchen radio brought news that the jihadists who had the previous day seized an ocean liner in the Mediterranean were now beheading passengers.

Years ago I stopped watching news programs on television. I can tolerate words and the knowledge they impart, but the images undo me.

Because he was an insomniac who went to bed at dawn, Hutch ate breakfast at noon. He paid me well, and he was kind, so I cooked to his schedule without complaint.

Hutch took his meals in the dining room, where the draperies were always closed. Not one bright sliver of any windowpane remained exposed.

He often enjoyed a film while he ate, lingering over coffee until the credits rolled. That day, rather than cable news, he watched Carole Lombard and John Barrymore in *Twentieth Century*.

Eighty-eight years old, born in the era of silent films, when Lillian Gish and Rudolph Valentino were stars, and having later been a successful actor, Hutch thought less in words than in images, and he dwelt in fantasy.

Beside his plate stood a bottle of Purell sanitizing gel. He lavished it on his hands not only before and after eating, but also at least twice during a meal.

Like most Americans in the first decade of the new century, Hutch feared everything except what he ought to fear.

When TV-news programs ran out of stories about drunk, drug-addled, murderous, and otherwise crazed celebrities—which happened perhaps twice a year—they sometimes filled the brief gap with a sensationalistic piece on that rare flesh-eating bacteria.

Consequently, Hutch feared contracting the ravenous germ. From time to time, like a dour character in a tale by Poe, he huddled in his lamplit study, brooding about his fate, about the fragility of his flesh, about the insatiable appetite of his microscopic foe.

He especially dreaded that his nose might be eaten away.

Long ago, his face had been famous. Although time had disguised him, he still took pride in his appearance.

I had seen a few of Lawrence Hutchison's movies from the 1940s and '50s. I liked them. He'd been a commanding presence on screen.

Because he had not appeared on camera for five decades, Hutch was less known for his acting than for his children's books about a swash-buckling rabbit named Nibbles. Unlike his creator, Nibbles was fearless.

Film money, book royalties, and a habit of regarding investment opportunities with paranoid suspicion had left Hutch financially secure in his old age. Nevertheless, he worried that an explosive rise in the price of oil or a total collapse in the price of oil would lead to a worldwide financial crisis that would leave him penniless.

His house faced the boardwalk, the beach, the ocean. Surf broke less than a minute's stroll from his front door.

Over the years, he had come to fear the sea. He could not bear to sleep on the west side of the house, where he might hear the waves crawling along the shore.

Therefore, I was quartered in the ocean-facing master suite at the front of the house. He slept in a guest room at the back.

Within a day of arriving in Magic Beach, more than a month previous to the red-tide dream, I had taken a job as Hutch's cook, doubling as his chauffeur on those infrequent occasions when he wanted to go out.

My experience at the Pico Mundo Grill served me well. If you can make hash browns that wring a flood from salivary glands, fry bacon to the crispness of a cracker without parching it, and make pancakes as rich as pudding yet so fluffy they seem to be at risk of floating off the plate, you will always find work.

At four-thirty that afternoon in late January, when I stepped into the parlor with Boo, my dog, Hutch was in his favorite armchair, scowling at the television, which he had muted.

"Bad news, sir?"

His deep and rounded voice rolled an ominous note into every syllable: "Mars is warming."

"We don't live on Mars."

"It's warming at the same rate as the earth."

"Were you planning to move to Mars to escape global warming?"

He indicated the silenced anchorman on the TV. "This means the sun is the cause of both, and nothing can be done about it. Nothing."

"Well, sir, there's always Jupiter or whatever planet lies beyond Mars."

He fixed me with that luminous gray-eyed stare that conveyed implacable determination when he had played crusading district attorneys and courageous military officers.

"Sometimes, young man, I think *you* may be from beyond Mars."

"Nowhere more exotic than Pico Mundo,

California. If you won't need me for a while, sir, I thought I'd go out for a walk."

Hutch rose to his feet. He was tall and lean. He kept his chin lifted but craned his head forward as does a man squinting to sharpen his vision, which might have been a habit that he developed in the years before he had his cataracts removed.

"Go out?" He frowned as he approached. "Dressed like that?"

I was wearing sneakers, jeans, and a sweatshirt.

He was not troubled by arthritis and remained graceful for his age. Yet he moved with precision and caution, as though expecting to fracture something.

Not for the first time, he reminded me of a great blue heron stalking tide pools.

"You should put on a jacket. You'll get pneumonia."

"It's not that chilly today," I assured him.

"You young people think you're invulnerable."

"Not this young person, sir. I've got every reason to be astonished that I'm not already permanently horizontal."

Indicating the words MYSTERY TRAIN on my sweatshirt, he asked, "What's that supposed to mean?"

"I don't know. I found it in a thrift shop."

"I have never been in a thrift shop."

"You haven't missed much."

"Do only very poor people shop there or is the criteria merely thriftiness?"

"They welcome all economic classes, sir."

"Then I should go one day soon. Make an adventure of it."

"You won't find a genie in a bottle," I said, referring to his film *The Antique Shop*.

"No doubt you're too modern to believe in genies and such. How do you get through life when you've nothing to believe in?"

"Oh, I have beliefs."

Lawrence Hutchison was less interested in my beliefs than in the sound of his well-trained voice. "I keep an open mind regarding all things supernatural."

I found his self-absorption endearing. Besides, if he were to have been curious about me, I would have had a more difficult time keeping all my secrets.

He said, "My friend Adrian White was married to a fortune-teller who called herself Portentia."

I traded anecdotes with him: "This girl I used to know, Stormy Llewellyn—at the carnival, we got a card from a fortune-telling machine called Gypsy Mummy."

"Portentia used a crystal ball and prattled a lot of mumbo jumbo, but she was the real thing. Adrian adored her."

"The card said Stormy and I would be together forever. But it didn't turn out that way."

"Portentia could predict the day and very hour of a person's death."

"Did she predict yours, sir?"

"Not mine. But she predicted Adrian's. And two days later, at the hour Portentia had foretold, she shot him."

"Incredible."

"But true, I assure you." He glanced toward a window that did not face the sea and that, therefore, was not covered by draperies. "Does it feel like tsunami weather to you, son?"

"I don't think tsunamis have anything to do with the weather."

"I feel it. Keep one eye on the ocean during your walk."

Like a stork, he stilted out of the parlor and along the hallway toward the kitchen at the back of the house.

I left by the front door, through which Boo had already passed. The dog waited for me in the fenced yard.

An arched trellis framed the gate. Through white lattice twined purple bougainvillea that produced a few flowers even in winter.

I closed the gate behind me, and Boo passed through it as for a moment I stood drawing deep breaths of the crisp salted air.

After spending a few months in a guest room at St. Bartholomew's Abbey, high in the Sierra, trying to come to terms with my strange life and my losses, I had expected to return home to Pico Mundo for Christmas. Instead, I had been called here, to what purpose I didn't know at the time and still had not deduced.

My gift—or curse—involves more than a rare prophetic dream. For one thing, irresistible intuition sometimes takes me places to which I would not go by choice. And then I wait to find out why.

Boo and I headed north. Over three miles long, the boardwalk serving Magic Beach was not made of wood but of concrete. The town called it a boardwalk anyway.

Words are plastic these days. Small loans made to desperate people at exorbitant interest rates are called payday advances. A cheesy hotel paired with a seedy casino is called a resort. Any assemblage of frenetic images, bad music, and incoherent plot is called a major motion picture.

Boo and I followed the concrete boardwalk. He was a German shepherd mix, entirely white. The moon traveling horizon to horizon moved no more quietly than did Boo.

Only I was aware of him, because he was a ghost dog.

I see the spirits of dead people who are reluctant to move on from this world. In my experience, however, animals are always eager to proceed to what comes next. Boo was unique.

His failure to depart was a mystery. The dead

don't talk, and neither do dogs, so my canine companion obeyed two vows of silence.

Perhaps he remained in this world because he knew I would need him in some crisis. He might not have to linger much longer, as I frequently found myself up to my neck in trouble.

On our right, after four blocks of beachfront houses came shops, restaurants, and the three-story Magic Beach Hotel with its white walls and striped green awnings.

To our left, the beach relented to a park. In the sunless late afternoon, palm trees cast no shadows on the greensward.

The lowering sky and the cool air had discouraged beachgoers. No one sat on the park benches.

Nevertheless, intuition told me that she would be here, not in the park but sitting far out above the sea. She had been in my red dream.

Except for the lapping of the lazy surf, the day was silent. Cascades of palm fronds waited for a breeze to set them whispering.

Broad stairs led up to the pier. By virtue of being a ghost, Boo made no sound on the weathered planks, and as a ghost in the making, I was silent in my sneakers.

At the end of the pier, the deck widened into an observation platform. Coin-operated telescopes offered views of ships in transit, the coastline, and the marina in the harbor two miles north.

The Lady of the Bell sat on the last bench,

facing the horizon, where the moth-case sky met the sullen sea in seamless fusion.

Leaning on the railing, I pretended to meditate on the timeless march of waves. In my peripheral vision, I saw that she seemed to be unaware of my arrival, which allowed me to study her profile.

She was neither beautiful nor ugly, but neither was she plain. Her features were unremarkable, her skin clear but too pale, yet she had a compelling presence.

My interest in her was not romantic. An air of mystery veiled her, and I suspected that her secrets were extraordinary. Curiosity drew me to her, as did a feeling that she might need a friend.

Although she had appeared in my dream of a red tide, perhaps it would not prove to be prophetic. She might not die.

I had seen her here on several occasions. We had exchanged a few words in passing, mostly comments about the weather.

Because she talked, I knew she wasn't dead. Sometimes I realize an apparition is a ghost only when it fades or walks through a wall.

On other occasions, when they have been murdered and want me to bring their killers to justice, they may choose to materialize with their wounds revealed. Confronted by a man whose face has imploded from the impact of a bullet or by a woman carrying her severed head, I am as quick as the next guy to realize I'm in the company of a spook.

In the recent dream, I had been standing on a beach, snakes of apocalyptic light squirming across the sand. The sea had throbbed as some bright leviathan rose out of the deep, and the heavens had been choked with clouds as red and orange as flames.

In the west, the Lady of the Bell, suspended in the air above the sea, had floated toward me, arms folded across her breast, her eyes closed. As she drew near, her eyes opened, and I glimpsed in them a reflection of what lay behind me.

I had twice recoiled from the vision that I beheld in her eyes, and I had both times awakened with no memory of it.

Now I walked away from the pier railing, and sat beside her. The bench accommodated four, and we occupied opposite ends.

Boo curled up on the deck and rested his chin on my shoes. I could feel the weight of his head on my feet.

When I touch a spirit, whether dog or human, it feels solid to me, and warm. No chill or scent of death clings to it.

Still gazing out to sea, the Lady of the Bell said nothing.

She wore white athletic shoes, dark-gray pants, and a baggy pink sweater with sleeves so long her hands were hidden in them.

Because she was petite, her condition was more apparent than it would have been with a larger woman. A roomy sweater couldn't conceal that she was about seven months pregnant.

I had never seen her with a companion.

From her neck hung the pendant for which I had named her. On a silver chain hung a polished silver bell the size of a thimble. In the sunless day, this simple jewelry was the only shiny object.

She might have been eighteen, three years younger than I was. Her slightness made her seem more like a girl than like a woman.

Nevertheless, I had not considered calling her the Girl of the Bell. Her self-possession and calm demeanor required *lady*.

"Have you ever heard such stillness?" I asked.

"There's a storm coming." Her voice floated the words as softly as a breath of summer sets dandelion seeds adrift. "The pressure in advance weighs down the wind and flattens the waves."

"Are you a meteorologist?"

Her smile was lovely, free of judgment and artifice. "I'm just a girl who thinks too much."

"My name's Odd Thomas."

"Yes," she said.

Prepared to explain the dysfunctional nature of my family that had resulted in my name, as I had done countless times before, I was surprised and disappointed that she had none of the usual questions.

"You knew my name?" I asked.

"As you know mine."

"But I don't."

"I'm Annamaria," she said. "One word. It would have come to you."

Confused, I said, "We've spoken before, but I'm sure we've never exchanged names."

She only smiled and shook her head.

A white flare arced across the dismal sky: a gull fleeing to land as the afternoon faded.

Annamaria pulled back the long sleeves of her sweater, revealing her graceful hands. In the right she held a translucent green stone the size of a fat grape.

"Is that a jewel?" I asked.

"Sea glass. A fragment of a bottle that washed around the world and back, until it has no sharp edges. I found it on the beach." She turned it between her slender fingers. "What do you think it means?"

"Does it need to mean anything?"

"The tide washed the sand as smooth as a baby's skin, and as the water winked away, the glass seemed to open like a green eye."

The shrieking of birds shattered the stillness, and I looked up to see three agitated sea gulls sailing landward.

Their cries announced company: footfalls on the pier behind us.

Three men in their late twenties walked to the

north end of the observation platform. They stared up the coast toward the distant harbor and marina.

The two in khakis and quilted jackets appeared to be brothers. Red hair, freckles. Ears as prominent as handles on beer mugs.

The redheads glanced at us. Their faces were so hard, their eyes so cold, I might have thought they were evil spirits if I hadn't heard their footsteps.

One of them favored Annamaria with a razor-slash smile. He had the dark and broken teeth of a heavy methamphetamine user.

The freckled pair made me uneasy, but the third man was the most disturbing of the group. At six four, he towered half a foot above the others, and had that muscled massiveness only steroid injections can produce.

Unfazed by the cool air, he wore athletic shoes without socks, white shorts, and a yellow-and-blue, orchid-pattern Hawaiian shirt.

The brothers said something to him, and the giant looked at us. He might be called handsome in an early Cro-Magnon way, but his eyes seemed to be as yellow as his small chin beard.

We did not deserve the scrutiny we received from him. Annamaria was an ordinary-looking pregnant woman, and I was just a fry cook who had been fortunate enough to reach twenty-one years of age without losing a leg or an eye, or my hair.

Malevolence and paranoia cohabit in a twisted mind. Bad men trust no one because they know the treachery of which they themselves are capable.

After a long suspicious stare, the giant turned his attention once more to the northern coast and the marina, as did his cohorts, but I didn't think they were done with us.

Half an hour of daylight remained. Because of the overcast, however, twilight seemed to be already upon us. The lampposts lining the pier brightened automatically, but a thin veil of fog had risen out of nowhere to aid and abet the coming dusk.

Boo's behavior confirmed my instincts. He had gotten to his feet. Hackles raised, ears flattened, he focused intently on the giant.

To Annamaria, I said, "I think we better go."

"Do you know them?"

"I've seen their kind before."

As she rose from the bench, she closed the green orb in her right fist. Both hands shrank back into the sleeves of her sweater.

I sensed strength in her, yet she also had an aura of innocence, an almost waiflike air of vulner-ability. The three men were the kind to whom vulnerability had a scent as surely as rabbits hidden in tall grass have a smell easily detected by wolves.

Bad men wound and destroy one another,

although as targets they prefer those who are innocent and as pure as this world allows anyone to
be. They feed on violence, but they *feast* on the
despoiling of what is good.

As Annamaria and I walked off the observation
deck and toward the shore, I was dismayed that no
one had come onto the pier. Usually a few evening
fishermen would already have arrived with rods
and tackle boxes.

I glanced back and saw Boo moving closer to
the three men, who were oblivious of him. The
hulk with the chin beard looked over the heads
of the other two, again staring at Annamaria
and me.

The shore was still distant. The shrouded sun
slowly sank behind a thousand fathoms of clouds,
toward the drowning horizon, and rising mist
damped the lamplight.

When I looked back again, the freckled pair
were approaching at a brisk walk.

"Keep going," I told Annamaria. "Off the pier,
among people."

She remained calm. "I'll stay with you."

"*No*. I can handle this."

Gently, I pushed her ahead of me, made sure
that she kept moving, and then turned toward
the redheads. Instead of standing my ground or
backing away, I walked toward them, smiling,
which surprised them enough to bring them to a
halt.

As the one with the bad teeth looked past me at Annamaria, and as number two reached inside his unzipped jacket, I said, "You guys know about the tsunami warning?"

Number two kept his hand in his jacket, and the poster boy for dental hygiene shifted his attention to me. "Tsunami?"

"They estimate twenty to thirty feet."

"They who?"

"Even thirty feet," I said, "won't wash over the pier. She got scared, didn't want to stay, but I want to ride it out, see it. We must be—what?—forty feet off the water. It could be cool."

Throughout all this, the big guy had been approaching. As he joined us, number two asked him, "You hear about a tsunami?"

I said with some excitement, "The break slope on the shore here is twenty feet, but the other ten feet of the wave, man, it's gonna wipe out the front row of buildings."

Glancing back, as if to assess the potential for destruction, I was relieved to see Annamaria reaching the end of the pier.

"But the pier has deep pilings," I said. "The pier will ride it out. I'm pretty sure. It's solid. Don't you think the pier will ride it out?"

The big guy's mother had probably told him that he had hazel eyes. Hazel is a light golden-brown. He did not have hazel eyes. They were yellow rather than golden, and they were more yellow than brown.

If his pupils had been elliptical instead of round, I could almost have believed that he was a humanoid puppet and that an intelligent mutant cat was curled up in his skull, peering at me through the empty sockets. And not a *nice* intelligent mutant cat.

His voice dispelled the feline image, for it had a timbre more suited to a bear. "Who're you?"

Instead of answering, I pretended excitement about the coming tsunami and looked at my wristwatch. "It could hit shore in like a few minutes. I gotta be on the observation deck when it comes."

"Who're you?" the hulk repeated, and he put his big right paw on my left shoulder.

The instant he touched me, reality flipped out of sight as if it were a discarded flashcard. I found myself not on the pier but on the shore instead, on a beach across which squirmed reflections of fire. A hideous bright something rose in a sea that pulsed with hellish light under an apocalyptic sky.

The nightmare.

Reality flipped into view again.

The hulk had snatched his hand back from my shoulder. With his wide eyes focused on his spread fingers, he looked as if he had been stung—or had seen the red tide of my dream.

Never before had I passed a dream or a vision, or a thought, or anything but a head cold, to someone else by a touch. Surprises like this spare me from a dull life.

Like the cold-jewel stare of a stone-temple god, the yellow gaze fixed on me again, and he said, "Who the *hell* are you?"

The tone of his voice alerted the redheads that an extraordinary event had occurred. The one with his hand inside his jacket withdrew a pistol, and the one with bad teeth reached into his jacket, most likely not for dental floss.

I ran three steps to the side of the pier, vaulted the railing, and dropped like a fry cook through mist and fading light.

Cold, dark, the Pacific swallowed me, my eyes burned in the brine, and as I swam beneath the surface, I fought the buoyant effect of the salt water, determined that the sea would not spit me up into a bullet-riddled twilight.

CHAPTER 2

S tung, my wide-open eyes salted the seawater with tears.

As I breast-stroked and frog-kicked, the marine murk at first seemed to be without a scintilla of light. Then I became aware of a sullen-green phosphorescence, universally distributed, through which faint amorphous shadows writhed, perhaps clouds of sand swept off the bottom or long undulant stalks and fronds of seaweed.

The green dismalness abruptly darkened into true gloom. I had swum under the pier, between two of the many concrete columns on which the timber support posts stood.

A blind moment later, I encountered another column bristling with barnacles. I followed it to the surface.

Gasping for air that smelled of iodine and tar, that tasted of salt and chalk, I clung to the encrusted concrete, the barnacles sharp and slick under my hands, and I pulled my sweatshirt sleeves down to protect against cuts as best I could.

At the moment low on energy, the ocean rolled rhythmically and without violence between the pilings, toward shore. Although tame, it nevertheless sought to pull me away from the column.

Every minute I strove to hold fast would drain my strength. My sodden sweatshirt felt like a heavy flak jacket.

The liquid soliloquy of the sea echoed in murmurs and whispers along the pier floor, which was now my ceiling. I heard no shouts from above, no thunder of running footsteps.

Daylight as clouded and as gray as bilge water seeped into this sheltered space. Overhead, an architecture of thick vertical posts, horizontal tie beams, struts, and purlins dwindled into shadows.

The top of this piling, on which one of the posts stood, lay less than three feet above my head. I toed and kneed and clawed upward, repeatedly slipping backward but stubbornly gaining more ground than I lost.

These barnacles were of the stalkless variety, snugged tight to the concrete. As inch by inch I pulled myself out of the water, the calcareous shells of the crustaceans cracked and splintered, so the air smelled and tasted chalkier than ever.

This was no doubt a cataclysm for the barnacle community. I felt some regret about the destruction I wreaked, although not as much as I would have felt if, weighed down and weakened by my sodden clothes, I had sunk deep into snares of seaweed, and drowned.

Seated on the thirty-inch-diameter concrete base, an eighteen-inch-diameter wooden column rose high into shadows. Thick stainless-steel pitons had been driven into the wood to serve as hand-holds and as anchors for safety lines during construction. Using these, I pulled myself onto the six-inch ledge that encircled the post.

Standing there on my toes, dripping and shivering, I tried to find the bright side to my current situation.

Pearl Sugars, my maternal grandmother, a fast-driving and hard-drinking professional poker player now deceased, always encouraged me to find the bright side of any setback.

"If you let the bastards see you're worried," Granny Sugars said, "they'll shake you, break you, and be walking around in your shoes tomorrow."

She traveled the country to high-stakes private games in which the other players were men, most of them not nice men, some of them dangerous. Although I understood Granny's point, her solemn advice conjured in my mind an image of scowling tough guys parading around in Granny's high-heels.

As my racing heart slowed and as I caught my breath, the only bright side I could discern was that if I lived to be an old man—a one-eyed, one-armed, one-legged, hairless old man without a nose—at least I wouldn't be able to complain that my life had lacked for adventure.

Most likely the mist and the murky water had prevented the hulk with the chin beard and the two gunmen from seeing that I had taken refuge under the pier. They would expect me to swim to shore, and they would by now be arrayed along the beach, searching the low swells for a swimmer.

Although I had leaped off the pier in the last quarter of its length, the tide had carried me closer to land as I'd been swimming for cover. I remained, however, seaward of the structure's midpoint.

From my current perch, I could see a length of the shore. But I doubted that anyone patrolling the beach would have been able to catch sight of me in the deepening gloom.

Nevertheless, when not throwing myself headlong into trouble and leaping off piers, I am a prudent young man. I suspected I would be wise to ascend farther into the webwork of wood.

In some cozy high redoubt, I would roost until the thugs decided that I had drowned. When they went away to raise a toast to my death in whatever greasy barroom or opium den their kind frequented, I would safely go ashore and return home, where Hutch would be washing his face in sanitizing gel and waiting for the tsunami.

Piton to piton, I climbed the pole.

During the first ten feet or so, those eyeletted

spikes were solidly planted. Perhaps the greater humidity near the water kept the wood swollen tight around them.

As I continued to ascend, I found some pitons that moved in my hands, the aged and drier wood having shrunk somewhat away from them. They bore my weight, did not pull loose.

Then under my right foot, a piton ripped from the post. With a clink, the spike bounced off the concrete below, and I could even hear the faint *plop* as it met the sea.

I have no incapacitating fear of either heights or darkness. We spend nine months in a nurturing darkness before we're born, and we aspire to the highest of all places when we die.

As the day faded and as I climbed into the substructure of the pier, the shadows grew deeper, more numerous. They joined with one another like the billowing black cloaks of *Macbeth*'s witches as they gathered around their cauldron.

Since going to work for Hutch, I had read some of the volumes of Shakespeare's plays that were in his library. Ozzie Boone, the famous mystery writer, my mentor and cherished friend in Pico Mundo, would be delighted if he knew that I was thus continuing my education.

In high school, I had been an indifferent student. In part, my lack of academic achievement could be attributed to the fact that while other kids were at home, dutifully poring through

their *Macbeth* assignment, I was being chained to
a pair of dead men and dumped off a boat in the
middle of Malo Suerte Lake.

Or I was bound with rope, hanging from a rack
in a refrigerated meat locker, beside a smiling
Japanese chiropractor, waiting for a quartet of
unreasonable men to return and torture us, as
they had promised to do.

Or I had stepped into the parked motor home
of an itinerant serial killer who might return at
any moment, where I had discovered two ferocious attack dogs that were determined to keep
me from leaving, against which I had no weapons
or defenses except one fluffy pink dust mop and
six cans of warm Coke, which when shaken
spewed foamy streams that terrified the killer
canines.

As a teenager, I always intended to do my
homework. But when the supplicant dead come
to you for justice and you also have occasional
prophetic dreams, life tends to interfere with your
studies.

Now, as I hung twenty feet above the surface
of the sea, the witchy shadows closed around me
so completely that I couldn't see the next piton
thrusting from the pole above my head. I halted,
pondering whether I could ascend safely in the
pitch dark or should retreat to the narrow concrete
ledge below.

The penetrating odor of creosote, applied to

preserve the wood, had grown thicker as I climbed. I could no longer smell the ocean or the wet concrete pilings, or even my sweat: only the astringent scent of the preservative.

Just as I decided that prudence—which, as you know, is one of my most reliable character traits—required me to go back down to the ledge, lights blinked on under the pier.

Fixed to numerous wooden posts, five feet below my position, floodlights were directed down toward the sea. A long line of them extended from one end of the structure to the other.

I could not recall if the underside of the pier had been illuminated on other nights. These lamps might be automatically activated every evening at dusk.

If the floodlights were only for emergency situations, such as in the event someone fell off the pier, then perhaps a responsible citizen had seen me go over the side and had alerted the authorities.

More likely, the hulk and the redheaded gunmen had known where to find the switch. In that case, they had glimpsed me underwater, making for cover, and they had wasted no time scanning the incoming tide for a shorebound swimmer.

As I hung there in a quandary, trying to decide whether this meant I should continue upward or perhaps return to the water, I heard what for a moment I thought was a chain saw in the distance.

Then I recognized the sound as that of an outboard engine.

After ten or fifteen seconds, the engine throttled back. The consequent throbbing chug could not be mistaken for anything but an outboard.

Cocking my head left, right, I tried to hear around the thick support to which I clung. Sounds bounced deceptively through the ranks of posts and crossbeams and ricocheted off the gently rolling water, but after half a minute, I was sure the craft was proceeding slowly shoreward from the ocean-end of the pier.

I looked westward but could not see the boat for the intervening substructure. The pilot might be cruising in open water, paralleling the pier, or he could be threading through the pilings to conduct a more thorough search.

Although the floodlamps were below my position and were directed downward, light bounced off the moving water. Shimmering phantoms swooped up the columns, across the horizontal beams, and fluttered all the way up against the underside of the pier deck.

In these quivering reflections, I was revealed. An easy target.

If I descended now, I would be going down to death.

Considering the events of the last couple of years, I was ready for death when my time came, and I did not fear it. But if suicide damns the soul, then I would never see my lost girl again. Peace is not worth the slightest risk of being denied that reunion.

Besides, I suspected that Annamaria was in trouble and that I had been drawn to Magic Beach, in part, to help her.

I climbed more rapidly than before, hoping to find a junction of beams or an angular nest between purlins and posts where I would be hidden not merely from the floodlamps reflecting off the water but also from probing flashlights, if the searchers had any.

Although I wasn't afraid of heights, I could have composed an almost infinite list of places that I would rather have been than up a pier post, much like a cat treed by wolves. I counseled myself to be grateful that, indeed, there were not vicious attack dogs below; although on the other hand, to assist in self-defense, I didn't have even so much as a fluffy pink dust mop or a six-pack of warm Cokes.

CHAPTER 3

Monkey-quick but clumsy in my desperation, I scrambled up the post, feet stepping where my hands had grasped a moment earlier.

A loose piton cracked out of dry wood underfoot and fell away, and rang off concrete below. The chug of the approaching outboard masked the sound of the water receiving the steel.

The post bypassed a massive crossbeam. I clambered and clawed sideways onto that horizontal surface with such an ungainly series of maneuvers that no observer would have mistaken me for a member of a species that lived in trees and ate bananas by the bunch.

Although the beam was wide, it was not as wide as I was. Like radiant spirits, the leaping bright reflections of floodlamps off the rolling sea soared and swooned over me, making of me a pigeon, easy plinking for a practiced gunman shooting from below.

Fleeing on all fours is fine if your four are all

feet, but hands and knees don't allow much speed. Grateful that I was not afraid of high places, wishing that my stomach shared my insouciance about heights, I stood and my stomach sank.

I peered down into the drink and grew a little dizzy, then glanced west toward the grumble of the outboard. The ranks of intervening pier supports hid the boat from me.

At once, I discovered why high-wire walkers use a balance pole. With my arms tucked close to my sides and hands tensely fisted, I wobbled as if I were a drunk who had failed out of a twelve-step program in just four steps.

Defensively, I spread my arms and opened my hands. I cautioned myself not to look down at my feet but, instead, at the beam ahead, where I wanted my feet to go.

Quivering specters of reflected light painted an illusion of water across the beam and the surrounding posts, raising in me the irrational feeling that I would be washed off my perch.

This high above the sea, under the cowl of the pier, the odor of creosote intensified. My sinuses burned, and my throat. When I licked my dry lips, the taste of coal tar seemed to have condensed on them.

I halted and closed my eyes for a moment, shutting out the leaping ghosts of light. I held my breath and pressed away the dizziness, and moved on.

When I had crossed half the width of the pier, the north-south beam intersected another running east-west.

The outboard had grown louder, therefore nearer. Still the searchers had not hoved into view below.

I turned east, onto the intersecting beam. Always putting foot in front of foot on the narrow path, I was not as fleet as a ballet dancer hurrying *en pointe* across a stage, but I made swift progress.

My jeans did not accommodate such movement as well as a pair of tights would have. Instead they kept binding where too much binding would squeeze my voice into a permanent falsetto.

I crossed another intersection, continuing east, and wondered if I might be able to flee through this support structure all the way to shore.

Behind me, the outboard growled louder. Above the buzz of the engine, I heard the boat's wake slapping against the concrete support columns twenty feet below, which suggested not just that the craft was making greater speed than previously but also that it was close.

As I approached another intersection, two radiant red eyes, low in front of me, brought me to a stop. The fairy light teased fitfully across the shape before me, but then revealed a rat sitting precisely where the two beams joined.

I am not afraid of rats. Neither am I so tolerant

that I would welcome a swarm of them into my home in a spirit of interspecies brotherhood.

The rat was paralyzed by the sight of me looming over it. If I advanced another step, it had three routes by which it could flee to safety.

In moments of stress, my imagination can be as ornate as a carousel of grotesque beasts, standing on end like a Ferris wheel, spinning like a coin, casting off kaleidoscopic visions of ludicrous fates and droll deaths.

As I confronted the rat, I saw in my mind's eye a scenario in which I startled the rodent, whereupon it raced toward me in a panic, slipped under a leg of my jeans, squirmed up my calf, squeaked behind my knee, wriggled along my thigh, and decided to establish a nest between my buttocks. Through all of this, I would be windmilling my arms and hopping on one foot until I hopped off the beam and, with the hapless rodent snugged between my cheeks, plunged toward the sea just in time to crash into the searchers' boat, smashing a hole in the bottom with my face, thereupon breaking my neck *and* drowning.

You might think that I have earned the name Odd Thomas, but it has been mine since birth.

The racket of the outboard sawed through the support posts, echoing and re-echoing until it seemed that legions of lumberjacks were at work, intent on felling the entire structure.

When I took a step toward the rat, the rat did

not relent. As I had nothing better to do, I took another step, then halted because the noise of the outboard abruptly became explosive.

I dared to look down. An inflatable dinghy passed below, wet black rubber glossy under the floodlamps.

The hulk in the Hawaiian shirt sat on the stern-most of two thwarts, one hand on the steering arm of the engine. He piloted the boat with expertise, weaving at speed between the concrete columns, as if late for a luau.

On the longer port and starboard inflation compartments that formed the rounded bulwarks of the craft, in yellow letters, were the words MAGIC BEACH/HARBOR DEPT. The dinghy must have been tied up to the pier; the giant had boldly stolen it to search for me.

Yet he never looked up between the floodlamps as he passed under me. If the dinghy doubled as a search-and-rescue craft, waterproof flashlights would be stowed aboard; but the hulk wasn't using one.

The small craft disappeared among the staggered rows of columns. The engine noise gradually diminished. The ripples and dimples of the dinghy's modest wake were smoothed away by the self-ironing sea.

I had expected to see three men in the boat. I wondered where the dead-eyed redheads had gone.

The other rat had vanished, too, but not up a leg of my blue jeans.

Exhibiting balletic poise, foot in front of foot, I stepped into the junction of beams, which the trembling rodent had once occupied. I meant to continue shoreward, but I stopped.

Now that the blond giant was under the pier, between me and the beach, I was not confident of continuing in that direction.

The mood had changed. An overwhelming sense of peril, of being in the mortal trajectory of a bullet, had propelled me into frantic flight. Now death seemed no less possible than it had before the passage of the dinghy, but less imminent.

The moment felt dangerous rather than perilous, characterized by uncertainty and by the tyranny of chance. If a bullet was coming, I now had hope of dodging it, though only if I made the right moves.

I looked north, east, south along the horizontal beams. West, over my shoulder. Down into floodlit tides. I looked up toward the underside of the pier deck, where the dancing sea translated itself into phrases of half-light that swelled and fluttered and shrank and swelled in an eerie choreography through geometric beams and braces.

I felt as indecisive as the feckless mob in *The Second Part of King Henry the Sixth*, Act 4, when they vacillate repeatedly between swearing loyalty to the grotesque Cade, then to the rightful king.

Shakespeare again. Once you let him into your head, he takes up tenancy and will not leave.

The sound of the outboard engine had been waning. Abruptly it cut out altogether.

Briefly the silence seemed perfect. Then the wordless whispering and the soft idiot chuckling of the sea began to echo off surrounding surfaces.

In the brief period since the dinghy had passed under me, it could not have traveled all the way to the beach. It had probably gone little more than half that distance.

The hulk at the tiller would not surrender steering to the sea and let it pinball the dinghy from post to post. He must have somehow tied up to one of the concrete columns.

He would not have moored the dinghy unless he intended to disembark from it. Already he must be climbing into the pier support structure ahead of me.

Certain that I knew where the redheaded gunmen were, I looked over my shoulder, through the labyrinth of posts and beams to the west. They were not yet in sight.

One in front of me. Two behind. The jaws of a nutcracker.

CHAPTER 4

While I dithered at the intersection of support beams, a pale form loomed out of the south, to my right.

Because occasionally spirits manifest suddenly, unexpectedly, with no regard for my nerves, I don't startle easily. I swayed on the timber but did not plummet from it.

My visitor proved to be Boo, good dog and former mascot of St. Bartholomew's Abbey in the California Sierra.

He could be seen by no one but me, and no touch but mine could detect any substance to him. Yet to my eyes at least, the shimmering reflections sprayed up by the rolling sea played off his flanks and across his face, as if he were as solid as I was.

Although he could have appeared in midair, he walked the crossbeam toward me, like the ghost of Hamlet's father approaching the doomed prince on the platform before the castle.

Well, no. Boo had a tail, soft fur, and a friendly smile. Hamlet's father had none of that, although Hollywood would no doubt eventually give him all three in some misguided adaptation.

I hoped that the *Hamlet* comparison was inappropriate in other ways. At the end of that play, the stage is littered with dead bodies.

Boo stopped when he knew that I had seen him, cocked his head, and wagged his tail. Suddenly facing away from me without having turned around, he padded south, paused, glanced back at me, and then continued.

Even if I had not watched a lot of old episodes of *Lassie*, I understood the dead well enough to know that I was expected to follow my dog. I took some small pride that, unlike young Timmy in the TV show, I didn't need to be barked into obedience.

The blond hulk had not appeared in the east, nor the redheads in the west, so I hurried, if gingerly, after the ghostly shepherd, who led me toward the south side of the pier.

At the end of the timber path, I came to a large railed landing that served two flights of ascending stairs, one to the left, one to the right. The landing might have been a staging platform for workers of one kind or another.

When Boo climbed the stairs to the left, I went after him. The flight was short, and at the top lay a four-foot-wide railed catwalk.

The underside of the pier deck hung little more than one foot above my head. In this high corridor, where only a storm wind could have stirred the air, the stink of creosote thickened.

Darkness pooled deeper here than elsewhere. Nevertheless, the quivering marbled reflections, ever-changing on the ceiling, revealed electrical conduits, junction boxes, and copper pipes that must have been water lines.

The conduits brought power to the lampposts topside and to the emergency floodlamps below me. The copper lines served the freshwater faucets provided at regular intervals for the anglers who, on most nights, fished from the pier.

This catwalk, along which Boo led me, would be used by plumbers and electricians when problems arose with pier utilities.

After we had proceeded some distance shoreward, we came to a two-foot-by-five-foot pop-out in the catwalk. A wooden storage chest with two padlocks filled this space.

In the poor light, I could not see any words or markings on the chest. Perhaps it contained maintenance supplies.

Or interred in the chest might have been the shrunken remains of the pier master's poor wife, Lorraine, who perhaps had been murdered twenty years ago when she complained once too often about a lingering creosote smell in his work clothes.

My eager imagination might have worked up a hair-raising image of Lorraine's shriveled cadaver, pickled in creosote, if I had been able to believe there was actually such a position as a pier master. I don't know where the name Lorraine came from.

Sometimes I am a mystery to myself.

Boo settled on the catwalk and rolled onto his side. He extended one paw toward me and raked the air—universal canine sign language that meant *Sit down, stay awhile, keep me company, rub my tummy.*

With three dangerous men searching for me, a tummy-rub session seemed ill-advised, like pausing in midflight across a howitzer-hammered battlefield to assume the lotus position and engage in some yoga to calm the nerves.

Then I realized that the brute in the orchid-pattern shirt was overdue for an appearance as he searched the support structure from east to west. The storage chest stood about two and a half feet high and offered cover that the open railing did not.

"Good boy," I whispered.

Boo's tail beat against the floor without making a sound.

I stretched out on the catwalk, on my side, left arm bent at the elbow, head resting on my palm. With my right hand, I rubbed my ghost dog's tummy.

Dogs know we need to give affection as much

as they need to receive it. They were the first therapists; they've been in practice for thousands of years.

After perhaps two minutes, Boo brought an end to our therapy session by rolling to his feet, ears pricked, alert.

I dared to raise my head above the storage chest. I peered down seven feet into the level of the support structure from which I had recently ascended.

At first I saw no one. Then I spotted the hulk proceeding along the series of east-west beams.

The eddying water far below cast luminous patterns that turned through the support structure like the prismatic rays from a rotating crystal chandelier in a ballroom. The hulk had no one to dance with, but he didn't appear to be in a dancing mood, anyway.

CHAPTER 5

The big man didn't walk the beams with reticence and caution, as I had done, but with such confidence that his mother must have been a circus aerialist and his father a high-rise construction worker. His powerful arms were at his sides, a gun in one and a flashlight in the other.

He paused, switched on the flashlight, and searched among the vertical posts, along the horizontal supports.

On the catwalk, I ducked my head behind the storage chest. A moment later the probing light swept over me, east to west, back again, and then away.

Although Boo had moved past me and stood with his head through a gap in the railing, watching the giant, he remained visible only to me.

When the searcher had moved out of sight into the labyrinth of posts and purlins and struts, I rose to my feet. I continued east.

Padding ahead of me, Boo dematerialized. He appeared solid one moment, then became transparent, faded, vanished.

I had no idea where he went when he was not with me. Perhaps he enjoyed exploring new places as much as did any living dog, and went off to wander previously unvisited neighborhoods of Magic Beach.

Boo did not haunt this world in the way that the lingering human dead haunted it. They were by turns forlorn, fearful, angry, bitter. Transgressively, they refused to heed the call to judgment, and made this world their purgatory.

This suggested to me that the free will they had been given in this life was a heritage they carried with them into the next, which was a reassuring thought.

Boo seemed to be less a ghost than he was a guardian spirit, always happy and ready to serve, still on the earth not because he had remained behind after death but because he had been sent back. Consequently, perhaps he had the power and permission to move between worlds as he wished.

I found it comforting to imagine that when I didn't urgently need him, he was in Heaven's fields, at play with all the good dogs who had brightened this world with their grace and who had moved on to a place where no dog ever suffered or lived unloved.

Evidently Boo believed that for the immediate future I could muddle on without him.

I continued east along the catwalk until, glancing down at the opportune moment, I glimpsed the inflatable dinghy tied to a concrete column far below, bobbing gently on the floodlit swells. Here the hulk had ascended and had begun searching westward.

At least one-quarter of the pier's length lay to the east of this position. I paused to brood about that.

As it turned out, Boo had been right to think that I would be able to puzzle my way through this development without his counsel. The hulk had not searched the last quarter of the support structure because he was confident that I could not have gone that far before he had climbed up here to look for me.

I did not believe, however, that he was as dumb as he was big. He would have left the last section unsearched only if, in the event that I slipped past him, someone waited on the shore to snare me.

Perhaps both redheads had not begun searching together from the west end of the pier, as I had imagined. One of them might be waiting ahead of me.

Had I been a dog and had Boo been a man, he would have given me a cookie, patted me on the head, and said, "Good boy."

After climbing over the catwalk railing, I lowered

myself onto a tie beam below, lost my balance, got it back. I went north toward the center of the pier.

Just before I reached the intersection with the east-west beam, I stepped off the timber, across a six-inch gap, and put one foot on a piton in one of the vertical supports. I grabbed another piton with one hand, and swung onto that post.

I descended to the concrete base column, slid down through the enshrouding colony of barnacles, breaking them with my jeans, taking care to spare my hands, and landed as quietly as I could on the sectioned floorboards of the inflatable dinghy. A softly rattling debris of broken crustacean shells arrived with me.

The boat bobbed under one of the floodlamps. I felt dangerously exposed and was eager to get out of there.

A mooring line extended from the bow ring to a cleat in the concrete: two horns of pitted steel that barely protruded past the barnacles. I did not dare untie the dinghy until I was prepared to struggle against the currents that would carry it toward land.

If I started the engine, the searchers would come at once. Considering the time that I, an inexperienced pilot, would need to negotiate among the pilings and into open water, I might not get out of pistol range before one of the gunmen arrived.

Therefore, I resorted to the oars. A pair were secured with Velcro straps against the starboard bulwark.

Because long oars were needed and space was at a premium in the dinghy, this pair had wooden paddles but telescoping aluminum poles. With a little fumbling and a lot of muttering—both activities at which I excel—I extended the oars and locked them at full length.

I fixed one oar in the port oarlock, but I kept the other one free. Because the staggered ranks of pilings would make it difficult if not impossible to paddle against the tide and also navigate around every column, I hoped to steer and propel the inflatable craft across the remaining width of the pier by pushing off one after another of those concrete impediments.

Finally I untied the belaying line from the cleat. Because the dinghy began at once to drift with the tide, I let the rope ravel on the floorboards as it wished.

Before the column receded beyond reach, I sat upon the forward thwart, seized the free oar, and used it to thrust off the concrete. Jaws clenched, pulse throbbing in my temples, I tried with all my strength to move the dinghy northward, across the shorebound tide.

And so it did, for a short distance, before the tide pulled it north-northeast, and then east. I corrected course by thrusting off the next piling, the next, the next, and although a couple of times the oar scraped or knocked the concrete, the sound was too brief and low to draw attention.

Inevitably, I could not entirely halt an eastward drift. But the distance to land remained great enough that I hoped the intervening supports would prevent anyone at that end of the pier from seeing me.

When open water lay ahead, I slipped the free pole into the starboard lock, and with both oars I rowed crosstide, pulling harder with the seaward paddle than with the landward.

In the open, I expected a bullet in the back. If it happened, I hoped that it would not cripple me, but cleanly kill me instead, and send me on to Stormy Llewellyn.

Full night had fallen while I had cat-and-moused through the support structure of the pier. The mist that had risen near dusk, just before I had decided Annamaria should leave the pier, was slowly thickening into a heartier brew.

The fog would cloak me quicker than the darkness alone. The poles creaked in the locks and the paddles sometimes struck splashes from the black water, but no one shouted behind me, and moment by moment, I felt more confident of escaping.

My arms began to ache, my shoulders and my neck, but I rowed another minute, another. I was increasingly impressed by the power of the sea, and grateful for the low sluggish waves.

When I allowed myself to look back, the shrouded glow of some of the pier lamps could still be discerned. But when I saw that the pier itself was lost to view in gray murk, I brought both oars aboard and dropped them on the sectioned floorboards.

Under a novice seaman, an inflatable dinghy can be a slippery beast, almost as bad as riding the back of an angry and intoxicated crocodile that wants to thrash you off and eat your *cojones*. But that's a story for another time.

Fearful of falling overboard or capsizing the craft, I crept on my hands and knees to the rear thwart. I sat there with one hand on the steering arm of the outboard.

Instead of a starter rope, there was an electronic ignition, which I found by reading the engine as a blind man reads a line of Braille. A push of the button brought a roar, and then a whoosh of propeller blades chopping surf.

The engine noise prevented me from hearing any shouts that rose from the pier, but now the demonic trinity knew where I had gone.

CHAPTER 6

Steering straight to shore seemed unwise. The gunman who had been positioned at the landward end of the pier would race north along the beach, using the engine noise to maintain a fix on me.

The fog was not dense enough to bury all of Magic Beach. I could see some fuzzy lights from shoreside businesses and homes, and I used these as a guide to motor north, parallel to the coast.

For the first time since it had happened, I allowed myself to wonder why the big man's hand upon my shoulder had cast me back into the previous night's apocalyptic dream. I couldn't be sure that he had shared my vision. But he had experienced *something* that made him want to take me somewhere private for the kind of intense questioning during which the interrogator acquires a large collection of the interrogee's teeth and fingernails.

I thought of those yellow eyes. And of the

voice that belonged to something that would eat Goldilocks with or without gravy: *Who the* hell *are you?*

My current circumstances were not conducive to calm thought and profound reasoning. I could arrive at only one explanation for the electrifying effect of his hand upon my shoulder.

My dream of that horrendous but unspecified catastrophe was not a dream but, beyond doubt now, a premonition. When the hulk touched me, he triggered a memory of the nightmare, which backwashed into him *because the mysterious cataclysm that I had inadequately foreseen was one that he would be instrumental in causing.*

The waves were too low to turn my stomach, but when my stomach turned nevertheless, it felt as viscous as an oyster sliding out of its shell.

When I had gone perhaps half a mile from the pier, I set the outboard's steering arm, locked the throttle, stripped off the sodden sweatshirt that had encumbered me on my previous swim, and dived overboard.

Having worked up a sweat with my exertions, I had forgotten how cold the water was: cold enough to shock the breath out of me. I went under. A current sucked me down. I fought upward, broke the surface, spat out a mouthful of seawater, and gasped for air.

I rolled onto my back, using a flutter kick and a modified butterfly stroke to make for land at an easy pace. If one of the redheads waited on the shore for me, I wanted to give him time to hear the dinghy proceeding steadily north and to decide either to follow it or to return to the pier.

Besides, maybe a shark, a really huge shark, a giant mutant shark of unprecedented size would surface under me, kill me with one bite, and swallow me whole. In that event, I would no longer have to worry about Annamaria, the people of Magic Beach, or the possible end of the world.

All but effortlessly afloat in the buoyant salt water, gazing up into the featureless yet ever-changing fog, with no sounds but my breathing and the slop of water washing in and out of my ears, having adjusted to the cold but not yet aching from it, I was as close to the experience of a sensory-deprivation tank as I ever wanted to get.

With no distractions, this seemed like an ideal moment to walk my memory through the red-tide dream in search of meaningful details that had not initially registered with me. I would have been relieved to recall a neon sign that provided the month, day, and hour of the cataclysm, the precise location, and a description of the event.

Unfortunately, my predictive dreams don't work that way. I do not understand why I have been given a prognostic gift vivid enough to make me feel morally obliged to prevent a foreseen evil—but not clear enough to allow me to act at once with force and conviction.

Because of the disturbing supernatural aspects of my life and because the weight of my unusual responsibilities outweighs my power to fulfill them, I risk being crushed by stress. Consequently, I have kept the nonsupernatural part of my life simple. As few possessions as possible. No obligations like a mortgage or a car payment to worry about. I avoid contemporary TV, contemporary politics, contemporary art: all too frantic, fevered, and frivolous, or else angry, bitter.

At times, even working as a fry cook in a busy restaurant became too complicated. I contemplated a less demanding life in tire sales or the retail shoe business. If someone would pay me to watch grass grow, I could handle that.

I have no clothes except T-shirts and jeans, and sweatshirts in cool weather. No wardrobe decisions to make.

I have no plans for the future. I make my life up as I go along.

The perfect pet for me is a ghost dog. He doesn't need to be fed, watered, or groomed. No poop to pick up.

Anyway, drifting through fog toward the shrouded shore, I was at first unable to fish new details of the dream from memory. But then I realized that in the vision, Annamaria had not worn the clothes I had seen her wear in life.

She had been pregnant, as in life, suspended

in the air above the luminous and crimson sea, a tempest of fiery clouds behind her.

As I stood on a beach crawling with snakes of light, she floated toward me, freed from the power of gravity, arms folded across her breast, eyes closed.

I recalled her garment fluttering, not as if billowing in the winds of a cataclysm, but as if stirred gently by her own magical and stately progress through the air.

Not a dress or gown. Voluminous but not absurdly so. A robe of some kind, covering her from throat to wrists, to ankles.

Her ankles had been crossed, her feet bare.

The fabric of the garment exhibited the softness and the sheen of silk, and it hung in graceful folds; yet there had been something strange about it.

Something extraordinary.

I was certain that it had been white at first. But then not white. I could not recall what color it had subsequently become, but the change of color hadn't been the strange thing.

The softness of the weave, the sheen of the fabric. The graceful draping. The slightest flutter of the sleeves, and of the hem above the bare feet . . .

Scissors-kicking, the heels of my sneakered feet bumped something in the water, and an instant later my stroking hands met resistance. I flailed once at an imagined shark before I realized I had reached shallow water and that I was fighting only sand.

I rolled off my back, rose into night air colder than the water. Listening to the outboard engine fade in the distance, I waded ashore through whispering surf and a scrim of sea foam.

Out of the white fog, up from the white beach came a gray form, and suddenly a dazzling light bloomed three inches from my face.

Before I could reel backward, the flashlight swung up, one of those long-handled models. Before I was able to dodge, the flashlight arced down and clubbed me, a glancing blow to the side of my head.

As he hit me, he called me a rectum, although he used a less elegant synonym for that word.

The guy loomed so close that even in the confusing fog-refracted slashes of light, I could see that he was a new thug, not one of the three miscreants from the pier.

The motto of Magic Beach was EVERYONE A NEIGHBOR, EVERY NEIGHBOR A FRIEND. They needed to consider changing it to something like YOU BETTER WATCH YOUR ASS.

My ears were ringing and my head hurt, but I was not dazed. I lurched toward my assailant, and he backed up, and I reached for him, and he clubbed me again, this time harder and squarely on the top of the head.

I wanted to kick his crotch, but I discovered that I had fallen to my knees, which is a position from which crotch-kicking is a too-ambitious offense.

For a moment I thought the faithful were being summoned to church, but then I realized the bell was my skull, tolling loudly.

I didn't have to be psychic to know the flashlight was coming down again, cleaving fog and air.

I said a bad word.

CHAPTER 7

Considering that this is my fourth manuscript, I have become something of a writer, even though nothing that I have written will be published until after my death, if ever.

As a writer, I know how the right bad word at a crucial moment can purge ugly emotions and relieve emotional tension. As a guy who has been forced to struggle to survive almost as long as he has been alive, I also know that no word—even a really, really bad word—can prevent a blunt object from splitting your skull if it is swung with enthusiasm and makes contact.

So having been driven to my knees by the second blow, and with my skull ringing as though the hunchback of Notre Dame were inside my head and pulling maniacally on bell ropes, I said the bad word, but I also lunged forward as best I could and grabbed my assailant by the ankles.

The third blow missed its intended target, and I took the impact on my back, which felt better than a whack on the head, although not as good as any moment of a massage.

Facedown on the beach, gripping his ankles, I tried to pull the sonofabitch off his feet.

Sonofabitch wasn't the bad word that I used previously. This was another one, and not as bad as the first.

His legs were planted wide, and he was strong.

Whether my eyes were open or closed, I saw spirals of twinkling lights, and "Somewhere over the Rainbow" played in my head. This led me to believe that I had nearly been knocked unconscious and that I didn't have my usual strength.

He kept trying to hit my head again, but he also had to strive to stay upright, so he managed only to strike my shoulders three or four times.

Throughout this assault, the flashlight beam never faltered, but repeatedly slashed the fog, and I was impressed by the manufacturer's durability standards.

Although we were in a deadly serious struggle, I could not help but see absurdity in the moment. A self-respecting thug ought to have a gun or at least a blackjack. He flailed at me as though he were an eighty-year-old lady with an umbrella responding to an octogenarian beau who had made a rude proposal.

At last I succeeded in toppling him. He dropped the flashlight and fell backward.

I clambered onto him, jamming my right knee

where it would make him regret having been born a male.

Most likely he tried to say a bad word, a very bad word, but it came out as a squeal, like an expression of consternation by a cartoon mouse.

Near at hand lay the flashlight. As he tried to throw me off, I snared that formidable weapon.

I do not like violence. I do not wish to be the recipient of violence, and I am loath to perpetrate it.

Nevertheless, I perpetrated a little violence on the beach that night. Three times I hit his head with the flashlight. Although I did not enjoy striking him, I didn't feel the need to turn myself in to the police, either.

He stopped resisting and I stopped hitting. I could tell by the slow soft whistle of his breathing that he had fallen unconscious.

When all the tension went out of his muscles, I clambered off him and got to my feet just to prove to myself that I could do it.

Dorothy kept singing faintly, and I could hear Toto panting. The twinkling lights behind my eyelids began to spiral faster, as if the tornado was about to lift us out of Kansas and off to Oz.

I returned voluntarily to my knees before I went down against my will. After a moment, I realized that the panting was mine, not that of Dorothy's dog.

Fortunately, my vertigo subsided before my

adversary regained consciousness. Although the flashlight still worked, I didn't think it could take much more punishment.

The cracked lens cast a thin jagged shadow on his face. But as I peeled back one of his eyelids to be sure that I had not given him a concussion, I could see him well enough to know that I had never seen him before and that I preferred never to see him again.

Eye of newt. Wool-of-bat hair. Nose of Turk and Tartar's lips. A lolling tongue like a fillet of fenny snake. He was not exactly ugly, but he looked peculiar, as if he'd been conjured in a cauldron by *Macbeth*'s coven of witches.

When he had fallen, a slim cell phone had slid half out of his shirt pocket. If he was in league with the trio at the pier, he might have called them when he heard me swimming ashore.

After rolling him onto his side, I took the wallet from his hip pocket. Supposing he had summoned help moments before I had come ashore, I needed to move on quickly and could not pore through his ID there on the beach. I left his folding money in his shirt pocket with his cell phone, and I took the wallet.

I propped the flashlight on his chest. Because his head was raised on a mound of sand, the bright beam bathed him from chin to hairline.

If something like Godzilla woke in a Pacific abyss and decided to come ashore to flatten our picturesque community, this guy's face would dissuade it from a rampage, and the scaly beast would return meekly to the peace of the deeps.

With the fog-diffused lights of town to guide me, I slogged across the wide beach.

I did not proceed directly east. Perhaps Flashlight Guy had told the pier crew that he was on the shore due west of some landmark, by which they could find him. If they were coming, I wanted to cut a wide swath around them.

CHAPTER 8

As I angled northeast across the strand, the soft sand sucked at my shoes and made every step a chore.

Wearing wet jeans and T-shirt on the central coast on a January night can test your mettle. Five weeks ago, however, I had been in the Sierra during a blizzard. This felt balmy by comparison.

I wanted a bottle of aspirin and an ice bag. When I touched the throbbing left side of my head, I wondered if I needed stitches. My hair felt sticky with blood. I found a lump the size of half a plum.

When I left the beach, I was at the north end of the shoreside commercial area, where Jacaranda Avenue dead-ended. From there, a mile of oceanfront houses faced the concrete boardwalk all the way to the harbor.

For its ten-block length, Jacaranda Avenue, which ran east from the boardwalk, was lined with ancient podocarpuses. The trees formed a canopy that cooled the street all day and shaded the streetlamps at night. Not one jacaranda grew along its namesake avenue.

Wisteria Lane boasted no wisteria. Palm Drive featured oaks and ficuses. Sterling Heights was the poorest neighborhood, and of all the streets in town, Ocean Avenue lay the farthest from the ocean.

Like most politicians, those in Magic Beach seemed to live in an alternate universe from the one in which real people existed.

Wet, rumpled, my shoes and jeans caked with sand, bleeding, and no doubt wild-eyed, I was grateful that the podocarpuses filtered the lamplight. In conspiracy with the fog, I traveled in shadows along Jacaranda Avenue and turned right on Pepper Tree Way.

Don't ask.

Three guys were hunting me. With a population of fifteen thousand, Magic Beach was more than a wide place in the highway, but it did not offer a tide of humanity in which I could swim unnoticed.

Furthermore, in my current condition, if an alert policeman spotted me, he would be inclined to stop and chat. He would suspect I had been the target or the perpetrator of violence—or both.

I had no confidence in my ability to convince him that I clubbed myself over the head as punishment for a wrong decision I had made.

I did not want to file a report regarding the

gunmen at the pier and the assault at the beach. That would take hours.

Already the three goons would be trying to determine who I was, describing me to people working in the commercial zone near the pier.

They might not get a lead. Having been in town little more than a month, having kept to myself as I waited to discover why I had been drawn there, I had remained a stranger to almost the entire populace.

Even an accurate description of me would not help them much. I am of average height, average weight. I have no distinguishing scars, birthmarks, tattoos, moles, warts, or facial mutations. I do not have a chin beard or yellow eyes. My teeth are not dissolving from meth addiction, but I also do not turn heads as would, say, Tom Cruise.

Except for the paranormal gifts with which I have been burdened, I was born to be a fry cook. Tire salesman. Shoe-store clerk. The guy who puts handbills under windshield wipers in the mall parking lot.

Give me an accurate and detailed description of at least one of the many fry cooks who has whipped up breakfast for you in a diner or coffee shop over the years, one tire salesman or shoe-store clerk who has served you. I know what comes to your mind: *nada*.

Don't feel bad. Most fry cooks and tire salesmen and shoe clerks never want to be famous or widely recognized. We just want to get along. We want to live quietly, avoid hurting anyone, avoid being hurt, provide for ourselves and for those we love, and have some fun along the way. We keep the economy humming, and we fight wars when we have to, and we raise families if we get the chance, but we have no desire to see our pictures in the newspaper or to receive medals, and we don't hope to hear our names as answers to questions on *Jeopardy!*

We are the water in the river of civilization, and those fellow citizens who desire attention, who ride the boats on the river and wave to admiring crowds along the shore . . . well, they interest us less than they amuse us. We don't envy them their prominence. We embrace our anonymity and the quiet that comes with it.

The artist Andy Warhol said that in the future everyone would be famous for fifteen minutes, and he implied that they would hunger for that fame. He was right, but only about the kind of people he knew.

And as for the guys who put handbills under windshield wipers in the shopping-mall parking lot: Man, they have *totally* got the anonymity thing right; they are as invisible as the wind, as faceless as time.

As I made my way through shadows and fog, along back streets more than main streets, I worried that the yellow-eyed man might have more muscle on his team than just the pair of redheads and Flashlight Guy. Depending on his resources, he could have people searching not just for me but also for Annamaria.

She had known my name. She must know more than that about me. I didn't think she would willingly give me up to the hulk; but he would break her like a ceramic bank to get at the coins of knowledge that she held.

I didn't want her to be hurt, especially not because of me. I had to find her before he did.

CHAPTER 9

By an alley I arrived at the back of Hutch Hutchison's house. A gate beside the garage opened to a walkway that led to a brick patio.

Glazed terra-cotta urns and bowls held red and purple cyclamens, but the bleach of fog and the stain of night left the blooms as colorless as barnacle shells.

On a glass-topped wrought-iron table, I put down my wallet and the one I had taken off the agitated man with the flashlight.

Toe to heel, I pried off my sand-caked sneakers. I stripped off my socks and then my blue jeans, which were crusted with enough sand to fill a large hourglass. With a garden hose, I washed my feet.

Mrs. Nicely came three days a week to clean, as well as to do the laundry and ironing. Her surname suited her even better than my first name suited me, and I did not want to cause her extra work.

The back door was locked. Among the cyclamens in the nearest bowl, in a Ziploc pill bag, Hutch kept a spare key. After retrieving the two wallets, I let myself into the house.

Fragrant with the cinnamony aroma of chocolate-pumpkin cookies that I had baked earlier in the afternoon, brightened only by the golden glow of string lights hidden in the recessed toe kick of the cabinets, the kitchen waited warm and welcoming.

I am no theologian. I would not be surprised, however, if Heaven proved to be a cozy kitchen, where delicious treats appeared in the oven and in the refrigerator whenever you wanted them, and where the cupboards were full of good books.

After blotting my wet feet on the small rug, I snatched a cookie from the plate that stood on the center island, and I headed for the door to the downstairs hall.

I intended to go upstairs with the stealth of a Ninja assassin, quickly shower, dress my head wound if it didn't need stitches, and put on fresh clothes.

When I was halfway across the kitchen, the swinging door opened. Hutch switched on the overhead lights, stork-walked into the room, and said, "I just saw a tsunami many hundreds of feet high."

"Really?" I asked. "Just now?"

"It was in a movie."

"That's a relief, sir."

"Uncommonly beautiful."

"Really?"

"Not the wave, the woman."

"Woman, sir?"

"Téa Leoni. She was in the movie."

He stilted to the island and took a cookie from the plate.

"Son, did you know there's an asteroid on a collision course with the earth?"

"It's always something," I said.

"If a large asteroid strikes land"—he took a bite of the cookie—"millions could die."

"Makes you wish the world was nothing but an ocean."

"Ah, but if it lands in the ocean, you get a tsunami perhaps a thousand feet high. Millions dead that way, too."

I said, "Rock and a hard place."

Smiling, nodding, he said, "Absolutely wonderful."

"Millions dead, sir?"

"What? No, of course not. The cookie. Quite wonderful."

"Thank you, sir." I raised the wrong hand to my mouth and almost bit into the two wallets.

He said, "Soberingly profound."

"It's just a cookie, sir," I said, and took a bite of mine.

"The possibility all of humanity could be exterminated in a single cataclysmic event."

"That would put a lot of search-and-rescue dogs out of work."

He lifted his chin, creased his brow, and drew his noble face into the expression of a man always focused on tomorrow. "I was a scientist once."

"What field of science, sir?"

"Contagious disease."

Hutch put down his half-eaten cookie, fished a bottle of Purell from a pocket, and squeezed a large dollop of the glistening gel into the cupped palm of his left hand.

"A terrible new strain of pneumonic plague would have wiped out civilization if not for me, Walter Pidgeon, and Marilyn Monroe."

"I haven't seen that one, sir."

"She was marvelous as an unwitting pneumonic-plague carrier."

His gaze refocused from the future of science and mankind to the glob of germ-killing goop on his palm.

"She certainly had the lungs for the role," he said.

Vigorously, he rubbed his long-fingered hands together, and the sanitizing gel made squishy sounds.

"Well," I said, "I was headed up to my room."

"Did you have a nice walk?"

"Yes, sir. Very nice."

"A 'constitutional' we used to call them."

"That was before my time."

"That was before *everyone's* time. My God, I am old."

"Not that old, sir."

"Compared to a redwood tree, I suppose not."

I hesitated to leave the kitchen, out of concern that when I started to move, he would notice that I was without shoes and pants.

"Mr. Hutchison—"

"Call me Hutch. Everyone calls me Hutch."

"Yes, sir. If anyone comes around this evening looking for me, tell them I came back from my walk very agitated, packed my things, and split."

The gel had evaporated; his hands were germ-free. He picked up his half-eaten cookie.

With dismay, he said, "You're leaving, son?"

"No, sir. That's just what you tell them."

"Will they be officers of the law?"

"No. One might be a big guy with a chin beard."

"Sounds like a role for George Kennedy."

"Is he still alive, sir?"

"Why not? I am. He was wonderfully menacing in *Mirage* with Gregory Peck."

"If not the chin beard, then maybe a redheaded guy who will or will not have bad teeth. Whoever—tell him I quit without notice, you're angry with me."

"I don't think I could be angry with you, son."

"Of course you can. You're an actor."

His eyes twinkled. He swallowed some cookie. With his teeth just shy of a clench, he said, "You ungrateful little shit."

"That's the spirit, sir."

"You took five hundred in cash out of my dresser drawer, you thieving little bastard."

"Good. That's good."

"I treat you like a son, I *love* you like a son, and now I see I'm lucky you didn't slit my throat while I slept, you despicable little worm."

"Don't ham it up, sir. Keep it real."

Hutch looked stricken. "Hammy? Was it really?"

"Maybe that's too strong a word."

"I haven't been before a camera in half a century."

"You weren't over the top," I assured him. "It was just too . . . fulsome. That's the word."

"Fulsome. In other words, less is more."

"Yes, sir. You're angry, see, but not furious. You're a little bitter. But it's tempered with regret."

Brooding on my direction, he nodded slowly. "Maybe I had a son I lost in the war, and you reminded me of him."

"All right."

"His name was Jamie, he was full of charm, courage, wit. You seemed so like him at first, a young man who rose above the base temptations of this world . . . but you were just a leech."

I frowned. "Gee, Mr. Hutchison, a leech . . ."

"A parasite, just looking for a score."

"Well, okay, if that works for you."

"Jamie lost in the war. My precious Corrina dead of cancer." His voice grew increasingly forlorn, gradually diminishing to a whisper. "So alone for so long, and you . . . you saw just how to take advantage of my vulnerability. You even stole Corrina's jewelry, which I've kept for thirty years."

"Are you going to tell them all this, sir?"

"No, no. It's just my motivation."

He snared a plate from a cabinet and put two cookies on it.

"Jamie's father and Corrina's husband is not the type of old man to turn to booze in his melancholy. He turns to the cookies . . . which is the only sweet thing he has left from the month that you cynically exploited him."

I winced. "I'm beginning to feel really bad about myself."

"Do you think I should put on a cardigan? There's something about an old man huddled in a tattered cardigan that can be just wonderfully pathetic."

"Do you have a tattered cardigan?"

"I have a cardigan, and I could tatter it in a minute."

I studied him as he stood there with the plate of cookies and a big grin.

"Look pathetic for me," I said.

His grin faded. His lips trembled but then pressed

together as if he struggled to contain strong emotion.

He turned his gaze down to the cookies on the plate. When he looked up again, his eyes glistened with unshed tears.

"You don't need the cardigan," I said.

"Truly?"

"Truly. You look pathetic enough."

"That's a lovely thing to say."

"You're welcome, sir."

"I better get back to the parlor. I'll find a deliciously sad book to read, so by the time the doorbell rings, I'll be fully in character."

"They might not get a lead on me. They might not come here."

"Don't be so negative, Odd. They'll come. I'm sure they will. It'll be great fun."

He pushed through the swinging door with the vigor of a younger man. I listened to him walk down the hallway and into the parlor.

Shoeless, pantless, bloody, I scooped some cubes from the icemaker and put them in a OneZip plastic bag. I wrapped a dishtowel around the bag.

Pretending the confidence of a fully dressed man, I walked down the hallway. Passing the open doors to the parlor, I waved to Hutch when, from the solace of his armchair, moored in melancholy, he waved listlessly at me.

CHAPTER 10

My scalp was abraded, not lacerated. In the shower, the hot water and shampoo stung, but I didn't begin to bleed freely again.

Unwilling to take the time to cautiously towel or blow-dry my hair, I pulled on fresh jeans and a clean T-shirt. I laced my backup pair of sneakers.

The MYSTERY TRAIN sweatshirt had been lost to the sea. A similar thrift-shop purchase featured the word WYVERN across the chest, in gold letters on the dark-blue fabric.

I assumed Wyvern must be the name of a small college. Wearing it did not make me feel any smarter.

As I dressed, Frank Sinatra watched me from the bed. He lay atop the quilted spread, ankles crossed, head propped on pillows, hands behind his head.

The Chairman of the Board was smiling,

amused by me. He had a winning smile, but his moods were mercurial.

He was dead, of course. He had died in 1998, at the age of eighty-two.

Lingering spirits look the age they were when death took them. Mr. Sinatra, however, appears whatever age he wishes to be, depending on his mood.

I have known only one other spirit with the power to manifest at any age he chose: the King of Rock 'n' Roll.

Elvis had kept me company for years. He had been reluctant to move on, for reasons that took me a long while to ascertain.

Only days before Christmas, along a lonely California highway, he had finally found the courage to proceed to the next world. I'd been happy for him then, to see his sorrow lift and his face brighten with anticipation.

Moments after Elvis departed, as Boo and I walked the shoulder of the highway, drawn toward an unknown destination that proved to be Magic Beach, Mr. Sinatra fell in step beside me. He appeared to be in his early thirties that day, fifty years younger than when he died.

Now, lying on the bed, he looked forty or forty-one. He was dressed as he had been in some scenes in *High Society*, which he had made with Bing Crosby in 1956.

Of all the spirits I have seen, only Elvis and Mr. Sinatra are able to manifest in the garments of their choice. Others haunt me always in whatever they were wearing when they died.

This is one reason I will never attend a costume party dressed as the traditional symbol of the New Year, in nothing but a diaper and a top hat. Welcomed into either Hell or Heaven, I do not want to cross the threshold to the sound of demonic or angelic laughter.

When I had pulled on the Wyvern sweatshirt and was ready to leave, Mr. Sinatra came to me, shoulders forward, head half ducked, dukes raised, and threw a few playful punches at the air in front of my face.

Because he evidently hoped that I would help him move on from this world as I had helped Elvis, I had been reading biographies of him. I did not know as much about him as I knew about the King, but I knew the right thing for this moment.

"Robert Mitchum once said you were the only man he was afraid to fight, though he was half again as big as you."

The Chairman looked embarrassed and shrugged.

As I picked up the cloth-wrapped bag of ice and held it against the lump on the side of my head, I continued: "Mitchum said he knew he could knock you down, probably more than once, but he also knew you would keep getting up and coming back until one of you was dead."

Mr. Sinatra gestured as if to say that Mitchum had over-estimated him.

"Sir, here's the situation. You came to me for help, but you keep resisting it."

Two weeks ago, he had gone poltergeist on me, with the result that my collection of books about him went twirling around my room.

Spirits cannot directly harm us, not even evil spirits. This is our world, and they have no power over us. Their blows pass through us. Their fingernails and teeth cannot draw blood.

Sufficiently malevolent, however, with bottomless depths of rage to draw upon, they can spin spiritual power into whips of force that lash inanimate objects into motion. Squashed by a refrigerator hurled by a poltergeist, you tend not to take solace in the fact that the blow was indirect, rather than from the ghostly hand itself.

Mr. Sinatra wasn't evil. He was frustrated by his circumstances and, for whatever reason, fearful about leaving this world—though he would never admit to the fear. As one who had not found organized religion highly credible until later in life, he was now confused about his place in the vertical of sacred order.

The biographies had not ricocheted from wall to wall with violent force, but had instead circled the room like the horses on a carousel. Every time I tried to pluck one of those books from the air, it had eluded me.

"Mr. Mitchum said you'd keep getting up and coming back until one of you was dead," I repeated. "But in *this* fight, sir, one of us is already dead."

His sunny smile grew wintry for a moment, but then thawed away. As dark as his bad moods could be, they were always short seasons.

"There's no point in you resisting me. No point. All I want to do is help you."

As was often the case, I could not read those extraordinary blue eyes, but at least they were not bright with hostility.

After a moment, he affectionately pinched my cheek.

He went to the nearest window and turned his back to me, a genuine spirit watching the fog haunt the night with its legions of false ghosts.

I recalled "It Was a Very Good Year," a song that could be read as the sentimental and boastful recollections of an irredeemable Casanova. The poignant melancholy of his interpretation had elevated those words and that music to art.

For him, the good and the bad years were gone, and what remained was merely forever. Maybe he resisted eternity out of fear based in remorse, though maybe not.

The next life promised to be without struggle, but everything I had learned about him suggested that he had *thrived* on struggle. Perhaps he could not imagine an interesting life without it.

I can imagine it easily enough. After death, whatever I might have to face, I will not linger on this side of the door. In fact, I might cross the threshold at a run.

CHAPTER 11

I did not want to leave the house by the front door. The way my luck was running, I would find the barbarian horde on the porch, about to pay a visit.

In my dictionary, three bad guys who between them have at least one chin beard, one set of rotten teeth, and three guns qualify as a horde.

Leaving by the back of the house meant I had to pass the parlor, where Hutch brooded about the wife and son he'd never had and about how lonely and vulnerable he was after losing them.

I did not mind if he called me an ungrateful little shit again; that was merely rehearsal for a possible visit from a representative of the horde. The quick shower, the change of clothes, and the chat in the kitchen with Hutch had cost me twenty minutes, however, and I was anxious to locate Annamaria.

"Odd," he said as I tried to move past the

open parlor doors with the stealth of a Special Forces op in camouflage and sound-suppressing footgear.

"Oh, hi."

Roosting in his armchair with a chenille throw across his lap, as if keeping eggs warm in a bird's nest, he said, "In the kitchen a little while ago, when we were talking about what a useful bit of wardrobe a cardigan can be . . ."

"A tattered cardigan," I qualified.

"This may seem a peculiar question. . . ."

"Not to me, sir. Nothing seems peculiar to me anymore."

"Were you wearing pants?"

"Pants?"

"Later, I had the strangest impression that you hadn't been wearing any pants."

"Well, sir, I never wear pants."

"Of course you wear pants. You're wearing them now."

"No, these are jeans. I only have jeans—and one pair of chinos. I don't consider them pants. Pants are dressier."

"You were wearing jeans in the kitchen?"

As I stood in the parlor doorway, holding a bag of ice to the lump on the side of my head, I said, "Well, I wasn't wearing chinos, sir."

"How very peculiar."

"That I wasn't wearing chinos?"

"No. That I can't remember them."

"If I wasn't wearing chinos, you wouldn't remember them."

He thought about what I had said. "That's true enough."

"Just enough, sir," I agreed, and changed the subject. "I'm going to leave you a note about the dinner casserole."

Putting aside the novel he had been reading, he said, "Aren't you cooking dinner?"

"I've already made it. Chicken enchiladas in tomatillo sauce."

"I love your tomatillo enchiladas."

"And a rice and green-bean salad."

"Does the rice have green sauce, too?"

"Yes, sir."

"Oh, good. Do I heat them in the microwave?"

"That's right. I'll leave a note about time and power."

"Could you put Post-its on the dishes?"

"Take the Post-its off before you put the dishes in the oven."

"Of course. I wouldn't make that mistake. Again. Going out?"

"Just for a little while."

"You aren't leaving for good, are you?"

"No, sir. And I didn't steal Corrina's jewelry, either."

"I was a diamond merchant once," Hutch said. "My wife conspired to have me killed."

"Not Corrina."

"Barbara Stanwyck. She was having an affair with Bogart, and they were going to run off to Rio with the diamonds. But, of course, something went very wrong for them."

"Was it a tsunami?"

"You have a sly sense of humor, son."

"Sorry, sir."

"No, no. I like it. I believe my career would have been much bigger if I'd been able to get roles in a few comedies. I can be quite funny in my own way."

"I'm well aware."

"Barbara Stanwyck was consumed by flesh-eating bacteria, and Bogart was hit by an asteroid."

"I'll bet the audience didn't see that coming."

Picking up the book again, Hutch said, "Do you enjoy the fog so much that you want to take a second walk in it, or is there something else I should know?"

"There's nothing else you should know, sir."

"Then I will wait for the doorbell and denounce you as a fiend to anyone who asks."

"Thank you."

In the kitchen, I emptied the ice-filled OneZip bag into the sink and tossed it in the trash.

The lump on my head remained the size of half a plum, but it no longer throbbed.

On two yellow Post-its, with a blue pen, I wrote directions for heating the enchiladas and the rice salad. With a red pen, I printed REMOVE THIS TAG BEFORE PUTTING IN OVEN.

Standing at the kitchen island, I went through the contents of the wallet that I had taken off Flashlight Guy.

In his California driver's-license photo, I recognized the man I had left lying on the beach, although he only slightly resembled something conjured out of a witch's cauldron. His name was Samuel Oliver Whittle. Thirty years old, he had an address in Magic Beach.

In his Nevada driver's-license photo, he smiled broadly at the camera, which was a mistake. His smile transformed his face, and not in a good way. He looked like a lunatic villain from a Batman movie.

Nevada, where he had an address in Las Vegas, knew him as Samuel Owen Bittel. In Vegas, he was two years older than he claimed to be in his California incarnation, but perhaps a Las Vegas lifestyle aged a person prematurely.

He had no credit cards. This made him suspicious in a country that not only looked to the future but lived on the earnings from it.

The wallet contained no insurance card, no Social Security card, nor any of the other ID you might have expected.

An employee-identification card revealed that he worked for the Magic Beach Harbor Department.

Suddenly a theme had developed. Perhaps the hulk with the chin beard had not taken the inflatable dinghy without permission; maybe he had the authority to use it because he, too, worked for the harbor department, which also had responsibility for the beaches and the town's one pier.

I found it difficult to believe that the redheads were also on the municipal payroll. Thugs who worked for the government usually tried not to *look* like thugs.

After returning the cards to Sam Whittle's wallet, I tucked it in my left hip pocket.

Whatever trouble I found in the coming hours, at least some of it would involve men with guns. I did not have a gun of my own and did not want one. On occasion I have used a bad guy's firearm after taking it away from him, but only in desperation.

When I was a child, my mother spoiled guns for me, not because she disapproved of them, but because she had a psychotic attachment to a pistol. Guns spook me.

In a clutch or a corner, I tend to make a weapon out of what is near at hand. That can be anything from a crowbar to a cat, though if I had a choice, I would prefer an angry cat, which I have found to be more effective than a crowbar.

Although weaponless, I left the house by the back door, with two chocolate-pumpkin cookies. It's a tough world out there, and a man has to armor himself against it however he can.

CHAPTER 12

Paw after paw silent on wet blacktop, the fog crept along the alleyway behind Hutch's house, rubbing its furry flanks against the garages on both sides, slipping through fence pickets, climbing walls, licking into every niche and corner where mouse or lizard might have taken shelter.

These earthbound clouds swathed nearby things in mystery, made objects half a block away appear to be distant, dissolved the world entirely past the one-block mark, and raised in the mind a primitive conviction that the edge of the earth lay near at hand, a precipice from which I would fall forever into eternal emptiness.

Slowly turning in a circle, turning again, I ate one cookie and concentrated on Annamaria: on her long hair the color of molasses, on her face, on her too-pale skin. In my mind, I saw her delicate hand close around the ocean-polished orb of green bottle glass and retreat with it into the long sleeve of her sweater. . . .

My imperfect gift has one more imperfect aspect, which I have discussed before, though not in this fourth manuscript. My lost girl, Stormy Llewellyn, had called it psychic magnetism.

If I wish to find someone whose whereabouts I don't know, I can surrender myself to impulse and intuition, drive or bicycle or walk around wherever my whims take me, concentrating on that person's face and name . . . and usually within half an hour, I will find him. Psychic magnetism.

This handy talent is problematic because I cannot control or foresee when or where the desired encounter will occur. I might spot my target across a busy street—or turn a corner and collide with him.

If I am seeking a bad guy, psychic magnetism might put me on his trail—or drop me into his talons.

And if I am in pursuit of someone who is no threat, someone I need to question or to sweep out of harm's way, I cannot be sure the search will be successful. I usually find the person I'm seeking, but not always. Once in a while, resorting to psychic magnetism in desperate circumstances can be a waste of precious minutes when I have not a second to spare.

I am a half-assed champion of the imperiled innocent: able to see the lingering dead, but unable to hear what of value they might wish to tell me;

informed by predictive dreams that never provide me with sufficient detail to be certain of what they predict, of when the event will occur, or of where the horror will go down; without gun or sword, armored only with cookies.

All of this fearsome uncertainty ought to have made a hermit of me, ought to have sent me fleeing to a cave or to a remote cabin, in curmudgeonly rejection of the dead and the living. But my heart tells me that the gift was given to be used, imperfect or not, and that if I deny it, I will wither away in despair and will earn no life after this one, no reunion with my lost girl.

At least this time, standing in the alleyway behind Hutch's house, I sought not someone who wanted me dead, but instead a young woman who might need me to keep her alive. I most likely would not blunder into the teeth of the tiger.

The thick muffling fog was a time machine that rolled the night back more than one hundred years, silencing all the sounds of modern civilization—car engines, radios, the TV voices that often leaked from houses. The peaceful quiet of the nineteenth century coddled Magic Beach.

One cookie finished, concentrating on Annamaria, I suddenly set off north along the alley, as if I were a milk-wagon horse following a route so familiar that I did not need to think about my purpose or my destination.

Windows, usually electric-bright, glowed softly, as if the rooms beyond were candlelit. At the end of the alleyway, the sodium-yellow streetlight appeared to throb subtly, like gas flames, as a thousand slowly pulsing moth wings of fog pressed against the lenses of the lamp.

Nibbling my last cookie, I turned east where the alley met the street, and headed inland.

At only 6:45 on a Wednesday evening, the town appeared to have gone to bed for the night, snuggled down in Nature's white blankets. The damp chill encouraged dog owners to take shorter walks than usual, and the blinding density of the fog dissuaded drivers from unnecessary trips.

By the time that I had gone three blocks east and one block north of Hutch's place, I had seen only two ghostly cars in motion, each at least half a block distant. They looked like deep-sea submersibles in a Jules Verne tale, quietly motoring through a murky oceanic abyss.

In that quaint residential neighborhood known as the Brick District, which had no brick streets and only two brick houses, a large vehicle turned the corner at the farther end of the block. A soft kaleidoscope of fog formed shifting white-on-white patterns in the headlights.

Deep inside me, a still small voice said *Hide*.

I left the sidewalk, jumped a waist-high plum-thorn hedge, and knelt behind that greenery.

I smelled woodsmoke from fireplaces, wet foliage, and garden mulch.

In the hedge, something smelled me and bolted from cover. I almost startled to my feet before I realized I had spooked a rabbit, which was already gone across the lawn.

The truck approached with the throttled growl of a prowling beast, traveling even slower than the low visibility required.

Oppressed by a feeling that a deadly threat loomed behind me, I glanced toward the house in front of which I had taken refuge. The windowpanes were dark. Except for the lazily billowing fog, nothing moved, and as far as I could tell, no watcher waited in either the scud or the shadows.

Still on my knees, I kept my head bowed behind the hedge while the truck growled closer.

The surrounding fog drank in the twin beams of the vehicle and glowed like swamp gas, yet contained the light within itself and brightened neither me nor the hedge.

I held my breath, though the driver could not have heard me exhale.

As the truck skulked past, seeming to sniff at the pavement for the scent of prey, the fog around me darkled with the passage of the headlamps.

I dared to rise just far enough to peer across the plum thorn toward the street.

Although the vehicle passed less than ten feet

away, the dashboard lights were not bright enough to reveal the driver, only a lumpish shadow. I was able, however, to make out the city seal emblazoned on the door. And black letters on an orange background announced MAGIC BEACH/HARBOR DEPARTMENT.

Fog folded the truck out of sight. Its engine faded to a distant guttural purr.

Rising to my feet, I breathed fog faintly scented with exhaust fumes. After my third inhalation, the last engine noise whispered away into another neighborhood.

I wondered what kind of corruption coiled in the heart of the harbor department.

Moving toward the break in the hedge that accommodated the front walkway, I heard a noise issue from the dark house. Not loud. The low *squeak-ping* of metal tweaking metal.

Although a sense of danger welled in me once more, I turned from the street and followed the walkway to the foot of the porch steps.

Intuition told me that pretending to have heard nothing would be taken as a sign of weakness. And weakness would invite attack.

The subtle sound was a kind of singing, still metallic but also reminiscent of an insect's clicking serenade.

No less than the world around it, the porch was filled with fog and shadows.

"Who's there?" I asked, but received no reply.

Climbing the steps, I saw movement to my right. The rhythmic sweep of a slatted form—forward, back—timed to the squeak-ping-click, drew me forward.

I found a bench swing suspended from ceiling hooks. The chains torqued as the bench came forward, and the torsion was released as it swung backward.

Someone must have been sitting here in the dark, not swinging but perhaps watching me as I hid from the truck. Judging by the size of the current arc, the watcher had shoved back with his feet and had gotten up mere seconds ago, leaving the swing in motion to attract my attention.

I stood alone on the porch.

If he had come down the steps as I ascended, I would have encountered him, and if he had vaulted over the porch railing, I would have heard him.

The front door, no matter how stealthily pulled open and drawn shut, would have made some noise if he had gone inside.

Four windows faced me. With no light to reflect, the glass was as black as the sky at the rim of the universe, beyond the light of all stars.

I took a moment to stare at each window. If someone had been observing me from the other side, I would have seen a form in a paler shade of black than that of the lightless room.

The swing continued to move.

For a moment I thought its arc had not diminished, as though an unseen occupant still powered it. The metallic song of the twisting chain links undeniably had subsided . . . and as I watched, the swing gradually slowed toward a stop.

I considered rapping softly on one of the windows, to see what I might stir up.

Instead, I retreated to the steps, descended.

Around me, fog and dark and quiet pooled.

On the porch, I had felt that I might be in the company of someone, something.

As one who sees the lingering dead, I had never imagined that a class of spirits might walk the earth invisible to me.

Now I considered that possibility—and rejected it. Something strange had occurred, but ghosts were not the explanation.

Concentrating once more on the face of Annamaria, I left the property of the porch-swing phantom, returned to the public sidewalk, and headed north. Soon I was in the grip of psychic magnetism.

No night birds sang. No dogs barked. No whiff of breeze, no roosting owl, no stalking cat rustled the leaves of any tree. I had gone too far inland to hear the susurration of the sea.

Although I repeatedly glanced behind, I caught no glimpse of anyone trailing me. Perhaps the skin on the back of my neck prickled not because someone might be following me but instead

because I was *so* alone, with no friend to turn to
except an eighty-eight-year-old actor who lived
inside himself to such an extent that he never
noticed the blood on my face or, later, the ice
pack held to my head.

CHAPTER 13

Hutch's predicted tsunami had swept across the town, if you allowed that the fog was the white shadow of the dark sea, because it inundated every neighborhood, imposing the stillness of drowned cities. For all I knew, it measured a thousand feet high.

As I sought Annamaria, the currents of opaque mist increasingly seemed to me not just the shadow of the sea, but a foreshadowing of a tide to come, the red tide of my dream.

Street after street, every tree stood turbaned, robed, and bearded—until I arrived at the foot of a broad-leafed giant from which the fog appeared to shrink. This specimen towered sixty or seventy feet, and it offered a magnificent architecture of wide-spreading limbs.

Because knowing the names of things is a way to pay respect to the beauty of the world, I know the names of many trees; but I did not know the

name of this one and could not recall having seen
one like it before.

The leaves had two lamina, each with four
lobes. Between thumb and forefinger, they felt
thick and waxy.

Among the black branches, white flowers as
large as bowls seemed radiant in the dark. They
were reminiscent of magnolia blooms, though
more imposing, but this was not a magnolia. Water
dripped from the petals, as if the tree had
condensed the fog to form these flowers.

Behind the tree stood a half-seen, two-story
Victorian house, dressed with less gingerbread
than was standard for the style, with a modest
porch rather than a grand veranda.

Although the fog seemed to retreat from the
tree, it conquered the house. The pale lights inside
were barely able to pierce the windowpanes.

I passed under the tree, and psychic magnetism
drew me not toward the residence but toward the
detached garage, where a ruddy glow pressed out
from the second-floor windows, tinting the fog.

Behind the garage, a flight of stairs led to a
landing. At the top, the four French panes in the
door were curtained with pleated sheers.

As I was about to knock, the latch slipped from
the striker plate in the jamb, and the door eased
inward a few inches. Through the gap, I could
see a plastered wall where soft ringlets of shadow
pulsed in a shimmerous coppery light.

I expected the door to be caught by a security chain and to see Annamaria peering warily past those links. But no chain was engaged, and no face appeared.

After a hesitation, I pushed the door open. Beyond lay a large room softly illuminated by five oil lamps.

One lamp rested on a dinette table at which stood two chairs. Annamaria sat facing the door.

She smiled as I crossed the threshold. She raised her right hand to motion me to the empty chair.

Pleased to be out of the dampness and chilly air, I closed the door and engaged the lock.

In addition to the table and two chairs, the humble furniture included a narrow bed in one corner, a nightstand on which stood a gooseneck desk lamp, a worn and sagging armchair with a footstool, and an end table.

Distributed around the room, the five oil lamps were squat, long-necked glass vessels in which floated burning wicks. Two were the color of brandy, and three were red.

When I sat across the table from her, I found dinner waiting. Two kinds of cheese and two kinds of olives. Tomatoes cut in wedges. Circlets of cucumber. Dishes of herb-seasoned yogurt glistening with a drizzle of olive oil. A plate of ripe figs. A loaf of crusty bread.

I didn't realize how thirsty I was until I saw

the mug of tea, which tasted as if it had been sweetened with peach juice.

As decoration, in a wide shallow bowl floated three of the white flowers from the tree at the front of the property.

Without a word, we began to eat, as if there were nothing unusual about my having found her or about her expecting me.

One of the oil lamps stood on the counter in the kitchenette, the others in the main space. On the ceiling above each lamp were circles of light and tremulous watery shadows of the glass vessels.

"Very nice," I said eventually. "The oil lamps."

She said, "The light of other days."

"Other days?"

"The sun grows the plants. The plants express essential oils. And the oils fire the lamps—giving back the light of other days."

I'd never thought of the light of an oil lamp being the stored, converted, and then liberated sunshine of years past, but of course it was.

"Lamplight reminds me of my parents."

"Tell me about them."

"You would be bored."

"Try me."

A smile. A shake of the head. She continued eating and said no more.

She wore the white tennis shoes, the dark-gray slacks, and the roomy pink sweater that she had worn earlier on the pier. The long sleeves were rolled up now to form thick cuffs, exposing her slender wrists.

The graceful silver bell gleamed on the silver chain.

"The pendant is lovely," I said.

She did not reply.

"Does it have any significance?"

She met my eyes. "Doesn't everything?"

Something in her stare made me look away, and fear found me. Not fear of her. Fear of . . . I knew not what. I felt a helpless sinking of the heart for reasons that eluded me.

She fetched a ceramic pitcher from the kitchen and refreshed my tea.

When she returned to her chair, I reached across the table to her, palm turned up. "Will you take my hand?"

"You want to confirm what you already know."

I continued to reach out to her.

She acquiesced, and took my hand.

The garage apartment vanished, and I no longer sat on a chrome-and-vinyl chair, but stood upon a beach in bloody light, with the sky afire and molten masses rising in the sea.

When she released my hand, the dream relented. The only fires were those burning on the lamp wicks, safely contained in glass.

"You're part of it," I said.

"Not like the big man on the pier is part of it."

He had been surprised by the vision that I had passed to him; but Annamaria was not surprised.

She said, "That man and I are in different camps. What camp are you in, Odd Thomas?"

"Have you had the dream, too?"

"It isn't a dream."

I looked into the palm of my hand, by the touch of which she had summoned the nightmare.

When I lifted my gaze, her dark eyes were ages older than her face, yet they seemed gentle and kind.

"What's going to happen? When? Where—here in Magic Beach? And how are you a part of it?"

"That isn't for me to say."

"Why not?"

"All things in their time."

"What does that mean?"

Her smile reminded me of the smile of someone else, but I could not remember who. "It means—all things in their time."

Perhaps because time was the subject, I glanced at the lighted wall clock in the kitchen. I compared its declaration to that of my wristwatch.

The correct time was one minute until seven. The kitchen clock showed one minute until midnight, a five-hour error.

Then I realized that the thin red hand counting off the seconds had frozen on the 12. The broken wall clock had stopped.

"Your clock doesn't work."

"That depends on what you want from a clock."

"The time," I suggested.

When I returned my attention to Annamaria, I discovered that she had unclasped the silver chain and had taken it from around her neck. She held it out to me, the tiny bell suspended.

"Will you die for me?" she asked.

I said at once, "Yes," and took the offered bell.

CHAPTER 14

We continued eating, as if the conversation and the events that had occurred since I had walked through the door were as ordinary as those of any dinner hour.

In fact, people were not in the habit of asking if I would die for them. And I was not accustomed to answering in the positive, without hesitation.

I would have died for Stormy Llewellyn, and she would have died for me, and neither of us would have needed to ask the other the question that Annamaria had posed to me. Stormy and I had understood, at a level more profound than mind or heart, at the level of blood and bone, that we were committed to each other at any cost.

Although I would have given my life for my lost girl, Fate had not allowed me to make that trade. Since the bullet-shattered day in which she died, I have lived a life I don't need.

Don't get me wrong. I do not seek death. I love life, and I love the world as its exquisite design is revealed in each small portion of the whole.

No one can genuinely love the world, which is too large to love entire. To love all the world at once is pretense or dangerous self-delusion. Loving the world is like loving the *idea* of love, which is perilous because, feeling virtuous about this grand affection, you are freed from the struggles and the duties that come with loving people as individuals, with loving one place—home— above all others.

I embrace the world on a scale that allows genuine love—the small places like a town, a neighborhood, a street—and I love life, because of what the beauty of this world and of this life portend. I don't love them to excess, and I stand in awe of them only to the extent that an architect might stand in the receiving room of a magnificent palace, amazed and thrilled by what he sees, while knowing that all this is as nothing compared to the wondrous sights that lie beyond the next threshold.

Since that day of death in Pico Mundo, seventeen months earlier, my life had not been mine. I had been spared for a reason I could not understand. I had known the day would come when I would give my life in the right cause.

Will you die for me?

Yes.

Instantly upon hearing the fateful question, I felt that I had been waiting to hear it since Stormy's death, and that the answer had been on my tongue before the question had been spoken.

Although I had committed myself to this cause with no knowledge of it, I was nevertheless curious about what the men on the pier were planning, how Annamaria figured in their plans, and why she needed my protection.

With the silver chain around my neck and the small bell pendant against my breastbone, I said, "Where is your husband?"

"I'm not married."

I waited for her to say more.

With her fork she held down a fig, and with her knife trimmed off the stem.

"Where do you work?" I asked.

Setting the knife aside, she said, "I don't work." She patted her swollen abdomen, and smiled. "I labor."

Surveying the modest accommodations, I said, "I suppose the rent is low."

"Very low. I stay here free."

"The people in the house are relatives?"

"No. Before me, a poor family of three lived here free for two years, until they had saved enough to move on."

"So the owners are just . . . good people?"

"You can't be surprised by that."

"Maybe."

"You have known many good people in your young life."

I thought of Ozzie Boone, Chief Wyatt Porter and his wife, Karla, Terri Stambaugh, and all of my friends in Pico Mundo, thought of the monks at St. Bartholomew's, of Sister Angela and the nuns who ran the orphanage and school for special-needs children.

"Even in this rough and cynical age," she said, "you're neither rough nor cynical yourself."

"With all due respect, Annamaria, you don't really know me."

"I know you well," she disagreed.

"How?"

"Be patient and you'll understand."

"All things in their time, huh?"

"That's right."

"I sort of think the time is now."

"But you are wrong."

"How can I help you if I don't know what kind of fix you're in?"

"I'm not in a fix."

"Okay, then what kind of mess, what kind of pickle, what kind of trap?"

Finished eating, she blotted her mouth with a paper napkin.

"No mess, pickle, or trap," she said, with a trace of amusement in her gentle voice.

"Then what would you call it?"

"The way of things."

"You're in the way of things? What things are you standing in the way of?"

"You misheard me. What lies before me is just the way of things, not a fix from which I need to be extricated."

Out of the shallow bowl, she retrieved one of the huge floating flowers, and she placed it on her folded napkin.

"Then why did you ask that question, why did you give me the bell, what do you need me to do for you?"

"Keep them from killing me," she said.

"Well, there you go. That sounds like a pickle to me."

She plucked one thick white petal from the flower and set it aside on the table.

I said, "Who wants to kill you?"

"The men on the pier," she replied, plucking another petal from the flower. "And others."

"How many others?"

"Innumerable."

"Innumerable—as in *countless,* as in the countless grains of sand on the oceans' shores?"

"That would be more like *infinite*. Those who want me dead can be counted, and have been, but there are too many for the number to matter."

"Well, I don't know. I think it matters to me."

"But you're wrong about that," she quietly assured me.

She continued to disassemble the flower. She had made a separate pile of half its petals.

Her self-possession and calm demeanor did not change when she spoke of being the target of killers.

For a while I waited for her eyes to meet mine again, but her attention remained on the flower.

I said, "The men on the pier—who are they?"

"I don't know their names."

"Why do they want to kill you?"

"They don't yet know they want to kill me."

After considering that response for a moment and being unable to make sense of it, I said, "When will they know that they want to kill you?"

"Soon enough."

"I see," I lied.

"You will," she said.

Impurities in the wicks periodically caused the flames to leap, flutter, and subside. The reflections on the ceiling swelled, shrank, shivered.

I said, "And when these guys finally realize that they want to kill you, *why* will they want to kill you?"

"For the wrong reason."

"Okay. All right. What would the wrong reason be?"

"Because they'll think that I know what horror they intend to perpetrate."

"Do you know what horror they intend to perpetrate?"

"Only in the most general terms."

"Why not share those general terms with me?"

"Many deaths," she said, "and much destruction."

"Those are some spooky terms. And way too general."

"My knowledge here is limited," she said. "I'm only human, like you."

"Does that mean—a little bit psychic like me?"

"Not psychic. It only means that I am human, not omniscient."

She had plucked all the petals from the flower, leaving only the fleshy green receptacle, the sepals that had protected the petals, a spray of stamens, and the pistil.

I plunged into our monkey-barrel conversation once more: "When you say they'll want to kill you for the wrong reason, that implies there's a right reason for them to want to kill you."

"Not a right reason," she corrected, "but from their point of view, a better one."

"And what would be that better reason?"

At last she met my eyes. "What have I done to this flower, odd one?"

Stormy and only Stormy had sometimes called me "odd one."

Annamaria smiled, as though she knew what thought had passed through my mind, what association she had triggered.

Indicating the pile of petals, I said, "You're just nervous, that's all."

"I'm not nervous," she said with quiet conviction. "I was not asking you why I did it, only to tell me what it is that I've done to the flower."

"You've trashed it."

"Is that what you think?"

"Unless you're going to make a potpourri with it."

"When the flower was floating in the bowl, although it had been cut from the tree, how did it look?"

"Beautiful."

"Lush and alive?" she asked.

"Yes."

"And now it looks dead."

"Very dead."

She propped her elbows on the table, rested her face in her cupped hands, and smiled. "I'm going to show you something."

"What?"

"Something with the flower."

"All right."

"Not now."

"When?"

"All things in their time," she said.

"I hope I live that long."

Her smile broadened, and her voice was soft with the affection of a friend. "You have a certain grace, you know."

I shrugged and shifted my attention to the flame within the red glass lamp between us.

She said, "Let's have no misunderstanding. I mean—a grace on which you can rely."

If she thought that she had distracted me with the flower and that I had forgotten the question that she had dodged, she was wrong. I returned to it:

"If they don't want to kill you right now but *will* want to kill you soon, and for the wrong reason—what is the right reason? I'm sorry. Excuse me. I mean, what is the *better* reason they might have for wanting you dead?"

"You will know when you will know," she said.

"And when will I know?"

As she replied, I answered my question in sync with her: "All things in their time."

Crazily, I did not believe that she was withholding information or was speaking in riddles either to deceive me or to entice me. She impressed me as being absolutely truthful.

Furthermore, I had the sense that everything she had said had carried more meaning than I had taken from it, and that eventually, when I looked back on our dinner, I would realize that on this night, in this hour, I should have known her for who she was.

With both hands, Annamaria picked up her mug of tea and sipped from it.

She looked no different in this flattering lamplight from the way that she had looked in the gray light of late afternoon, on the pier. Neither beautiful nor ugly, and yet not merely plain. Petite yet somehow powerful. She had a compelling presence for reasons that I could not define, a presence that was not as magnetic as it was humbling.

Suddenly my promise to keep her safe was a weight on my chest.

I raised one hand to the pendant that I now wore.

Lowering the mug of tea, she looked at the bell captured between my thumb and forefinger.

I said, " 'The bell invites me . . . it is a knell that summons me to Heaven or to Hell.' "

"Shakespeare," she said. "But that's not quite the quote. And a man like you doesn't need to doubt his ultimate destination."

Again I lowered my gaze to the oil lamp. Perhaps because my imagination is so rich, I saw the leaping flame fashion itself, for just a moment, into the image of a dragon rampant.

Together, without more talk, we quickly cleared the table, hastily put away the uneaten food, rinsed and stacked the dishes.

Annamaria retrieved a car coat from a closet and pulled it on as I employed a long-handled wick pincher to snuff the flame in the kitchen lamp, and also the one in the lamp by which we had eaten dinner.

She came to me with just a purse, and I said, "You may need more than that."

"I don't have much else," she said, "some clothes, but suddenly I don't think we have time."

The same hunch had harried me into quickly cleaning off the dinner table.

"Put out the other lamps," she said, withdrawing a flashlight from the purse. "Quickly."

I extinguished the remaining three flames.

As she played the flashlight across the floor, toward the door, out of the silent night came the roar of an approaching vehicle, a truck by the sound of it.

At once, she hooded the beam to prevent it from brightening the windows.

Brakes barked in the night, and the previously racing engine only idled now—in the driveway in front of the garage above which we waited.

A truck door slammed. And then another.

CHAPTER 15

"This way," she said, and with the flashlight still hooded, Annamaria led me to a door that I assumed must open on a closet.

Instead, a landing lay beyond, and narrow interior stairs went down to the garage.

Although sturdy, the stairhead door could be locked only from inside the apartment. If the hulk and his friends got into the apartment, we could not foil their pursuit.

Because Annamaria was pregnant and because I was afraid that, in a rush, she might trip and fall, I took the flashlight and urged her to hold fast to the railing and to follow me with caution.

Filtering the beam through fingers, holding the light behind me to illuminate her way more than mine, I descended into the garage less quickly than I would have liked.

I was relieved to see that the roll-up door featured no glass panels. Two windows, one in the north wall and one in the south, were small and set just below the ceiling.

Our light was not likely to be seen through those high dusty panes. Nevertheless, I continued to keep the lens half covered.

Two vehicles were parked in the garage: facing out, a Ford Explorer; facing in, an older Mercedes sedan.

As Annamaria reached the bottom of the stairs, she whispered, "There's a way out, along the south wall."

From above came the knock of knuckles on the door to her tiny apartment.

Through the smell of grease and oil and rubber, wary of putting a foot in a slippery spot on the floor, we moved past the SUV, past the sedan, and found the side exit.

Overhead, a second round of knocking sounded more insistent than the first. Definitely not just a pizza delivery.

With the thumb-turn knob, I disengaged the deadbolt. Because the door opened inward, it did not block my view in any direction when I leaned through to have a look outside.

The Victorian house stood to the north side of this building, out of sight. Here, a narrow walkway lay between the south wall of the garage and the high hedge that defined the property line.

If we stepped outside and went east, toward the front of the garage, we would find our visitors' truck in the driveway. If we went west, toward the back of the structure, we would be at the foot of the stairs that led up to the landing, where someone had just been knocking.

Even in the dense fog, I did not want to place a bet on our chances of getting off the property without encountering trouble. Two doors had slammed, so two men were out there—at least two—and I did not think they would both have gone up the outer stairs, since they had not arrived with a large gift basket, wine, and flowers. One of them would remain behind to snare us if we escaped from the man now knocking upstairs.

Turning from the door, leaving it open, I scanned the shadowy ceiling and saw no fluorescent fixtures, only one bare incandescent bulb. Another light would be built in to the chain-drive mechanism that raised the large roll-up, but it would come on only when that door was up.

When I guided Annamaria toward the Mercedes sedan, she trusted me at once. She neither resisted nor asked what I intended.

The knocking had stopped. From above came a subtle crack of breaking glass, which the visitor could not entirely muffle.

As I took hold of the handle on the rear passenger-side door, I was suddenly afraid that the car would be locked. Our luck held, and the door opened.

Overhead, the footsteps were so heavy that I

would not have been surprised if they had been accompanied by a giant's voice chanting, "Fee, fi, fo, fum," and promising to grind up our bones to make his bread.

The interior lights of the Mercedes were not bright. We had no choice but to risk them.

As I encouraged Annamaria into the backseat of the sedan, I saw in my mind's eye the modest apartment above us. The intruder would see the stacked dishes in the sink: two mugs, two sets of flatware. Sooner than later, he would touch the long neck of one of the oil lamps.

The glass would not be merely warm, but hot. With a smile, he would snatch back his stung fingers, certain that we had fled only as he had arrived.

I glanced toward the south-wall door that I had left standing open to the walkway alongside the property-line hedge. Tendrils of fog crept across the threshold and probed around the jamb, like the fingers of a blind ghost, but no one had yet appeared in the doorway.

Annamaria slid across the backseat, and I climbed into the sedan after her. I pulled the door shut firmly without slamming it, though with more noise than I would have liked. The interior car lights winked out.

The Mercedes was at least twenty years old, maybe twenty-five, from the era when the Germans still made them big, boxy, and not in the least aerodynamic. We were able to slide down in that roomy space, heads below the windows.

This was not quite Poe's purloined-letter trick, but something similar. Our pursuers would expect us to flee, and the open south-side door would suggest that we had done just that.

In the heat of the moment, believing they were close on our heels, they were not likely to suspect that we would risk hiding in what was virtually plain sight.

Of course, they *might* find the open door and the in-creeping fog to be a tad too obvious. They might decide to search the garage, and if they did, we were doomed.

They were not fools, after all. They were serious men. I had it on good authority that they were planning many deaths and much destruction; and men don't get much more serious than that.

CHAPTER 16

Huddling in the back of the Mercedes, we had arrived at one of those moments of extreme stress that I mentioned earlier, one of those awkward situations in which my imagination can be as ornate as a carousel of grotesque beasts, standing on end like a Ferris wheel, vigorously spinning off visions of ludicrous fates and droll deaths.

If we were found, these men could shoot us through the windows. They could open the doors and shoot us point-blank. They could bar the doors, set the car on fire, and roast us alive.

Whatever they chose to do to us, we would not die as easily as any of those scenarios allowed. They would first need to find out who we were and what we knew about their plans.

Torture. They would torture us. Pliers, sharp blades, needles, red-hot pokers, nail guns, garlic presses applied to the tongue. Blinding bleach, caustic acids, unpleasant-tasting elixirs, secondhand smoke. They would be enthusiastic torturers. They would be relentless. They would enjoy it so much that they would take videos of our suffering to play later for their adoring mothers.

I had told Annamaria that I was prepared to die for her, and I had told the truth, but my vow had come with the implicit promise that I would also not lead her to her death *before* I died for her. At least not in the same hour that I had solemnly sworn to be her protector.

Someone switched on the single bare bulb in the garage ceiling. The car was parked nose-in, which meant we were at the front of the garage, farther from the stairs than anywhere else we could have hidden. The light proved too weak to penetrate to our dark little haven.

Mercedes' engineers could be proud of their skill at providing sound attenuation. If someone was poking around the garage, opening the door to the water-heater closet or peering behind the furnace, I could not hear him.

Silently I counted sixty seconds, then another sixty, and then a third set.

Timing our confinement proved to whittle my nerves, so I stopped counting minutes and waited, trying not to think about torture.

The interior of the old Mercedes smelled of well-worn leather, mentholated liniment, gardenia-based perfume, cat dander, and dust.

An urge to sneeze overcame me. In a spirit of

Zen stoicism, I meditated on transforming the urge
to sneeze into an itch between my shoulder blades,
which I would have been more able to endure.
When that did not work, I meditated on transforming the urge to sneeze into a benign colon polyp.

After tightly pinching my nose and breathing
through my mouth for a while, I began to believe
that the agents of the nefarious harbor department would have by now concluded that
Annamaria and I had escaped. They must have
gone away.

As I cautiously raised my head, intending to
scope the garage, two male voices rose nearby,
one deep-toned and the other full of wheedle. I
dropped back into my hole as though I were a
jack-in-the-box.

Annamaria reached out of the shadows and
found my hand. Or maybe I reached out and
found hers.

I could not discern what the men were saying.
Clearly, however, one of them was angry, and the
other was making excuses.

A loud crash followed by a diminishing clatter
suggested that the deep-voiced one had knocked
over something or had thrown a heavy object at
the excuse-maker.

As the argument continued, I realized that
Annamaria's hand in mine seemed to give me
courage. My racing heart began to slow and my
teeth unclenched.

The two men proved to be closer than I had first realized. To make a point, the angrier one pounded a hand three times on the hood or on a front fender of the sedan in which we had taken refuge.

CHAPTER 17

The deep-voiced thug, who most likely had yellow eyes and a chin beard and a reservation for a bed of nails in Hell, pounded on the Mercedes again.

In our inadequate hidey-hole in the backseat of that very sedan, Annamaria squeezed my hand gently, reassuringly.

My eyes had adapted to the gloom. I could see her face just well enough to know that she was smiling as though to say that this would prove to be a temporary setback in our escape, that soon we would be skipping through meadows full of flowers, where iridescent butterflies would dance through the air to the sweet songs of larks and robins and bright yellow warblers.

I knew that she was not stupid, and I doubted that she would prove to be foolish. Consequently, I assumed that either she knew something that I did not or that she had more faith in me than my survival skills justified.

As the argument subsided, the voices grew quieter. Then they moved away from the Mercedes.

The garage light went off.

A door closed.

I could no longer see Annamaria's face. I hoped that she was not smiling at me in the dark.

Although it is not a full-blown phobia, I am made uncomfortable by the thought of people smiling at me in the dark, even people as benign—and even as good-hearted—as this woman seemed to be.

In the movies, when a character in a pitch-black place strikes a match and finds himself face to face with someone or something that is grinning at him, the someone or something is going to tear off his head.

Of course, movies bear virtually no resemblance to real life, not even the kind that pile up awards. In movies, the world is either full of fantastic adventure and exhilarating heroism—or it's a place so bleak, so cruel, so full of treachery and vicious competition and hopelessness that you want to kill yourself halfway through a box of Reese's miniature peanut-butter cups. There's no middle ground in modern movies; you either save a kingdom and marry a princess or you are shot to death by assassins hired by the evil corporation that you are trying to bring to justice in the courtroom of a corrupt judge.

Outside, a truck engine started. The noise ebbed, and silence flowed back into the night.

I remained slouched in the dark car for a minute, perhaps being smiled at, perhaps not, and then said, "Do you think they're gone?"

She said, "Do *you* think they're gone?"

Over dinner, I had agreed to be her paladin, and no self-respecting paladin would decide on a course of action based on a majority vote of a committee of two.

"All right," I said, "let's go."

We climbed out of the sedan, and I used the flashlight to find our way to the man-size door in the south wall. The hinges creaked when it swung open, which I had not noticed previously.

In the narrow passage between the garage and the tall hedge, no one waited to tear off our heads. So far so good. But they would be waiting elsewhere.

After dousing the flashlight, I hesitated to lead her out to the driveway and the street, for fear that a sentinel had been stationed there.

Intuiting my concern, Annamaria whispered, "At the back, there's a gate to a public greenbelt."

We went to the rear of the building. Passing the steps that led to her apartment, I glanced up, but no one was looking down at us.

We crossed the foggy yard. Slick yellow leaves littered the wet grass: fall-off from sycamore trees that held their foliage longer on this stretch of the central coast than elsewhere.

In a white fence with scalloped pickets stood a gate with carved torsades. Beyond lay the green-belt. A sward of turf vanished into the mist to the south, west, and north.

Taking Annamaria's arm, I said, "We want to go south, I think."

"Stay near the property fences here along the east side," she advised. "The greenbelt borders Hecate's Canyon to the west. It's narrow in some places, and the drop-off can be sudden."

In Magic Beach, Hecate's Canyon was legendary.

Along the California coast, many ancient canyons, like arthritic fingers, reach crookedly toward the sea, and any town built around one of them must unite its neighborhoods with bridges. Some are wide, but more of them are narrow enough to be called defiles.

Hecate's Canyon was a defile, but wider than some, and deep, with a stream at the bottom. Flanking the stream—which would become a wilder torrent in the rainy season—grew mixed-species junk groves of umbrella pine, date palm, *Agathis*, and common cypress, gnarled and twisted by the extreme growing conditions and by the toxic substances that had been illegally dumped into the canyon over the years.

The walls of the defile were navigable but steep. Wild vines and thorny brush slowed both erosion and hikers.

In the 1950s, a rapist-murderer had preyed on the young women of Magic Beach. He had dragged them into Hecate's Canyon and forced them to dig their own graves.

The police had caught him—Arliss Clerebold, the high-school art teacher—disposing of his eighth victim. His wispy blond hair had twisted naturally into Cupid curls. His face was sweet, his mouth was made for a smile, his arms were strong, and his long-fingered hands had the gripping strength of a practiced climber.

Of the previous seven victims, two were never found. Clerebold refused to cooperate, and cadaver dogs could not locate the graves.

As Annamaria and I walked south along the greenbelt, I dreaded encountering the spirits of Clerebold's victims. They had received justice when he had been executed in San Quentin; therefore, they had mostly likely moved on from this world. But the two whose bodies had never been found might have lingered, yearning for their poor bones to be reinterred in the cemeteries where their families were at rest.

With Annamaria to protect and with the responsibility to thwart whatever vast destruction was on the yellow-eyed hulk's agenda, I had enough to keep me busy. I could not afford to be distracted by the melancholy spirits of murdered girls who would want to lead me to their long-hidden graves.

Concerned that even thinking about those sad victims would draw their spirits to me, if indeed they still lingered, I tried to elicit more information from Annamaria as we proceeded cautiously through the nearly impenetrable murk.

"Are you originally from around here?" I asked softly.

"No."

"Where are you from?"

"Far away."

"Faraway, Oklahoma?" I asked. "Faraway, Alabama? Maybe Faraway, Maine?"

"Farther away than all of those. You would not believe me if I named the place."

"I would believe you," I assured her. "I've believed everything you've said, though I don't know why, and though I don't understand most of it."

"Why do you believe me so readily?"

"I don't know."

"But you do know."

"I do?"

"Yes. You know."

"Give me a hint. Why do I believe you so readily?"

"Why does anyone believe anything?" she asked.

"Is this a philosophical question—or just a riddle?"

"Empirical evidence is one reason."

"You mean like—I believe in gravity because if I throw a stone in the air, it falls back to the ground."

"Yes. That's what I mean."

"You haven't been exactly generous with empirical evidence," I reminded her. "I don't even know where you're from. Or your name."

"You know my name."

"Only your first name. What's your last?"

"I don't have one."

"Everybody has a last name."

"I've never had one."

The night was cold; our breath smoked from us. She had such a mystical quality, I might have been persuaded that we had exhaled the entire vast ocean of fog that now drowned all things, that she had come down from Olympus with the power to breathe away the world and, out of the resultant mist, remake it to her liking.

I said, "You had to have a last name to go to school."

"I've never gone to school."

"You're home-schooled?"

She did not reply.

"Without a last name, how do you get welfare?"

"I'm not on the welfare rolls."

"But you said you don't work."

"That's right."

"What—do people just give you money when you need it?"

"Yes."

"Wow. That would be even less stressful than the tire life or shoe sales."

"I've never asked anyone for anything—until I asked you if you would die for me."

Out there in the dissolved world, St. Joseph's Church tower must have remained standing, for in the distance its familiar bell tolled the half-hour, which was strange for two reasons. First, the radiant dial of my watch showed 7:22, and that seemed right. Second, from eight in the morning till eight in the evening, St. Joe's marked each hour with a single strike of the bell and the half-hour with two. Now it rang three times, a solemn reverberant voice in the fog.

"How old are you, Annamaria?"

"In one sense, eighteen."

"To go eighteen years without asking anyone for anything—you must have known you were saving up for a really big request."

"I had an inkling," she said.

She sounded amused, but this was not the amusement of deception or obfuscation. I sensed again that she was being more direct than she seemed.

Frustrated, I returned to my former line of inquiry: "Without a last name, how do you get health care?"

"I don't need health care."

Referring to the baby she carried, I said, "In a couple months, you'll need it."

"All things in their time."

"And, you know, it's not good to go to term without regularly seeing a doctor."

She favored me with a smile. "You're a very sweet young man."

"It's a little weird when you call me a young man. I'm older than you are."

"But nonetheless a young man, and sweet. Where are we going?" she wondered.

"That sure is the million-dollar question."

"I mean right now. Where are we going now?"

I took some pleasure in answering her with a line that was as inscrutable as anything that she had said to me: "I have to go see a man with hair like wool-of-bat and tongue like fillet of fenny snake."

"*Macbeth,*" she said, identifying the reference and robbing me of some of my satisfaction.

"I call him Flashlight Guy. You don't need to know why. It's liable to be dicey, so you can't go with me."

"I'm safest with you."

"I'll need to be able to move fast. Anyway, I know this woman—you'll like her. No one would think of looking for either of us at her place."

A growling behind us caused us to turn.

For an instant it seemed to me that the hulk had followed us and, while we had been engaged in our enigmatic conversation, had by some magic separated himself into three smaller forms. In the fog were six yellow eyes, as bright as road-sign reflectors, not at the height of a man's eyes but lower to the ground.

When they slunk out of the mist and halted just ten feet from us, they were revealed as coyotes. Three of them.

The fog developed six more eyes, and three more rangy specimens arrived among the initial trio.

Evidently they had come out of Hecate's Canyon, on the hunt. Six coyotes. A pack.

CHAPTER 18

Having lived where prairie met Mojave, in Pico Mundo, I had encountered coyotes before. Usually the circumstances were such that, being skittish about human beings, they wanted to avoid me and had no thought of picking my bones.

On one late-night occasion, however, they had gone shopping for meat, and I had been the juiciest item in the display case. I barely escaped that situation without leaving behind a mouthful of my butt.

If I had been Hutch Hutchison and had found myself on the menu of a coyote pack twice within seventeen months, I would have viewed this not as an interesting coincidence but as irrefutable scientific proof that coyotes as a species had turned against humanity and were intent on exterminating us.

In the fog, on the greenbelt, alongside Hecate's Canyon, the six prime specimens of *Canis latrans* had none of the appeal of any of the various species and breeds that pet shops put in their windows.

This was unusual, believe it or not, because coyotes sometimes can have a goofy charm. They are more closely related to wolves than to dogs, lean and sinewy, efficient predators, but with feet too big for their bodies and ears too big for their heads, they can appear a little puppylike, *at least* as cute as Iran's homicidal dictator when he puts on a leisure suit and has his photo taken eating ice-cream cones with grade-school children whose parents have volunteered them to be suicide bombers.

With narrow faces, bared fangs, and radiant-eyed intensity, these current six coyotes confronting Annamaria and me did not have what it took to be featured in a Purina Puppy Chow commercial. They looked like fascist jihadists in fur.

In most perilous moments, I can put my hands on a makeshift weapon, but on this empty greensward, the only possibility seemed to be a wooden fence pale if I could break one of them loose. No rocks. No baseball bats, buckets, brooms, antique porcelain vases, frying pans, shovels, pop-up toasters, or angry cross-eyed ferrets, which had proved to make effective impromptu weapons in the past.

I began to think I really needed to get over my gun phobia and start packing heat.

As it turned out, I had a weapon of which I was unaware: one young, pregnant, enigmatic woman. As I urged her to back slowly away from the toothy pack, she said, "They are not only what they appear to be."

"Well, who is?" I said. "But I think these guys are *largely* what they appear to be."

Instead of cautiously retreating from the beasts and hoping to discover an unlocked gate in a fenced backyard, Annamaria took a step toward them.

I said what might have been a bad word meaning excrement, but I hope that I used a polite synonym.

Quietly but firmly, she said to the coyotes, "You do not belong here. The rest of the world is yours . . . but not this place at this moment."

Personally, I did not think it was good strategy to tell a pack of hungry carnivores that would-be diners without the proper attire would not be served.

Their hackles were raised. Their tails were tucked. Their ears were flat to their heads. Their bodies were tense, muscles tight.

These guys were up for a meal.

When she took another step toward them, I said nothing because I was concerned my voice would sound like that of Mickey Mouse, but I reached after her and put a hand on her arm.

Ignoring me, she said to the coyotes, "I am not yours. He is not yours. You will leave now."

In some parts of the country, coyotes are called prairie wolves, which sounds much nicer, but even if you called them fur babies, they would not be cuddly bundles of joy.

"You will leave now," she repeated.

Astonishingly, the predators seemed to lose their confidence. Their hackles smoothed down, and they stopped baring their teeth.

"Now," she insisted.

No longer willing to meet her eyes, they pricked their ears and looked left, right, as though wondering how they had gotten here and why they had been so reckless as to expose themselves to a dangerous pregnant woman.

Tails in motion, ducking their heads, glancing back sheepishly, they retreated into the fog, as if they had previously been foiled by Little Red Riding Hood and now *this*, leaving them deeply unsure of their predatory skills.

Annamaria allowed me to take her arm once more, and we continued south along the greenbelt.

After some fruitless reflection on the meaning of what had just transpired, I said, "So, you talk to animals."

"No. That's just how it seemed."

"You said they were not only what they appeared to be."

"Well, who is?" she asked, quoting me, which will never be as enlightening as quoting Shakespeare.

"What were they . . . in addition to what they appeared to be?"

"You know."

"That's not really an answer."

She said, "All things in their time."

"That's not an answer, either."

"It is what it is."

"Yes, I see."

"Not yet. But you will."

"I never saw the White Rabbit, but we've fallen out of the world into Wonderland."

She squeezed my arm. "The World itself is a wonderland, young man, as you well know."

Off to our right, visible only now and then as shadowy forms along the edge of Hecate's Canyon, the coyotes skulked parallel to us, and I called them to her attention.

"Yes," she said, "they will be persistent, but do they dare look toward us?"

As we proceeded, I watched them for a while, but not once did I glimpse the faintest flicker of a radiant yellow eye in the murk. They seemed to be focused strictly on the ground before them.

"If you can handle a coyote pack," I said, "I'm not sure you really need me."

"I have no influence over people," she said. "If they wish to torture and murder me, and they are determined to shatter all my defenses, then I will suffer. But coyotes—even beasts like these—don't concern me, and they shouldn't worry you."

"You seem to know what you're talking about," I said. "But I'm going to worry a little about the coyotes anyway."

"'Virtue is bold, and goodness never fearful.'"

I said, "Shakespeare, huh?"

Measure for Measure."

"I don't know that one."

"Now you do."

As much as I admired the Bard of Avon, it seemed to me that goodness needed to be fearful of those slouching shapes in the fog if goodness wanted to avoid being chewed up and swallowed.

CHAPTER 19

A few blocks before we arrived at the Cottage of the Happy Monster, our skulking escorts faded away into the fallen clouds and did not return, although I suspected that we had not seen the last of them.

The house stood alone at the end of a narrow lane of cracked and runneled blacktop. Huge deodar cedars flanked the road, their drooping branches seeming to carry the fog as if it had the weight of snow.

With a thatched and dormered roof, cedar-shingle walls, trumpet vines espaliered along the roof line, and a bougainvillea-covered porte-cochere, the large cottage could have been copied from one of the romantic paintings of Thomas Kinkade.

Like curious spooks, pale shapes of curdled mist pressed to the casement windows, gazing in, as though deciding whether the rooms inside were conducive to haunting.

A dark amber glow of considerable appeal shone through those phantom spirits. As we drew closer, I saw that this cheerful light glimmered and twinkled along the beveled edges of the diamond-shaped panes of glass, as though a person of magical power resided within.

As we had approached along the lane, I had prepared Annamaria for Blossom Rosedale, with whom she would be staying for an hour or two. Forty-five years ago, when Blossom had been six years old, her drunk and angry father dropped her headfirst into a barrel in which he had been burning trash primed with a little kerosene.

Fortunately, she had been wearing tightly fitted glasses, which spared her from blindness and saved her eyelids. Even at six, she'd had the presence of mind to hold her breath, which saved her lungs. She managed to topple the barrel and quickly crawl out, though by then aflame.

Surgeons saved one ear, rebuilt her nose—although not to the extent that it resembled a normal nose—and reconstructed her lips. Blossom never had hair thereafter. Her face remained forever seamed and puckered with keloid scars too terrible to be addressed by any surgical technique.

Out walking a week previously, I had encountered her as, with a flat tire, she pulled to the side of the road. Although she insisted that she could change the tire herself, I did the job because Blossom stood under five feet, had only a thumb and forefinger on her burned left hand, and had not been dressed for the rain that threatened.

With the spare tire in place, she had insisted that I come with her for coffee and a slice of her incomparable cinnamon-pecan cake. She called her home the Cottage of the Happy Monster, and though the place was a cottage and she was a deeply happy person, she was no more a monster than was Spielberg's E.T., whom she somewhat resembled.

I had visited her once again in the week since we had met, for an evening of five-hundred rummy and conversation. Although she had won three games out of three, with stakes of a penny for every ten points of spread, she and I were on the way to becoming good friends. However, she did not know about the supernatural side of my life.

Now, when she opened the door in answer to my knock, Blossom said, "Ah! Come in, come in. God has sent me a sucker to fleece at cards. Another prayer answered. I'll have my Mercedes yet."

"You won fifty cents the last time. You'll need to beat me every day for a thousand years."

"And won't that be *fun*!" Blossom closed the door and smiled at Annamaria. "You remind me of my cousin Melvina—the married Melvina, not the Cousin Melvina who's an old maid. Of course, Cousin Melvina is crazy, and presumably you are not."

I made introductions while Blossom helped Annamaria out of her coat and hung it on a wall peg.

"Cousin Melvina," Blossom said, "has a problem with a time traveler. Dear, do you believe time travel is possible?"

Annamaria said, "Twenty-four hours ago, I was in yesterday."

"And now here you are in today. I'll have to tell my cousin about you."

Taking Annamaria by the arm, Blossom walked her toward the back of the cottage.

"Cousin Melvina says a time traveler from 10,000 A.D. secretly visits her kitchen when she's sleeping."

As I followed them, Annamaria asked, "Why her kitchen?"

"She suspects they don't have cake in the far future."

The cottage was magically lit by Tiffany-inspired stained-glass lamps and sconces, the shades of which Blossom had crafted herself.

"Does Melvina have a lot of cake in her kitchen?"

"She's a positive fanatic for cake."

On a living-room wall hung a colorful and intricately detailed quilt of great beauty. Blossom's quilts sold in art galleries; a few museums had acquired them.

"Perhaps her husband is having midnight snacks," Annamaria said.

"No. Melvina lives in Florida, and her husband, Norman, he lives in a former Cold War missile silo in Nebraska."

From a kitchen cabinet, Blossom took a container of coffee and a package of filters, and gave them to Annamaria.

As Annamaria began to prepare the brewer, she said, "Why would anyone want to live in an old missile silo?"

Opening a tin of cookies, Blossom said, "To avoid living with Melvina. She'd go anywhere with him, but not into a missile silo."

"Why wouldn't there be cake in the far future?" Annamaria asked.

With pastry tongs, Blossom transferred cookies from the tin to a plate. "Melvina says maybe they lost all the best recipes in a world war."

"They had a war over cake?"

"Probably the war was for the usual reasons. Cake would have been collateral damage."

"She does sound kind of crazy."

"Oh, yes," said Blossom, "but not in a bad way."

Standing in the open door, I said, "Annamaria is in a little trouble—"

"Pregnancy isn't trouble," Blossom said, "it's a blessing."

"Not that. Some bad guys are looking for her."

"Bad guys?" Blossom asked Annamaria.

"Nobody's inherently bad," said Annamaria. "It's all about the choices we make."

"And the Deceiver," said Blossom, "is always there to whisper the wrong choice in your ear. But I believe remorse can lead to redemption."

"Some people," I said, "the only way they get around to remorse is after you break a baseball bat over their head."

"When he sobered up, my father regretted what he did to me," said Blossom.

"Some people," I testified, "they lock you in a car trunk with two dead rhesus monkeys, put the car in one of those huge hydraulic crushers, push the SQUISH-IT button, and just laugh. They don't even know the word *regret*."

"Did you forgive your father?" Annamaria asked.

"He's eighty-two," Blossom said. "I pay his nursing-home bills. But I don't see him."

"Some people," I said, "they lose their temper and you have to take a gun away from them, and you give them a chance to rethink what they did, and they *say* they were wrong, they're remorseful, but then they let you walk into a room where they *know* there's a crocodile that hasn't been fed in a week."

Both women gave me the kind of look you usually reserve for a two-headed man walking a blue dog.

"I'm not saying everyone," I clarified. "Just *some* people."

To Blossom, Annamaria said, "But you forgave your father."

"Yes. A long, long time ago. It wasn't easy. The reason I don't see him is because he can't take it. Seeing me tears him apart. The guilt. It's too hard on him."

Annamaria held out a hand, and Blossom took it, and then they hugged each other.

I said, "So, these bad guys looking for Annamaria and me—I need to poke around, learn more about them. I thought she'd be safe here with you for a couple hours, if you're cool with that."

To Annamaria, Blossom said, "We could play cards or Scrabble or backgammon or something."

"I like backgammon," Annamaria said. "Do you ever add a little vanilla to your coffee when you brew it?"

"Sometimes vanilla, sometimes cinnamon."

"Cinnamon. That sounds good."

"Cousin Melvina—not the one married to Norman in the missile silo, the other one—she likes to add a half-teaspoon of cinnamon and a full teaspoon of cocoa to a twelve-cup pot."

"That sounds good to me. Let's do that. Why would parents name both daughters Melvina?"

"Oh," said Blossom, fetching the can of cocoa powder, "they aren't sisters. They're cousins to each other. They were both named after our maternal grandmother, Melvina Belmont Singleton, who was famous in her time."

"Famous? For what?"

"For living with gorillas."

"What gorillas did she live with?"

"Oh, anywhere they had gorillas, sooner or later, she went there to live with them."

"What was she—a naturalist or an anthropologist?"

"No, she wasn't any of that. She just thought the world and all of gorillas, couldn't get enough of watching them, and the gorillas didn't seem to mind."

"I'd think they would mind," Annamaria said.

"Well, when scientists move in to study them, the gorillas sometimes give them a lot of grief, but they didn't object to Grandma Melvina."

"She must have been a formidable person."

"We have strong women in our family," said Blossom.

"I can see that," said Annamaria, and they smiled at each other.

Blossom said, "Grandma Melvina taught a gorilla named Percy to write poetry."

Annamaria said, "Free verse, I imagine."

"No sane person would have paid for it," Blossom said, and they both laughed.

I wanted to hear more about Grandma Melvina and the gorillas, but I needed to have a serious talk with Flashlight Guy. Blossom and Annamaria were having such a good time, I didn't interrupt to tell them that their Odysseus was about to set sail on his warship.

Crossing the living room, I noticed that the mantel clock read one minute till midnight.

According to my wristwatch, the time was 7:52.

At the mantel, I put one ear to the clock, but it seemed to have spent its treasure of time, and it did not pay out a single tick.

Throughout my life, when the supernatural had become apparent to me in the natural world, it had always been through my paranormal senses, shared by no one else: the ability to see the lingering spirits of the dead, the frustrating gift of enigmatic predictive dreams, and psychic magnetism.

The stopped clock in Annamaria's one-room apartment had not been a vision but a reality, seen not just by me, but visible to her as well. I had no doubt that if I were to call her and Blossom from the kitchen, they would see what I saw on the mantel.

One clock frozen at a minute until midnight is nothing more than a broken clock. In this night of fog and spellbound coyotes and porch swings that swung themselves, however, meaning could not be denied upon the discovery of a second timepiece with its hands fixed at the very minute of the same hour.

The supernatural had entered the natural world

in ways new to my experience, and this development struck me as ominous.

I could think of only one interpretation to be made of broken but synchronized clocks. Only a little more than four hours remained for me to prevent the many deaths and the vast destruction planned by the yellow-eyed giant and his associates.

CHAPTER 20

A dove descending through candescent air, a bush bursting into fire and from the fire a voice, stars shifting from their timeless constellations to form new and meaningful patterns in the heavens . . .

Those were some of the signs upon which prophets historically had based their predictions and their actions. I received, instead, two stopped clocks.

If I am not just a freak whose extrasensory perceptions are the result of a few mutated synapses making strange connections in my brain, if my gift has a giver other than indifferent Nature and comes with a purpose, then the angel in charge of the Odd Thomas account must be operating on a shoestring budget.

Making my way through Magic Beach, toward the address I had found in the wallet of Sam Whittle—alias Sam Bittel, known to me affectionately as Flashlight Guy—I felt as if the fog drowning the town had flooded into my head. In that internal mist, my thoughts were as disconnected as, in the outer world, houses on the same block seemed to be separate islands, each a stranger to the other, in a white sea.

More traffic rolled through the quiet night than I had seen earlier.

Some of the vehicles were at such a distance, passing across the streets on which I traveled, that I could make out little more than the submerged glow of their headlights. Perhaps some were driven by ordinary men and women engaged upon the mundane tasks of daily life, with neither an unworthy thought nor an evil purpose among them.

At the first sight of any vehicle that shared a street with me, I hid behind the nearest cover and, from concealment, watched as it drifted past. One after another proved either to be labeled HARBOR DEPARTMENT or to be a police car.

Perhaps the police had put their entire motor pool on the streets because the cloaking fog facilitated burglary and other crimes. Call me paranoid, but I suspected the authorities were out in force only to support certain friends in the harbor department.

Through windshields and side windows, I glimpsed a few faces barely and queerly revealed in the glow of instrument panels and computer screens. None looked suitable for a poster celebrating the friendliness and selflessness of our public servants.

I felt as though extraterrestrial seeds, come quietly to Earth behind the curtains of fog, had grown swiftly into large pods that had been busily disgorging men who were not men.

Sam Whittle lived on Oaks Avenue, which was not grand enough to warrant being called an avenue, and was not shaded by oaks. Formerly called Founders Street, it had been renamed in honor of John Oaks, a sports star who never lived in Magic Beach or even visited, but whose cousin— or a woman who claimed to be his cousin—served on the city council.

Whittle lived in a bungalow as unremarkable as a cracker box, graced by no ornamental millwork, as plain as the fog that embraced it. The front porch was unfurnished, the yard devoid of landscape lighting, and the back porch as empty as the front.

No light brightened any window. No vehicle stood in the carport.

At the back door, I took a laminated driver's license from Sam Whittle's wallet and used it to loid the lock. The deadbolt had not been engaged, and when the license pressed back the latch, the door swung inward with a faint creak of hinges.

For a moment I remained on the porch, letting the fog precede me, searching the perfect darkness within, listening for the telltale sound of an impatient adversary shifting his weight from one foot to the other as he waited for the fly to come into the web.

Warily I stepped across the threshold. I left the door open for the moment, to facilitate sudden flight.

The digital clocks on the oven and the microwave had not frozen at a minute until midnight, but neither did the green glow of those numbers alleviate the gloom.

I smelled some kind of whiskey, and I hoped that it didn't come to me on the exhalations of a man with a gun.

When I held my breath, I heard nothing— except perhaps another man holding his breath.

Finally I committed. I closed the door behind me.

Had someone been in the room, he would have switched on a light just then, and I would have seen my fate in the muzzle of his gun.

Perhaps I had done more damage to Flashlight Guy than he had done to me, requiring him to visit a hospital emergency room for a few stitches in the scalp. The suturing would not have taken long, but the emergency-admissions clerk would have required him to fill out, read, and sign six pounds of paperwork, including ninety legal disclaimers and liability-release forms; thereafter, they might keep him an hour or two for observation. In any case, he would be home soon.

Counseling myself to be out of this house in five minutes or less, I switched on Annamaria's flashlight, with which I had led the way from her apartment into the garage below it.

Narrowing the beam with two spread fingers, I sectioned the room—a kitchen—left to right. The blade of light, in the fourth slice, found the source of the whiskey smell.

A bottle of Jack Daniel's and a glass stood on the dinette table. The cap was off the bottle, and the glass held bourbon that appeared to have been watered down, perhaps by melted ice.

Another glass lay on its side. A small puddle of spilled bourbon glistened on the table.

The evidence suggested Whittle had returned home after regaining consciousness, and had left again in too much of a hurry to clean up the spill.

Two chairs stood away from the table. Before leaving, the drinkers had not taken time to tuck the chairs where they belonged.

A pair of unlaced men's shoes were under the table, one lying on its side. Whittle could have changed shoes before leaving. Or he might still be here.

Because vinyl blinds had been drawn down tight at every window, I stopped pinching the flashlight beam and let it flourish.

A narrow hallway led from the kitchen past a living room full of lifeless furniture, where the draperies were drawn shut and where no art adorned the walls.

I had been in the house approximately one minute.

Across the hall from the living room lay a study with a couch, a desk, a chair, bookshelves. Here, too, the blinds allowed no view of the night.

The desk top had been swept bare. The bookshelves were empty.

I suspected that this place had been rented furnished and that Sam Whittle had not lived here more than a few weeks, having made no plans to settle in long-term.

Nevertheless, I wanted to search the desk drawers, although not until I determined Whittle was not here, either awake or sleeping.

In the final room, the bedclothes were disheveled. A pillow had fallen to the floor.

On the carpet, a damaged earthworm slowly writhed. It must have been brought in on someone's shoe or pants leg. If it had been there more than a little while, it would already have died.

Outside, a truck engine growled in the distance and swiftly approached. I switched off the flashlight, although the windows were covered.

The vehicle seemed to take forever to pass, but eventually the engine noise faded.

When I switched on the flashlight, the dying earthworm had nearly finished flexing.

Although the house was small, I felt that I was a long way from an outside door and a quick escape.

I clicked off the light again, drew open a set of draperies, and unlatched the double-hung window. Concerned that the wood might be swollen in the humid night, I was relieved when the bottom sash slid up with little noise.

I closed the window but did not lock it. I pulled the draperies across the window before switching on the flashlight again.

Two minutes.

The sliding doors of the closet were shut. I disliked turning my back on them.

Yet intuition drew me toward the bathroom. The gap at the base of that door admitted no light from the other side; but I have not survived by ignoring intuition.

When I put my hand on the knob, a shiver of trepidation climbed my spine, from sacrum to topmost vertebrae, and it seemed like a worm wriggled in the very axis on which my head turned.

Without realizing what I was doing, I had raised my left hand to my chest. Through the sweatshirt and the T-shirt, I could feel the thimble-size bell that hung from the silver chain around my neck.

I turned the knob. The door opened inward. No one flung himself at me or struck out.

The flashlight played across the surfaces of a

bathroom from the 1940s: a field of glossy white ceramic tiles on the floor, enhanced with inlays of small pastel-green tiles, the grout cracked with age and dirty; a reversal of that scheme on the walls, a pale-green field punctuated by white inlays.

From directly ahead came a silvery splash of flashlight flaring off a mirror, then my reflection uplighted by the beam bouncing off the floor.

To my left a shower stall featured a frosted-glass door in an aluminum frame crusted with white corrosion.

To my right lay a bathtub, and in the tub a dead man languished, he who had been Flashlight Guy.

The shock of such a discovery would provide the ideal moment for an assailant to strike. Glancing at myself in the mirror, I saw with relief that no one loomed in the bedroom behind me.

Sharing this small space with a corpse, I wanted more light than the flashlight could provide. A shutter covered the only window in the bathroom, so I risked switching on the over-head light.

Sam Whittle had died in a sitting position. He remained that way because his shirt collar was snared on the hot-water faucet. His head lolled to the left.

Duct tape sealed his mouth, and something—most likely a rag—bulged behind it. They had gagged him because they had not killed him quickly.

His wrists had been taped together in front of him, and his shoeless feet had been fettered at the ankles with tape, as well.

Bathed in blood, he apparently had been shot once in each leg, once in each arm, and—after writhing not unlike a dying worm—had finally been shot in the forehead.

In the cauldron tub, he was as fearsome as any witch's brew.

A starburst hemorrhage obscured his left eye, but the right stared at me, wide in the expression of disbelief with which he must have regarded his murderer. He had not expected death to come in the form of whoever had killed him.

No matter how many dead bodies one has discovered—and I have found more of them than has the average fry cook—the sight instantly focuses the mind, draws the nerves taut, and puts a sharp point on instinct.

Almost three minutes.

When I glanced at the mirror again and saw a man behind me, I ducked and turned and punched.

CHAPTER 21

The punch landed but had no effect, for the man behind me was Sam Whittle, who had been shot five times. His bullet-riddled body sat in the bathtub, and his lingering spirit implored rather than threatened me.

Although he had manifested without the bullet wounds, he stood before me in a state of high agitation. He exhibited none of the rage that is the mark of a potential poltergeist. The desperation that gripped him was so intense that he possessed no remaining emotional capacity for anger.

He grabbed at me, and I seemed to feel as solid to him as he felt to me, but he could not gather fistfuls of my shirt. His hand, when cupped around the back of my neck, could not pull my head toward him and compel my attention.

Although he could pass through walls and closed doors and all that had substance in this world, he could not pass through me, yet neither could he so much as muss my hair. By sight and touch, the form and substance of his spirit were real to me, as they would be real to no one else on the earth, but Sam Whittle could not have any physical effect on me.

When he realized his limitations, Whittle spoke urgently but produced no sound. Perhaps he heard himself and thought that I could hear him, because I had to speak up and tell him that his voice would never reach me regardless of the force with which he shouted.

I suspect that lingering spirits are restrained from speech because they know in fullness the true nature of death and at least something about what lies beyond this world. This is knowledge that might corrupt the living and misdirect us in one way or another if we were to receive it.

Denied speech, Whittle quickened into an even more frantic state of desperation, moving past me into the bathroom, to stand before his corpse. The spirit beat its fists against its chest, against its temples, as if to argue that it felt solid to itself and thus could not believe that it was in fact only a disembodied soul, that all life had bled out of its earthly shell.

Wild-eyed, Whittle surveyed the room, as though seeking a route of escape, a return door to life. Across his face writhed a series of expressions, each more despairing and more anguished than the one that preceded it.

Desperation is energized despair, and despair is the abandonment of hope. Without hope, he had no defense against fear, which quickly swelled into a purity of terror from which I had to look away.

Over the years I have had reason to believe that most of the lingering dead are those who are destined for a better world than this one, if only they will receive it. They resist moving on for a variety of reasons, none of them rational.

Elvis had loved his mother so profoundly and had lost her so early, that after his death he longed to leave this world and to be in her company once more. But because he felt that he had not lived his life in a manner that she would have approved, because he was loath to face her judgment of his drug use and his promiscuity and his general dissolution, he had lingered here until at last he became convinced that what waited for him was forgiveness that surpassed understanding.

Those whose lives had included insufficient acts of kindness and good will to outweigh the evil they had done, or who had done nothing but evil, did not often linger here after death. And those of their kind who did linger were not here for years, but usually for days or hours.

Because they never believed in hope while alive, I assumed their hopelessness stayed with them after death. Maybe they traveled into darkness eternal without protest because they lacked the imagination to envision anything else.

Another possibility was that, upon death, they had a debt to pay. I could envision a collector of those debts who had no patience for lingering debtors.

Whittle's behavior suggested that he faced something worse than an easy passage into peaceful darkness. As he accepted mortality and could no longer deny the corpse in the bathtub, his terror escalated.

Perhaps half a minute or forty seconds had passed since he had first appeared in the bathroom doorway.

What happened next happened fast, and it was a center-stage moment worthy of Second Witch, she who had no other name in *Macbeth*.

Whittle moved around the bathroom with the frenzied urgency of a bird that, having flown in through an open window, could not detect the draught that would lead it back to freedom.

In the play, Second Witch had stood over a cauldron, squeezing drops of her blood into the brew: *By the pricking of my thumbs* . . .

Desperately circling the room, Whittle made no sound equivalent to the swoop-and-flutter of a bird, and in fact no sound whatsoever. Yet I half thought there were wings that I *should* hear if only I knew how to listen.

By the pricking of my thumbs, something wicked this way comes.

Enter a player more terrible than Macbeth.

The bathroom light dimmed as if a great machine had surged on elsewhere in town, drawing power from the grid.

In half-light halved again, shadows swelled and swooned, and I thought I felt the wings that I could not hear, the rhythmic pulses of pressure from air beaten by great pinions.

I cannot testify with certainty to what I saw, because it defied interpretation both by my five senses as well as by those perceptions of mine that might be called extrasensory. I had never seen anything like it before—and hoped never to see its like again.

The spirit of Sam Whittle might have thrown itself against the mirror above the sink, but I think not. What seems more true is that the mirror reached out to seize the spirit of Sam Whittle.

Further: that the mirror was for a moment more than a mirror, that it unfolded from the wall, that the glass unfurled like fabric, forming mercurial membranes full of dark reflections of both the bathroom and of some more fantastical place.

Also: that those undulant plumes were simultaneously as reflective as polished silver and yet dark with tarnish, that they embraced Whittle's spirit and swept it up into the chaos of images that swarmed across their fluttering surfaces.

And finally: that his spirit was gathered into the membranes, that the membranes furled into the mirror, and that as the mirror quivered into stillness like a pond after swallowing a stone, there was for only an instant a face peering out at me, not Whittle's face but another so hideous that I cried in alarm and reeled back.

The Presence appeared so briefly that I cannot remember the grisly details of it, so briefly that it was only my reflection at which I shouted, from which I stumbled backward.

I almost fell, reached for something to steady myself, and grabbed the handle of the shower door. The latch released. The door came open. I stood face to face with another corpse.

CHAPTER 22

Four minutes.

In the kitchen, the man's shoes had been under that side of the table on which the glass of bourbon had been overturned. This woman must have been drinking from the other glass.

The killers had cinched a braided-leather belt around her neck and had hung her from the shower head. Her feet dangled two inches off the floor.

Ceramic tiles had cracked under the strain of her suspended weight. Ancient grout had crumbled to the floor of the shower stall. The water pipe had bent, but no leak had sprung.

Fortunately, I didn't have to examine the victim to see how she had died. Her face was a ghastly portrait of strangulation. Perhaps her neck had broken, too.

In life, she must have been attractive. She might have been in her twenties; but in one brutal minute, she had aged a decade.

Like Whittle, she had been bound with duct tape at the ankles and the wrists, and also gagged.

The line of sight between the tub and the shower stall made it likely that Sam Whittle had been forced to watch them hang the woman.

I had seen enough, too much.

The irrational conviction arose that if I looked at the cadavers again, their eyes would roll in their sockets to fix on me, and they would smile and say, *"Welcome."*

Above the sink, the streaked mirror appeared to be an ordinary looking-glass, but it had transformed once, so might transform again.

I was alive, not a lingering spirit, but I could not be sure that the collector who had taken Whittle lacked the power to take me.

Leaving the bathroom, I did not turn off the lights, but pulled the door tight shut.

For a few seconds I stood in the bedroom with the flashlight extinguished, less afraid of the dark than of the sights that light could show me.

They would not have killed Flashlight Guy merely because he had failed to subdue me on the beach when I had swum to shore from the inflatable dinghy. Whittle and the woman must have disagreed with the other conspirators about something, and must not have foreseen the ferocity with which their associates would settle a difference of opinion.

Usually I am pleased when bad guys fall out

with one another, because disharmony in their ranks can make them easier to defeat. But if this crew was planning many deaths and vast destruction such that the sky and sea would burn with bloody light, as in my dream, I would feel better if they were not also hair-trigger hotheads in addition to being criminal scum.

I switched on the flashlight and hurriedly searched the dresser drawers. They contained only clothes, and not many of those.

Although I had been in the house no more than five minutes, the time had come to get out. Maybe these murders had been impromptu; if so, the killers might return to remove the bodies and clean up the evidence of violence.

Twitching as if electrical impulses short-circuited through the frayed fibers of my nerves, I thought that I heard stealthy noises elsewhere in the house.

Chastising myself for being too easily spooked, I nevertheless decided not to leave by the way I had entered.

Dousing the flashlight, I swept aside the draperies. The window sash slid up as smoothly as it had moved previously.

From the back of the bungalow came the crash of a door being kicked open, and an instant later the front door was booted in as well.

I had spoken of one devil, and another had arrived. Murderers, returning to the scene of a crime, intent on removing the evidence, would never call attention to themselves by kicking down the doors any more than they would arrive blowing party horns.

From within the house, men shouted: *"Police!"*

I slipped out of the bungalow as quickly and as quietly as an experienced sneak thief, which is perhaps not a skill that I should trumpet with pride.

As though it were a living entity that could reproduce itself, the fog seemed to have fathered new generations of fog, crowding the night more completely than when I'd gone inside five minutes earlier.

The police had arrived without sirens and also without switching on the emergency-light arrays on their patrol cars. No revolving red or blue beacons stained the fog.

Again I thought of seed pods from outer space disgorging men who were not men. Although I didn't believe that the Magic Beach Police Department was staffed by extraterrestrials passing for human, I did suspect that at least some of them were less than exemplars of law enforcement.

Because I had taken Sam Whittle's wallet on the beach but had not taken his money, they had thought I might look him up to ask a few questions. They had entered the bungalow as if they knew two bodies were stashed there—which meant I had been lured inside to take the fall for the murders.

As I came out the window, the police were entering the bungalow by the front and the back. Not all of them would go inside.

Foiled by the density of the fog, a flashlight appeared at the front corner of the house.

The beam could not reach me. While I was still unable to see the officer behind the light and while I was likewise invisible, I moved blindly away from him, across a lawn.

Another flashlight quested through the murk at the back of the bungalow.

Turning from that one, as well, I headed toward what I thought must be the property next door, although I could see no house lights. The men inside the bungalow would soon find the window that I had left open, and upon making that discovery, they would focus all their resources in this direction.

When I walked boldly into a chain-link fence that marked the property line, the shaken barrier seemed to sing *here he is, here he is, here he is.*

CHAPTER 23

In defense of my sneak-thief reputation, I must point out that no shrubs fronted the fence to warn me of it. No climbing vine grew on it, the tendrils of which might have brushed my face, halting me inches short of the collision. The steel chain was pretty much the color of the fog.

I am not one who believes that life is unfair or that we are all victims of a cruel or indifferent universe, but *this fence* struck me as unfair to the extent that I might have sat down and pouted about it if my freedom and possibly even my life hadn't been in jeopardy.

As soon as the chain-link announced my ineptitude, one of the men behind me said "What was that?" and the other one said "Yancy, is that you?" and both flashlights probed toward the source of the chain song.

I had nowhere to go but up, so I climbed, strumming a harpist-from-Hell tune from the chain-link, hoping I would not encounter coils of lacerating razor wire at the top.

Behind me, entirely comfortable with clichés, a cop shouted, "Stop or I'll shoot!"

I doubted they could see me yet, and I didn't believe they would lay down a barrage of random fire in a residential neighborhood.

As I climbed, however, I tightened my sphincter muscles against the prospect of a bullet in the spine, because you never know what might happen in a universe that, at a critical moment, throws an invisible chain-link fence in front of you.

Sometimes when people are shot in the spine and take more than an instant to die, they lose control of their bowels. I tightened my sphincter so that my corpse would not be an embarrassment to me or to those who had to deal with it. While I am ready to die if I must, I have an aversion to dying filthy.

Good fences make good neighbors, and these were apparently good enough that they had not felt the need for razor wire at the top. I crested the fence, threw myself into the yard beyond, fell, rolled to my feet, and ran with the expectation of being garroted by a taut clothesline.

I heard panting, looked down, and saw a golden retriever running at my side, ears flapping. The dog glanced up at me, tongue lolling, grinning, as though jazzed by the prospect of an unscheduled play session.

Because I did not think a dog would run head-on into a fence or into the side of a house, or into a tree, I sprinted boldly through the clotted clouds, eyes directed down at my guide, acutely alert to his body language. I broke left and right each time that he did, keeping him close, though it occurred to me that if he was a dog with a sense of humor, he would race past a tree with no room to spare and leave me with my face embedded in bark.

Dogs do laugh, as any true dog lover knows. In my blind run, I took courage from the knowledge that dogs do not have a cruel sense of humor. They will laugh at human folly and stupidity, but they will not encourage it.

To my surprise, as I ran with the retriever, through my mind flew a fragment of my conversation with Annamaria as we had walked the greensward along Hecate's Canyon, when she had tried to help me understand why I believed everything she told me even though I had not understood most of it:

Why do you believe me so readily?

I don't know.

But you do know. . . .

Give me a hint. Why do I believe you so readily?

Why does anyone believe anything?

With the retriever, I ran headlong into a white opacity because I trusted in the essential goodness and the instincts of dogs. *Trust.* I also trusted

Annamaria, which was why I believed what she told me, as cryptic and evasive as her words sometimes seemed.

Trust, however, could not be the answer. If trust was the reason I believed her, that raised a subsequent question equal to the first: If I believed her because I trusted her, then why did I trust her, considering that she was a virtual stranger and that she seemed to be calculatedly mysterious?

The golden retriever was having so much fun that I wondered if he might be running me in circles around his master's house. But my trust in him proved well placed when he brought me to a gate in the chain-link fence.

I tried to keep him from getting out of the yard, but he proved too agile to be blocked. Free, he did not sprint away into the night but stayed nearby, waiting to see what fun thing I might want to do next.

To the south, swords of light dueled in the fog, seeking me. The dog and I went north.

CHAPTER 24

A universal solvent poured through the world, dissolving the works of man and nature.

Shapes like buildings loomed in vague detail. Geometric fence rows separated nothing from nothing, and their rigid geometry melted into mist at both ends.

Portions of trees floated into and out of sight, like driftwood on a white flood. Gray grass spilled down slopes that slid away as though they were hills of ashes too insubstantial to maintain their contours.

The dog and I ran for a while, changed direction several times, and then we walked, out of nil and into naught, through vapor into vapor.

At some point I became aware that the weather was something more than mere weather. The stillness and the fog and the chill were not solely the consequences of meteorological systems. I began to suspect and soon felt certain that the condition of Magic Beach on this night was a presentiment, a symbolic statement of things to come.

The dog and I journeyed through a dreamscape where thick smoke smoldered from fires long extinguished, and the fumes had no odor in a world purged of every stink and fragrance.

The air pooled in stillness because the winds had died and would never breathe again, and the silence betold a world of solid stone, where the planetary core had gone cold, where no rivers ran and seas no longer stirred with tides, where no clocks existed because no time remained to be counted.

When the dog and I stopped and stood entirely still, the white *nada* settled under us, no longer disturbed by our passage, and the pavement began to disappear beneath my feet, beneath his paws.

Such a terror rose in me that I exhaled explosively with relief when the sudden swish of his tail disturbed the bleached void and revealed, after all, the texture of the blacktop.

Yet a moment later, I felt that I had entered the Valley of Death and at once had passed into some place beyond even that, into an emptiness of such perfection that it contained no atom of the world that had been, not even a memory of nature or of the things of man, a place that lacked the substance to be a place, that was more accurately a condition. Here no hope existed for the past or for a future, no hope of the world that had been or of the world that might have been.

I was not *having* a premonition; instead, I was walking through a night that had *become* a premonition. Black is the combination of all colors, and white is the utter absence of color. The fog foretold the nullity of nonbeing, a vacuum within a vacuum, the end of history following the ultimate annihilation.

So much death was coming that it would be the end of death, such absolute destruction that nothing would escape to be destroyed hence. The terror that the dog's tail briefly brushed away returned to me and would not be dispelled again.

For a while I was aware of proceeding from nothing into nothing, my mind a deep well from the bottom of which I tried to scream. But like the lingering dead who came to me for assistance, I was not able to make a sound.

I could only pray silently, and I prayed to be led to a haven, a place with shape and color and scent and sound, a refuge from this awful nothingness, where I could press back the terror and be able to *think*.

Like a dreamer aware of dreaming, I knew that a geometric shape half resolved out of the amorphous clouds. And I was conscious of the exertion of climbing steps, though I never saw them.

I must have found the heavy door and pulled it wide, but even after I had crossed the threshold into shadow and light, with the golden retriever still at my side, and even after I had closed out the foreboding mist, I did not immediately realize the nature of the refuge into which I had been led by providence or by canine.

After the whiteness that denied all senses, the fragrances of wood polish and candle wax were so poignant that they brought tears to my eyes.

I passed through a low-ceilinged, wood-paneled room into a much larger and somewhat brighter space before realizing that I had gone from the narthex into the nave of a church.

Beside me, the dog panted with thirst, anxiety, or both.

The side aisles were softly lighted, but the main aisle lay in shadow as I followed it to the chancel railing.

Although I intended to sit in the front pew until my braided nerves untwisted, I settled on the floor because the dog needed to have his tummy rubbed. He had earned all the affection— and more—that I could give him in my current distracted state of mind.

When I am battered and oppressed by the world that humanity has made—which is different from the world that it was given—my primary defense, my consolation, is the absurdity of that world.

The given world dazzles with wonder, poetry, and purpose. The man-made world, on the other hand, is a perverse realm of ego and envy, where power-mad cynics make false idols of themselves and where the meek have no inheritance because they have gladly surrendered it to their idols in return not for lasting glory but for an occasional parade, not for bread but for the promise of bread.

A species that can blind itself to truth, that can plunge so enthusiastically along roads that lead nowhere but to tragedy, is sometimes amusing in its recklessness, as amusing as the great movie comedians like Buster Keaton, Laurel and Hardy, and the many others who knew that a foot stuck in a bucket is funny, that a head stuck in a bucket is funnier, and that trying stubbornly to move a grand piano up a set of stairs obviously too steep and narrow to allow success is the hilarious distillation of the human experience.

I laugh with humanity, not at it, because I am as big a fool as anyone, and bigger than most. I style myself as a paladin for both the living and for the lingering dead, but I have been stuck in more than my share of buckets.

At that moment in the church with the dog, recalling the dead bodies in the bungalow bathroom, worrying about the meaning of the premonition of total destruction, I could not work up a smile.

I might have fallen into depression; but experience had taught me that another foot-and-bucket moment would come along soon.

When after a few minutes the dog continued

panting, I told him to stay, and I went in search of water.

A glance toward the back of the nave confirmed that no holy-water font stood at the entrance.

Behind the altar hung a big abstract sculpture that might have been a winged spirit soaring, but only if you cocked your head to the left, squinted, and thought about Big Bird from *Sesame Street.*

I opened the gate in the chancel railing and stepped into the sanctuary.

To the right stood a plain marble baptismal font. It was dry.

On reflection, I realized that appropriating cere-monial water for a thirsty dog might be disrespectful if not even sacrilegious.

I moved deeper into the sanctuary, toward a door that I assumed opened into the sacristy, where the vestments were kept and where the minister prepared before a service. In St. Bartholomew's Church in Pico Mundo, where Stormy Llewellyn's uncle had been the priest, the sanctuary had included a small lavatory with a sink.

When I opened the door, I surprised a fiftyish man who seemed to be ordering the contents of a closet. Chubby but not fat, well barbered but not in an affected way, possessed of quick reactions but not of good balance, he startled backward at the sight of me, stepped on his own foot, and fell on his rump.

I apologized for frightening him, and he apologized for using foul language, but he must only have cursed me in his mind because he had said nothing in his startlement except *ook*.

By the time I had helped him to his feet and he had twice nearly pulled me off mine, I explained that I was seeking water for my dog, and he identified himself as Reverend Charles Moran. His eyes were merry, and when he assured me that his fall had not been as terrible as Satan's, I saw that he amused himself, and I liked him for that.

From a mini-refrigerator, he withdrew a bottle of water and from the closet a shallow dish. Together we went to the golden retriever, where he lay obediently in front of the chancel railing.

Reverend Moran did not suggest that I had been wrong to bring the dog into the church, but only asked his name. I didn't know the name and didn't want to explain how the retriever and I had come to be together, so I said his name was Raphael.

For an instant, I did not understand why I had chosen Raphael instead of Fido. Later, I would realize what had inspired the name.

When asked *my* name, I said it was Todd.

This was not exactly a lie. My parents insisted that they meant to name me Todd but a mistake had been made on my birth certificate—which did not explain why they had called me Odd forever thereafter.

Besides, when I say that my name is Odd, a series of tiresome misunderstandings and explanations ensues. After my adventures since late afternoon, I did not have the patience to thread the needle of my true name for the minister.

We knelt by the dog as he drank, and Reverend Moran asked if I was new in town.

I said that I had been there about a month, and he asked if I was looking for a church to join. I told him that I had stopped in this evening to pray because my life had taken a wrong turn.

The reverend proved discreet enough not to press me about the nature of my troubles, trusting in his counseling skills to tease my story from me in the course of easy conversation.

Although I had come to Magic Beach alone—but for Boo and Frank Sinatra—I was incomplete without a family of close friends. I am no good alone. I need bonds, vows real if unspoken, shared laughter, and people who depend on me as I depend on them.

Hutch was turned too far inward to be more than a casual friend. I had not known the wonderful Blossom Rosedale long enough to share the truest things with her.

At ease on the floor with the dog, the reverend had a relaxed manner and an open heart. Speaking with him for a few minutes made me feel less alone.

I did not tell him more about myself, but

somehow we got around to the subject of Armageddon. That was not surprising. These days, with most people, doomsday seemed to crop up in conversation more than it once did.

Eventually Reverend Moran asked if Raphael might be as hungry as he had been thirsty, and I said maybe so, but I did not want him to bother himself about it. He said it was no bother, he had a dog of his own, and he went away to get some biscuits from the pantry in the rectory.

Charles Moran's companionship had taken the edge off the fear that my premonition of total destruction had aggressively sharpened.

The dog solicited more attention, and I was pleased to respond, because in the human-dog relationship, both are therapists.

After a few minutes, however, Raphael scrambled to his feet. His ears lifted as much as a retriever's ears could lift. He stood alert, staring at the sacristy door at the back of the sanctuary.

I assumed that Reverend Moran must be returning with biscuits and that the dog had smelled them at a distance.

When Raphael shifted his attention from the sacristy door to the back of the church, peering toward the narthex, toward the main door through which we had earlier entered, I got up from the floor.

EVERYONE A NEIGHBOR, EVERY NEIGHBOR A FRIEND.

Maybe the community motto did not apply to

newcomers until they had been in residence a year. I had not read the fine print on the sign that welcomed visitors at the town limits. Maybe during your first year, you were fair game.

Life had not taught me to distrust ministers, but it had taught me to trust no one more than dogs.

I went to the third pew on the right. A long wooden pocket on the back of the second-row pews held hymnals for use by those who sat in the third row.

From my left hip pocket, I fished out Sam Whittle's wallet, the possession of which would be incriminating now that he lay dead in his bathtub. Hymnals were lined up in the holding pocket, but there were spaces between them. I dropped the wallet in one of those gaps.

Nothing would be gained by revealing more about myself than the name Todd. I fished my wallet from my other hip pocket and secreted it with Whittle's.

I returned to the dog and stood with him, glancing from the sacristy door to the narthex, sacristy to narthex. . . .

The first two police officers came through the main entrance, crossed the narthex, and stepped into the nave. They did not draw their pistols, but they approached along the center aisle with their hands on the butts of those weapons.

A policeman also stepped out of the sacristy,

onto the altar platform. He was in his late forties, a decade older than the two officers in the center aisle. His prematurely gray hair was shorn close on the sides, as flat on top as brush bristles.

He possessed an air of authority that had nothing to do with his uniform. If you encountered him in his undershorts, you would still call him sir and do what he told you to do—or be prepared to pay a high price for disobedience.

Reverend Charles Moran followed Brush Cut out of the sacristy. He met my gaze and did not look away, but his eyes were not as merry as they had been earlier.

I asked him why, and when he did not answer, I asked him again, but the reverend seemed not to hear me, and he would not speak to me, though we were both alive and neither of us governed by the law of silence imposed on the lingering dead.

CHAPTER 25

I had ridden in a squad car before, back in Pico Mundo. Although this was not my first time, it was still kind of cool.

Police headquarters—which included a small jail—was a Greek Revival building that stood adjacent to the courthouse, on the park, in one of the most picturesque parts of town. Now it beetled in the fog like a medieval fortress.

The watch officer's desk, the booking station, and all of that would be on the main floor at the front of the building. The two young officers parked in an alleyway behind the building and took me in through a back door.

Earlier at the church, they had searched me for weapons. Here, I expected them to take my wristwatch and the silver-bell pendant, and ask me to sign a receipt acknowledging that they had confiscated no additional items of value.

I also expected them to fingerprint me and take my photo. And it was my understanding that they might allow me to call an attorney if not book an appearance on a reality-TV courtroom show.

Instead, they escorted me along a hallway with depressing blue-speckled linoleum and walls the color of tubercular phlegm, through a door, down two flights of stairs, along another hallway with an intriguingly stained concrete floor, through another door, and into a bleak windowless room that smelled of a pine-scented disinfectant strong enough to kill asthmatics and, under that, subtly of vomit.

This chamber measured about twelve by fifteen feet. A concrete floor, concrete walls, and a low concrete ceiling offered little to work with for even the most talented interior designer.

A square metal table and two chairs stood in the center of the room.

A third chair had been placed in a corner. Maybe that was where they would make me sit if I didn't behave.

One of the officers pulled out a chair for me, which seemed to be a hopeful sign that they were respectful of a prisoner's innate human dignity.

But then the other guy shackled my right ankle to a ringbolt that was built in to the table leg. Although he did not handle me roughly, he did seem to be contemptuous of me.

Without informing me of what crime I was suspected of having committed, not bothering to explain the system for ordering a snack if I should want one, they went out and closed the door, leaving me alone.

Coming in, I had noticed that the door was so thick it must have been designed by a paranoid. It closed with the solid clunk of one thousand pounds of steel.

They had left me with nothing to do except contemplate my pain threshold and my mortality, which was probably their intention.

The table to which I had been shackled seemed heavy but not immovable. I felt sure that I could drag it around my windowless prison, but as the room offered nothing to see or do, I remained seated.

When I peered under the table, I noted an eight-inch-diameter drain with a slotted grille. Considering that Magic Beach had no history of floods, I supposed that this design feature facilitated the hosing-out of the room after unfortunate accidents.

This was one of those sobering circumstances in which my overheated imagination, if I were not careful, could cause a portion of my cerebellum to melt down, and set my hair on fire. I counseled myself that I remained in the United States, which was not Cuba or Venezuela, or even Mordor.

I consulted my watch—8:56. I still had a few minutes more than three hours to save the world or a significant portion thereof. No problem.

Because I had firm control of myself, I did not care when nothing happened by 8:57 or by 8:58, although I was within seconds of shouting strident demands for justice when the door finally opened at 8:59.

One man entered the room, but he was enough. At the church, I had thought of him as Brush Cut, but I had since learned that his name was Hoss Shackett and that he was the chief of police.

Hoss must have been the short form of a longer name, but I didn't know what that might be. I had asked the younger officers in the car but they had twice refused to answer me; and the third time that I asked, they had advised me to perform an act of reproduction with myself.

After closing the blastproof door—of which Norman must have several in his Cold War missile silo in Nebraska—the chief came to the table and stood staring down at me. He didn't say anything. He just stared.

I smiled and nodded. He didn't.

After I had busied myself for a while staring at my hands and wondering what they would look like after being smashed with a tire iron, the chief pulled out the other chair and sat down across the table from me.

When I looked up, ready to parry his questions, he still did not speak. He continued to stare at me.

He had ugly green eyes colder than those of a snake, although I would not have made this observation to his face or, for that matter, within one hundred miles of his jurisdiction.

I am not a stickler for etiquette, but I did not feel that it was my place to initiate our conversation.

After a while, I could not bear to stare into his venomous eyes any longer. Either I had to look away from him, which he would take as a sign of weakness, or I had to say something that would force him to speak.

"I imagine," I said with a relaxed affability that surprised me, "you've mistaken me for someone else."

He neither replied nor broke eye contact.

"I have never been in trouble with the law," I told him.

He remained fixated on me and was so still that I could not be sure that he breathed—or needed to.

If there was a Mrs. Hoss, she was either psychological wreckage or one tough mama.

"Well," I said, and could think of nothing to add.

At last he blinked. It was a slow blink, as if he were an iguana dazed by desert sun.

He held out his right hand and said, "Take my hand."

I knew what this was about, and I wanted no part of it.

His hand remained above the table, palm up.

He had hands big enough to play professional basketball, although the most sporting thing he had probably ever done with them was bash suspects' heads together.

Over the years, I had read thrillers in which the authors wrote things like "the air was full of violence" and "the pending violence hung over the scene like black thunderheads." I had always judged this to be clumsy writing, but maybe they should have won Nobels and Pulitzers.

"Take my hand," Hoss Shackett repeated.

I said, "I'm already dating someone."

"What's the point of dating if your pecker's broken off?"

"It's a platonic relationship, anyway."

My hands were folded on the table. Viper-quick, he struck, seizing my left hand, folding it tight enough in his to make me wish I'd had my knuckles surgically removed.

The grim concrete cell vanished, and I stood once more on Armageddon Beach, in a tempest of crimson light.

Chief Hoss Shackett was not a man who lightly revealed what he was feeling or thinking. But when he dropped my hand, returning me to reality, and leaned back in his chair, I could tell from a slight widening of his pupils that he had shared my nightmare vision.

"So," I said, "what was *that* about?"

He did not reply.

"Because," I said, "that has only happened to me once before, and it freaks me out."

He had a hard strong face that Stalin would have envied. His jaw muscles were so knotted at the hinges that he appeared able to crack walnuts in his teeth.

"Nothing like this—sharing a dream—has ever happened to me before," I assured him. "It's every bit as awkward for me as it is for you."

"Sharing a dream."

"I had this dream, and now people touch me and I'm thrown back into it. What is this—the Twilight Zone?"

He leaned forward, a small move, but it was like being in a Jurassic meadow when the *T. rex* that has its back to you casually looks over its shoulder.

"Who are you?" he asked.

"I have no idea."

"I won't keep asking nice like this."

"Sir, I appreciate how nice you've been. I really do. But I'm serious. I have amnesia."

"Amnesia."

"Yes."

"That's pathetic."

"It really is. Not knowing my past, my name, where I'm from, where I'm going. It's totally pathetic."

"You told Reverend Moran your name was Todd."

"Sir, I swear, it was just a name to tell him. I could have said Larry or Vernon, or Rupert, or Ringo. I could be anybody. I just do not know."

He did the staring thing again. It was as effective as it had been previously. Second by second, I became increasingly convinced that if I didn't spill everything about myself, he would bite off my nose. For starters.

Although he would infer weakness if I looked away from him, I had to break the stare before his eyes sucked out my soul. I examined my left hand to confirm that he had returned it with all my fingers.

With the solemnity of Darth Vader, the chief said, "You aren't carrying any identification."

"Yes, sir. That's right. If I had some identification, I'd know who I was."

"I don't like people in my town not carrying ID."

"No, sir, you wouldn't like that, you being a man of the law. I wouldn't like it if I were in your shoes, even if there's nothing in the Constitution that requires a person to carry ID."

"You're a constitutional scholar, are you?"

"No. Well, I guess I could be. I won't know until I recover my memory. What I think happened was somebody mugged me."

Gingerly I felt the lump on the side of my head, which Whittle had raised with his flashlight earlier in the night.

The chief watched me rub the lump, but he said nothing.

"Whoever mugged me and gave me amnesia, he must have taken my wallet."

"When were you mugged? Tonight on the beach?"

"On the beach? Tonight?" I frowned. "No, sir. I think it must have been a lot earlier in the day."

"People don't get mugged in my town in broad daylight."

I shrugged.

Clearly, he did not like the shrug. I couldn't take it back.

"So you're saying you were mugged before you jumped off the pier this afternoon?"

"Yes, sir. In fact the first thing I remember is walking along the boardwalk toward the pier, wondering who I am and where I am and whether I had lunch or not."

"Why did you jump off the pier?"

"Since being mugged unconscious, sir, my behavior hasn't been entirely rational."

"Why did you tell Utgard that a thirty-foot tsunami was coming?"

"Utgard?"

"Utgard Rolf."

"Is that a person, sir?"

"You'll remember him. A walking mountain with a chin beard."

"Oh, yes. He seemed nice. Excellent taste in Hawaiian shirts. I don't remember telling him about a tsunami, though. I must have been delirious from the mugging."

"Utgard put a hand on your shoulder—and saw the very thing I just saw when I touched your hand. He described it to me."

"Yes, sir. You and him. It happened twice now. It's the dream I had while I was mugged unconscious, before I found myself on the boardwalk, heading toward the pier."

"Tell me about your dream."

"There's not much to tell, sir. You saw it. The red sky, the sea full of light, the sand so bright, very scary."

The pupils of his eyes grew wider, as if he intended to switch off the lights and hunt me down like a serpent chasing a mouse.

"Very scary," I repeated.

"What do you think it means?"

"Means? The dream, sir? I've never had a dream mean anything. That's for those old movies with Gypsies."

Finally he looked away from me. He stared so long at the third chair in the corner that I turned my head to look at it.

Mr. Sinatra sat there. I don't know how long he had been in the room. He pointed at me as if to say *Looking good, kid.*

Hoss Shackett did not see the Chairman of the Board. He was staring into space, perhaps envisioning my evisceration.

The chief bent his fingers and studied his well-manicured nails as though checking to be sure that no dried blood remained under them from his most recent interrogation session.

He gazed at the massive door for a while, and I suppose he was recalling how effectively it had contained the screams of those who had been in this room before my visit.

When he shifted his attention to the oppressively low ceiling, he smiled. He had the kind of smile that, if he turned it on the sky, would cause birds to fall dead in flight.

He looked down at the steel top of the table. He leaned forward to consider his blurry image in the surface, which had been burnished by years of wear and by a multitude of sweaty hands.

His reflection was not recognizable as his face or as a face at all. It was a series of smears, dark whorls, lumpy and distorted.

He seemed to like himself that way, however, because he smiled once more.

Chief Hoss was making me so crazy that I wished he would look at me again.

My wish was answered. He met my eyes.

He said, "Kid, what do you say—let's you and me be friends?"

I said, "That would be swell, sir."

CHAPTER 26

Chief Hoss Shackett underwent a change worthy of one of those intelligent alien machines in that toy-based movie, *Transformers*, that can morph from an ordinary period Dodge into a giant robot with a hundred times the mass of the vehicle from which it unfolded.

I do not mean that the chief suddenly filled the cell and left me without elbow room. He metamorphosed from Mr. Hyde, if Mr. Hyde had been a sadistic warden in a Soviet gulag, into the benign Dr. Jekyll, if Dr. Jekyll had been a folksy sheriff from a small town where the biggest crime in twenty years had been when Lulamay copied Bobbijune's rhubarb-jam recipe and passed it off as her own in the county-fair competition.

The eat-your-liver-with-fava-beans grin melted into the smile of any grandfather in any TV commercial featuring cute little kids frolicking with puppies.

The knotted muscles in his face relaxed. The

tension went out of his body. As if he were a chameleon moving from gray stone to a rose, a touch of pink appeared in his skin.

Amazingly, the venomous green shade of his eyes changed, and they were now Irish eyes, happy and full of delight. Even his eyes were smiling, his lips and his eyes, his entire face, every line and plain and dimple of his countenance marshaling into a spectacle of sublime good will.

The previous Hoss Shackett could never have become the chief of police of Magic Beach, which was an elected position. Before me now was Hoss Shackett, the politician.

I was dismayed that he wasn't up for election this year, because I wanted to go out right this minute and work in his campaign, put up some signs, canvass a few neighborhoods, help paint his portrait on the side of a four-story building.

Mr. Sinatra came to the table to stare more closely at the chief. He looked at me, shook his head in amazement, and returned to the corner.

Slumped in his chair, so relaxed that he seemed to be in danger of sliding onto the floor, Chief Hoss said, "Kid, what do you want?"

"Want, sir?"

"Out of life. What do you want out of life?"

"Well, sir, I'm not sure I can answer that question accurately since at the present time I don't know who I am."

"Let's suppose you don't have amnesia."

"But I do, sir. I look in the mirror, and I don't know my face."

"It's your face," he assured me.

"I look in the mirror, and I see that actor, Matt Damon."

"You don't look anything like Matt Damon."

"Then why do I see him in the mirror?"

"Let me hazard a guess."

"I'd be grateful if you would, sir."

"You saw those movies where he has amnesia."

"Was Matt Damon in movies where he had amnesia?"

"Of course, you wouldn't remember them."

"Gone," I agreed. "It's all gone."

"*The Bourne Identity.* That was one of them."

I considered it. Then: "Nope. Nothing."

"Kid, you're genuinely funny."

"Well, I'd like to think I might be. But there's as good a chance that when I find out who I am, I'll discover I'm humorless."

"What I'm saying is, I'm willing to stipulate that you have amnesia."

"I sure wish I didn't, sir. But there you are."

"For the purpose of facilitating our discussion, I accept your amnesia, and I will not try to trip you up. Is that fair?"

"It's fair, sure, but it's also the way it is."

"All right. Let's suppose you don't have amnesia. I know you *do* have it, I know, but so you can answer questions with more than gone-it's-all-gone, let's just suppose."

"You're asking me to use my imagination."

"There you go."

"I think I might've been a guy with a good imagination."

"Is that what you think, huh?"

"It's just a hunch. But I'll try."

This new Chief Hoss Shackett radiated affability so brightly that being in his company too long might involve a risk of melanoma.

He said, "So . . . what do you want out of life, son?"

"Well, sir, I imagine a life in tire sales might be nice."

"Tire sales?"

"Putting people back on good rubber, getting them rolling again, after life threw a blow-out at them. That would be satisfying."

"I can see your point. But since we're just imagining here, why don't we imagine big?"

"Big. All right."

"If you had a big dream in life, what would it be?"

"I guess maybe . . . having my own ice-cream store."

"Is that as big as you can go, son?"

"My best girl at my side and an ice-cream shop we could work in together all our lives. Yes, sir. That would be terrific."

I was serious. That would have been some life, me and Stormy and an ice-cream shop. I would have loved that life.

He regarded me pleasantly. Then: "Yes, I see, with a little one coming along, it would be nice to have a business you could rely on."

"Little one?" I asked.

"The baby. Your girl is pregnant."

Bewilderment is, for me, a natural expression. "Girlfriend? You know my girlfriend? Then you must know who I am. You mean . . . I'm going to be a father?"

"You were talking to her this afternoon. Utgard saw you. Before you jumped off the pier."

I looked disappointed, shook my head. "That was crazy—jumping off the pier, talking tsunamis. But the girl, sir, I don't know her."

"Maybe you just don't remember knowing her."

"No, sir. When I came on the pier after being mugged, and I had amnesia, I saw her and thought, well, maybe I often went to the pier and she would know who I was."

"But she didn't know you."

"Not a clue."

"Her name's Annamaria," he said.

"That's a pretty name."

"Nobody knows her last name. Not even the people letting her live above their garage rent-free."

"Rent-free? What lovely people they must be."

"They're do-gooder morons," he said in the nicest way, with his warmest smile yet.

"The poor girl," I sympathized. "She didn't tell me that she had amnesia, too. What're the odds of that, huh?"

"I wouldn't take the bet. The thing of it is— the same day, here you are with no first name or last, and here she is with no last name."

"Magic Beach isn't a big city, sir. You'll help us find out who we are. I'm confident of that."

"I don't believe either of you is from around here."

"Oh, I hope you're wrong. If I'm not from around here, how will I find out where I'm from? And if I can't find out where I'm from, how will I find anyone who knows who I am?"

When the chief was in his charming-politician mode, his good humor was as unshakeable as the Rocky Mountains. He kept smiling, though he did close his eyes for a moment, as if counting to ten.

I glanced at Mr. Sinatra to see how I was doing.

He gave me two thumbs up.

Hoss Shackett opened his warm Irish eyes. Regarding me with delight, as if I were the leprechaun he had longed all his life to encounter, he said, "I want to go back to the big-dream question."

"Still an ice-cream parlor for me," I assured him.

"Would you like to hear my big dream, son?"

"You've accomplished so much, I'd guess your

big dream already came true. But it's good always to have new dreams."

Chief Hoss Shackett the Nice remained with me, and there was no sign of Chief Hoss Shackett the Mean, though he resorted to the silence and the direct stare with which he had regarded me when he had first entered the room.

This stare had a different quality from the previous one, which had been crocodilian. Now the chief smiled warmly, and as Frankie Valli sings in that old song, his eyes adored me, as though he were looking at me through a pet-shop window, contemplating adopting me.

Finally he said, "I'm going to have to trust you, son. Trust isn't an easy thing for me."

I nodded sympathetically. "Being an officer of the law and having to deal every day with the scum of the earth . . . Well, sir, a little cynicism is understandable."

"I'm going to trust you totally. See . . . my big dream is one hundred million dollars tax-free."

"Whoa. That is big, sir. I didn't know you meant *big* big. I feel a little silly now, saying an ice-cream parlor."

"And my dream has come true. I have my money."

"That's wonderful. I'm so happy for you. Was it the lottery?"

"The full value of the deal," he said, "was four hundred million dollars. My cut was one of the two largest, but several others here in Magic Beach have become very rich."

"I can't wait to see how you're going to spread the good fortune around, sir. 'Everyone a neighbor, every neighbor a friend.' "

"I'm adding four words to the motto—'Every man for himself.' "

"That doesn't sound like you, sir. That sounds like the other Chief Shackett."

Sitting forward on his chair, folding his arms on the table, virtually sparkling with bonhomie, he said, "Happy as I am to be stinking rich, I'm not without problems, son."

"I'm sorry to hear that."

Such a wounded look of disappointment came over his face that you would have wanted to hug him if you had been there.

"*You* are my biggest problem," he said. "I don't know who you are. I don't know *what* you are. That *dream,* the vision, whatever it was that you passed to me and Utgard."

"Yes, sir. I'm sorry. It's a very disturbing little dream."

"And so spot-on accurate. Clearly you know too much. I could kill you right now, bury you somewhere like Hecate's Canyon, and nobody would find you for years."

In his Chief Hoss Shackett the Nice persona, he had brought to the moment such a spirit of camaraderie and such fine intentions that the low concrete ceiling had seemed to expand into a high vault. Now it so suddenly crashed down again that I ducked my head a little.

Once again I could detect the smell of vomit under the pine disinfectant.

"If I have a vote, sir, I'm opposed to the kill-and-bury-in-Hecate's-Canyon solution."

"I don't like it, either. Because maybe that fake-pregnant girlfriend of yours is expecting you to report in."

"Fake-pregnant?"

"That's what I suspect. Good cover. The two of you come into town like vagrants, the kind nobody looks at twice. You're like some surf bum, she's like a runaway. But you work for somebody."

"Sounds like you have someone in mind."

"Maybe Homeland Security. Some intelligence agency. They have a slew of them these days."

"Sir, how old do I look to you?"

"Twenty. You might look younger than you are, might be twenty-three, twenty-four."

"A little young to be an undercover spy, don't you think?"

"Not at all. Navy SEALs, Army Rangers, the best of the best—some of them are twenty, twenty-one."

"Not me. I have a gun phobia."

"Yeah. Right."

I had leaned on the table, as well. He reached out and patted my arm affectionately.

"Suppose you don't check in with your partner, this Annamaria, at the appointed hour, and she gets on the horn to your controllers back in Washington or wherever."

Amnesia no longer served me well. I would do better being a cool and deadly government agent. I said only, "Suppose."

"In a spirit of trust, which I sincerely hope you genuinely do appreciate, I'll tell you—the job that made me rich, my part of that is done tonight. In two weeks, I'll be living in another country, under a new identity so tightly guarded I'll never be found. But leaving the right way, the careful way, is going to take two weeks."

"During which you're vulnerable."

"So I have only three options I can see. One— I have to find your Annamaria real quick, before she squawks, and kill you both."

I consulted my watch, as if in fact I had a pending report time with my undercover co-agent. "You won't be able to pull that off."

"That's what I figured. Option two—I kill you here, now. When you don't report to Annamaria, she sends the alarm, your agency comes storming into town. I play dumb, tough it out. Never saw you, don't know what happened to you."

I said, "I'm sorry to hear . . . this must mean Reverend Moran is in this with you."

"He's not. He found you in his church, you said your life had taken a wrong turn. Then you started talking Armageddon, the end of the world, you made him nervous. You told him the retriever's name was Raphael, but he knew who owned the dog, and its name is Murphy."

I said, "Gee, a troubled young man worried about the end of the world, maybe on drugs, has a dog isn't his . . . I'd think a preacher would try some counseling and prayer before turning me in."

"He feels comfortable calling me about small stuff, and don't pretend you don't know why."

"Are you a member of his parish?" I guessed.

"You know I am."

I hesitated, then nodded. "We know." I made the *we* sound like eight thousand bureaucrats in a block-square building near the CIA. "And don't forget—the reverend knows you arrested me."

He smiled and dismissed my concern with a wave of his hand. "That doesn't matter if before morning the reverend kills his wife and commits suicide."

"I gather you're not a *believing* member of the parish."

"Do I sound like a Christian to you?" he asked, and laughed softly, not as if he were remarking on his ruthless criminality but as if *Christian* were a synonym for *brain-dead troglodyte*.

I said, "Back to your second option. You remember that?"

"I kill you now, play dumb, say I never met you."

"Won't work," I told him. "They know I'm here right now."

"They who?"

"My handlers in . . . the agency."

He looked dubious. "They can't know."

"Satellite tracking."

"You aren't carrying a transponder. We searched you at the church."

"Surgically implanted."

A little venom seeped into his twinkling Irish eyes. "Where?"

"Very tiny, efficient device. Could be my right buttocks. Could be my left buttocks. Could be in an armpit. Even if you found it, cut it out, and crushed it, *they already know I'm here.*"

He sat back in his chair and gradually repaired the politician demeanor that had begun to break down. He took an Almond Joy from his shirt pocket and began to unwrap it. "You like half?"

"No."

"You don't like Almond Joy?"

"You were going to kill me."

"Not with poison candy."

"It's the principle of the thing," I said.

"You don't take sweets from men who threaten to kill you."

"That's right."

"Well . . . more for me." After he had enjoyed a bite of the Almond Joy, he said, "So there's only option three. This is where I figured we would wind up. Which is why I had to trust you and tell you my situation. I can make you very rich."

"What happened to 'Every man for himself'?"

"Son, I like you, I do, and I see my best option is co-opting you, but I wouldn't in a million years give you a piece of my cut. I'm surprised I offered you half of the candy bar."

"I appreciate your honesty."

"If I'm to trust you, then you've got to have good reason to trust me. So from now on, only truth between us."

Because he smiled at me so sincerely and because it would have been rude not to reciprocate, I returned his smile.

In the spirit of frankness that the chief encouraged, I felt it necessary to say, "In all honesty, I don't believe that Utgard Rolf is the kind of generous fellow who would share *his* cut with me."

"You're right, of course. Utgard would kill his own mother for a thousand dollars. Or maybe it was five thousand."

He ate more candy, and I digested the proposition that he had made to me.

After what seemed enough time for serious consideration, I said, "So, supposing I have a price—"

"Everyone has a price."

"Who would meet mine?"

"The men backing this operation have some of

the deepest pockets on the planet. They have a contingency fund. At this late hour, with so much on the line, if you join us *and* share what your agency knows or suspects, tell us the reason you were sent here, and if you feed them false information, you can be a very rich man, too, living in a wonderful climate under a name no one will ever discover."

"How rich?"

"I don't know the size of the contingency fund. And I would have to speak with a representative of our financiers, but I suspect they would consider you so valuable to this enterprise that they would find twenty-five million for you."

"What about my partner? Annamaria?"

"Do you have a thing for her?"

"No. We just work together."

"Then you tell us where she is, we kill her tonight. We put the body through a meat grinder, dump the sludge at sea, gone forever."

"Let's do it."

"That was quick."

"Well," I said, "I don't see an alternative, because I'm not giving her a piece of *my* cut."

"No reason you should."

"In the right part of the world," I said, "twenty-five million is like a hundred million here."

"Live like a king," the chief agreed, finishing his candy. "So, my new rich friend, what's your name?"

"Harry Lime," I said.

He held out his hand. I reached across the table and shook it.

I was not thrown back into the dream. Evidently, it happened only on first contact with one of these conspirators.

The chief said, "I've got to go talk to the money man, close the deal. I'll be back in five minutes. One thing he'll want to know."

"Whatever. We're partners."

"How the hell did you do that?"

"Do what?"

"How did you pass the dream to Utgard and me? The dream, the vision, whatever you want to call it."

"I don't know exactly how. You triggered it, I think. Because you're the people going to make it come true."

Wide-eyed, a third Hoss Shackett sat before me now, neither the hard-case sadist nor the charming politician. This chief possessed a capacity for wonder that neither the baby-killer nor the baby-kisser shared.

This chief might have had the ability to commit a selfless act or an uncalculated kindness, because wonder admits to the existence of mystery, and the recognition of mystery in the world allows the possibility of Truth. The other two wouldn't let this chief surface often. I was surprised that they had not already drowned him forever.

He said, "What are you, anyway? Some kind of psychic? I never believed in psychics, but what you put in my head, that was for damn sure real."

Recognizing that we live in a distressed culture where anything like a conspiracy theory will be embraced by more people than will the simple and obvious truth, I tried to make it easier for Hoss Shackett to accept my otherness:

"The government has a drug that facilitates clairvoyance," I lied.

"Sonofabitch."

"It doesn't work with everyone," I said. "You have to carry a certain combination of genes. There aren't many of us."

"You see the future?"

"Not really, not directly. Things come in dreams. And they're never complete. Just pieces of a puzzle. I have to do police work, just like you, to fill in what's missing."

"So you saw Magic Beach in your dream, and the nukes."

Trying not to react to the word *nukes*, I said, "Yeah." I suppose I had known all along.

"But in the dream, you didn't see me or Utgard?"

"No."

"What you put in my head, the sea all red and the sky—it seemed like the nukes were going off right here on the beach. That's not how it'll be."

"The dreams are fragmentary, sometimes more

symbolic than full of real details. Where will the bombs be detonated?"

He said, "Where it matters. In cities. In a few weeks. All on the same day. We're just bringing them ashore and distributing. The major seaports and airports, they're blanketed with radiation detectors."

In addition to lingering spirits of the dead, I once in a while see other supernatural entities, about which I have written in the past. Ink-black, with no facial features, fluid in shape, sometimes catlike, sometimes wolflike, they can pass through a keyhole or through the crack under a door.

I believe they are spiritual vampires and possess knowledge of the future. They swarm to places where extreme violence or a natural catastrophe will soon occur, as though they feed on human suffering, to which they react with frenzied ecstasy.

Now I realized why none of these creatures had appeared in Magic Beach. The suffering would occur elsewhere. Already, legions of those ghoulish entities must be swarming through the target cities, relishing the prospect of the death and misery to come.

As Shackett rose from the table, I said, "Good thing for me that I had a price. Sounds like, a month from now, this'll be a country nobody will want to live in."

He said, "How do you feel about that?"

I could not tell which of the three Hoss Shacketts regarded me at the moment.

Playing to the savagery of the sadist, to the megalomania of the politician, to the bitterness in both of them, I invented something that he would believe. Remembering my advice to Hutch, I strove not to let my performance become fulsome, to keep it subdued and real.

"They lied to me about the effects of the drug. They said it facilitated clairvoyance for twelve to eighteen hours. But they knew. One dose is all you ever need. They knew it would change me forever. I rarely have a night of restful sleep anymore. Visions, nightmares, more vivid than reality. There's a thousand kinds of hell on earth that could be coming. Sometimes I can't wake from them. Hour after hour in those horrors. When at last I wake up, my bed is soaked with sweat, I'm swimming in it. Throat raw from screaming in my sleep."

Through all of that, I had met his stare, daring him to see any lie in my eyes. Evil men are often easy to mislead, because they have spent so long deceiving that they no longer recognize the truth and mistake deception for it.

Now I gazed at the ceiling, as if seeing beyond it a nation that had betrayed me. Line by line, my voice grew quieter, less emotional, even as my words grew more accusatory.

"They lied to me. Now they say that after I've

served them for five years, they'll give me the antidote. I don't believe there is one. They lie not just for advantage but for sport. Five years will become ten. They can all go to hell."

I met his eyes again.

He was silent, not because he suspected deception but because he was impressed.

He was, after all, a man who would sell out his country to terrorists, who could conspire to murder millions of innocents in a nuclear holocaust and to condemn millions more to death in the chaos that would follow the day of detonations. A man who could believe in the rightness of such a scenario was one who could believe anything, even my little exercise in science-fiction paranoia.

At last he said, "You're a good hater, kid. That'll take you a long way in life."

"What now?"

"I go talk to the man, get our deal confirmed. Like I said—five minutes, ten at most."

"My leg is half numb. How about unshackling me from the table so I can walk around while I wait."

"As soon as Utgard and I get back with the polygraph," he said. "We'll have to unshackle you for that."

As if I had anticipated that they would want to confirm the sincerity of my conversion by any means available to them, I did not react to the word *polygraph*. Lie detector.

"You have a problem with that?" the chief asked.

"No. If our situations were reversed, I'd play it the same way you are."

He left the room and closed the half-ton door behind him.

The silence of tranquility lies light upon a room, but this was the silence of apprehension, heavy enough to press me down on the chair in paralytic stillness.

So saturated was the air with the stink of pine disinfectant that I could taste the astringent chemical when I opened my mouth, and the underlying scent of other prisoners' vomit was not conducive to a calm stomach.

The concrete walls were not mortared blocks, but solid, poured in place, reinforced with rebar, as was the ceiling.

One vent, high in a wall, brought air to the room and carried it away. No doubt any sound that passed through the vent would diminish as it followed a long insulated duct, and would be stifled entirely in whatever machine exchanged the air.

When I turned to look at Mr. Sinatra, he was sitting in the third chair, bent forward at the waist, elbows on his thighs, his face buried in his hands.

I said, "Sir, I'm in a real pickle here."

CHAPTER 27

Because my fettered ankle would not allow me to go easily to Mr. Sinatra, he came to me. He sat in the chair that Chief Hoss Shackett had occupied, across the table from me.

In the ceiling, the light fixture was recessed behind a flush-mounted sheet of plastic. That panel was frosted, a blind eye.

The only place in the room where a camera could have been concealed was in the duct that provided fresh air. Through the slots in the vent grille, I could not see any telltale gleam of a lens.

Considering the brutal interrogations that the chief had surely conducted in this room and that he would soon conduct again, I did not believe he would have installed a camera. He would be concerned that it would accidentally— or by the intention of a whistle-blower—record crimes that might lead to his imprisonment.

For the same reason, I doubted that the room was fitted with listening devices. Besides, as far as the chief knew, I had no one to whom I could talk.

Mr. Sinatra had lost his cocky air. He appeared distraught.

Throughout his life, he had been a patriot, in love with America both for what she was and for her potential. The plot that he had heard described in this room had clearly devastated him.

In December 1941, after the attack on Pearl Harbor, "the Voice" had been drafted. But at his physical, he was rejected and classified 4-F because of a punctured eardrum that he had suffered during birth. Subsequently, he tried four times to enlist. He used every person of influence he knew—they were numerous—to get the army to reclassify him and to accept him for service, but he never succeeded.

Although he weighed 135 pounds in those days, he had been a scrapper from childhood, quick to defend himself or a friend, making up in heart and temper for what he lacked in size. He never walked away from a fight and would have made a good soldier, though he might have been a discipline problem from time to time.

I said, "When you were born in your parents' Hoboken tenement, you weighed thirteen and a half pounds. Your grandma Rose was an experienced midwife, but she'd never seen a baby as big as you."

He looked puzzled, as though he wondered if

I was in denial of what I had heard from Hoss Shackett.

"The physician in attendance had never seen a baby so big, either. Your mother, Dolly, was under five feet tall, petite, and because of your size, the doctor had trouble delivering you."

Frowning with impatience, Mr. Sinatra waved a hand dismissively, as though brushing aside the subject of his entry into the world, and he pointed to the steel door to focus my attention on what mattered.

"Sir, I'm going somewhere with this," I promised him.

He looked dubious but remained attentive.

Because the circumstances of his birth were family legend, he knew what I told him: "The doctor used forceps, and didn't use them well. He ripped your ear, cheek, and neck, puncturing your eardrum. When he finally got you out of your mother, you weren't breathing."

His grandmother took him from the doctor, rushed him to a sink, and held him under cold running water until he gasped for air.

"The doctor would likely have certified you as born dead. You entered the world fighting, sir, and you never really stopped."

I glanced at my watch. I had a lot to achieve in five minutes, but Mr. Sinatra's fate and my life depended on getting it done.

Because his parents had worked and because

his mother had been a committeewoman for the Democratic party, with many outside interests, young Frank was a latchkey kid before the term was coined. From the age of six, he often made his own dinner—and sometimes had to scavenge for it when his mom had been too busy to go food shopping.

Lonely, almost desperately so at times, he drifted to the homes of other family members and friends. People said he was the quietest kid they knew, content to sit in a corner and listen to the adults.

"In your teens, your mother was in your life more. Always she was demanding. She set high standards, had a dominant personality."

She belittled his hope of a singing career, and was not entirely convinced even after he became the most famous singer in the world.

"But, sir, you're not like Elvis. You aren't lingering here because you're reluctant to face your mother in the next world."

A combative expression hardened his features, as if, ghost or not, he would punch me for ever thinking that his beloved mother *might* have been the reason he lingered in this world.

"Your mom could be exasperating, contentious, opinionated—but loving. Eventually you realized that your ability to stand up for yourself arose from the need to hold your own in arguments with her."

Mr. Sinatra glanced at the door and made a hurry-up gesture.

"Sir, if I'm going to die here tonight, at least I'm going to help you move on from this world before I leave it myself."

That was indeed my motive for this short session of straight talk. But I also had another.

Although Dolly's steel will led to contention between them, Mr. Sinatra honored her without fail and took good care of her. Unlike Elvis's mother, Dolly lived a long life. The Chairman was sixty-one when she died, and he had no reason to regret anything between them.

He had adored his gentle father, Marty, who died eight years before Dolly passed. If anything, his deep love for his dad should have made him rush away into the next life.

"No disrespect, sir, but you could sometimes be a bastard, hot-headed and even mean. But I've read enough about you to know those faults were more than balanced by loyalty and generosity."

In sickness and in hard times, friends received his devotion, not just significant money sent unsolicited but also daily calls for weeks, to give emotional support. He was capable of reaching out to a deserving stranger and changing a life with a generous gift.

He never mentioned these kindnesses and was embarrassed when his friends spoke of what he had done. Many of these stories surfaced after his death; the number of them is both inspiring and humbling.

"Whatever waits beyond this world, sir, is nothing you need to fear. But you fear it, and I think I know why."

The suggestion that he feared anything whatsoever annoyed him.

Acutely aware of how little time remained before Shackett would return, I said, "Almost died at birth. Lived in a bad neighborhood, they called you a wop. Walking home from grade school, you had to fight. Always had to struggle for what you got. But, sir, you got it all—fortune, fame, acclaim, more than any entertainer in history before you. And now what keeps you in this world is *pride*."

My statement compounded Mr. Sinatra's annoyance. With one cocked eyebrow and a gesture, he seemed to say *So what's wrong with pride?*

"Nothing is wrong with pride based on accomplishment, and your life was packed full of accomplishments. But justifiable pride can sometimes mutate into arrogance."

Mouth tight, he stared at me. But then he nodded. He knew that in life he had sometimes been guilty of arrogance.

"I'm not talking about then. I mean now. You don't want to move on to the next world because you're afraid you won't be special over there, that you'll just be equal to everyone else."

Although he resisted moving on, he wanted to make the journey, as do all of the lingering dead. He seriously considered my words.

I needed to channel him from polite consideration to a strong emotional response. I regretted what I was about to do, but his soul and my neck were on the line. Extreme measures were required.

"But it's worse than that. You're *afraid* to move on because you think maybe you'll be starting over from nothing, with nothing, just a nobody, and all the struggle will begin again. You're as scared as a little boy."

His face knotted with offense.

"Your first breath was a struggle. Will it be again? To win any respect, you had to fight. You can't stand the idea of being a nobody again, but you don't want to fight your way to the top like you had to do the last time."

He put up his fists.

"Sure, threaten to fight me. You know I can't hurt a ghost, what courage does it take to threaten me?"

He rose from the chair and glared down at me.

"You want all the respect you won in this world, but you don't have the guts to earn it again, if that's the way it is over there."

Never would I have believed that those warm blue eyes could have produced such an icy stare as the one with which he skewered me.

"You know what you've become in death?

You're a scared little *punk* like you never were in life."

In anger, hands fisted at his sides, he turned away from me.

"Can't handle the truth, huh?"

Treating him with such disrespect, when in fact I respected him, was difficult, and I was particularly afraid of revealing the falsity of my contempt by using the word *sir*.

I believed that I had in fact arrived at the reason that he lingered in this world, but I did not despise him for it. In other circumstances, I would have led him gently to accept the truth and to see that his fears were ungrounded.

Certain that Hoss Shackett would come through the door at any moment, I said witheringly, "Chairman of the Board, Old Blue Eyes, the Voice, famous big-shot singer, big cheese of the Rat Pack—and now all you are is another gutless punk from Hoboken."

He turned toward me once more.

His mottled face, his dead-cold stare, his lips skinned back from clenched teeth, his head lowered like that of a bull that sees not one red cape but a hundred: As lingering spirits go, this one was as pissed off as any I had ever seen.

The steel door opened.

Chief Hoss Shackett entered. Utgard Rolf followed him, rolling a cart on which was mounted the polygraph.

CHAPTER 28

In my room at Hutch's house, when Mr. Sinatra had levitated all the biographies of him and had spun them slowly around the room, out of my reach, he had shown poltergeist potential.

In my experience, only deeply malevolent spirits had been able to conjure the dark energy necessary to cause havoc. Mr. Sinatra had his moods, but he harbored no true malevolence.

Judging by the evidence of his life, however, his was a powerful spirit that might be able to bend the rules as I knew them.

The thing most certain to light a short fuse with Mr. Sinatra was unfairness. From his early years as an unknown singer, he had been angered by bigotry and had taken risks with his career to open doors and gain opportunities for black musicians in an era when many white performers were cool with the status quo.

The attack I had launched on him—calling him a gutless punk—qualified as grossly unfair. My first hope was that he would seethe as hotly when he was the target of unfairness as he did when he saw it being directed against others.

My second hope was that I had not cranked him so hard, so fast that he would blow like Vesuvius while I remained locked to the table.

As Utgard Rolf closed the steel door behind him and wheeled the polygraph, Mr. Sinatra turned his furious glare from me to the chin-bearded hulk.

"Spoke to the man," Chief Shackett told me. "The money's yours, as long as the machine says you're the real deal."

Because being shackled to the table would raise my stress levels and affect the reading, the chief kept his promise to free me. The cuff fell away from my ankle.

As Utgard readied the polygraph and the chief went around to the other side of the table, I said, "What do you think of Sinatra?"

"Think of what?" the chief asked.

Getting to my feet, I said, "Sinatra, the singer."

The tone of Utgard's bearish voice suggested that he did not like me, did not trust me, and did not want me in their game, no matter how much top-secret intelligence from Homeland Security I might be able to share with them: "What the hell do you care what we think?"

"Sinatra," the chief said dismissively. "Who listens to that crap anymore?"

The Voice, voiceless since death, pivoted toward Shackett.

"I had this girlfriend," I said, "she swooned for Sinatra, but I say he was just a gutless punk."

"They're all punks," the chief said. "Fact is, they're all pansies."

"You think so?" I asked.

"Sure. The big rock stars, the heavy-metal idiots, the lounge lizards like Sinatra, they all act tough, want you to believe they're true wise guys who made their bones, but they're all light in the loafers."

Here was contempt, bigotry, and insult served up steaming on a platter, and I was so grateful to the chief that I almost cried.

"In World War Two," I told Shackett, "Sinatra dodged the draft."

Mr. Sinatra snapped his head toward me so fast that had he been alive, he would have broken his neck. He knew that *I* knew this was a lie, which made my attack on his character especially unfair. His face contorted so extremely that it conveyed both astonishment and rage at the same time.

"Of course he dodged," the chief said. "What would he have done if he'd come up against Nazi badasses—slap them with his perfumed handkerchief?"

Concentric rings of power, visible only to me, began to radiate from Mr. Sinatra's fists.

"So," I said to Hoss Shackett as, in blissful ignorance of the building storm, he settled on his chair, "then you think maybe he and Dean Martin were more than just friends?"

Utgard Rolf stepped around the polygraph, scowling. "What're you going on about?"

In the corner, the third chair began to rock slowly side to side as the pulses of power from Mr. Sinatra disturbed it.

"I'm just saying he was a gutless punk," I replied, wishing I could think of a new insult.

"Anyway," the chief volunteered, "that old music—Rod Stewart sings it better."

"That should just about do it," I said.

Utgard's yellow eyes were not half as scary as Mr. Sinatra's blues had become. Looming over me, he said, "Why don't you shut up?"

"Why? Are you a big Rod Stewart fan or something?"

He was such a solid package of bone and beef that most punches he took probably resulted in shattered hands for those who threw them.

With the menace of a grizzly suffering a toothache, he growled, "Sit down."

"Hey, pal, take it easy, okay? We want the same thing. Don't you want this stinking country nuked to its knees?"

Perhaps one of Grandma Melvina Belmont Singleton's gorillas had been an ancestor of Utgard's, because the big man's instincts were closer to the jungle than were the chief's. He knew something about me was wrong, and he acted on it.

Utgard backhanded me across the face so quick I hardly saw his arm move, and so hard that gorillas in Africa would be looking up in surprise from their bananas when the crack of the blow reached them at the speed of sound.

I thought I had taken the hit without losing my footing, but when I tried to run, I discovered that I was sprawled on the floor.

Licking my lips, tasting blood, I shouted inspiration to Mr. Sinatra: "God bless America!"

Denied the chance to fight for his country in World War II, Old Crazy-Whirling-Blue Eyes seized this opportunity. He went ballistic.

He opened his fists and held his arms out straight, palms bared, fingers spread. Pulses of power, pale-blue rings, flew from him and animated the inanimate.

In the corner, the third chair started spinning on one leg, striking from the concrete a shriek as shrill as a drill bit might have made.

Instead of decorating my face with repeated impressions of his shoe tread, Utgard turned toward the whirling chair.

Chief Hoss Shackett, about to face the consequences of comparing Rod Stewart and Mr. Sinatra to the latter's disadvantage, rose from his chair in astonishment.

As a first strategic step toward the door, toward freedom, toward the hope of living to eat another bacon cheeseburger, I crawled under the table with the expectation that it would provide a temporary shelter while I calculated my next move.

The whirling chair exploded to the ceiling, ricocheted off the concrete, and bounced off the table with a *boom!* that made me feel as if I had taken refuge inside a drum.

A greater clatter arose, and I figured all three chairs must now be whacking around the room, a disturbing amount of crazed furniture in such a small space.

Hoss Shackett cursed, and Utgard topped him in the potty-mouth competition, and the chief followed his expletive with a grunt of pain that suggested justice was sometimes done in this world, after all.

As the metal table began to levitate off the floor, I scuttled on my hands and knees between its turning legs, which an instant later began to revolve so fast that they cut the air with a whirring worthy of a descending plague of locusts.

I abandoned my half-formed plan to reach the door in cautious stages, and I crawled as fast as a cockroach, eager to escape before the heavy table and the heavier wheeled polygraph began to carom from wall to wall with lethal enthusiasm.

Behind me, the chief spat out several astonishing words strung together in an order that was too imaginative for me to recall with accuracy, and Utgard Rolf shouted a bizarre knot of syllables that I had never heard before, though I knew at once that this, too, was not very suitable for print. I heard less anger than terror in their cursing.

As I reached the door, something slammed into the plastic panel that covered the ceiling fixture. The panel cracked, and the slamming something slammed again. Light bulbs shattered, and the interrogation room went dark.

Clawing up the slab of steel, I found the handle, levered it down, and pushed on the door. Ball-bearing hinges carried the great weight with ease, and I opened the door only wide enough to slip into the basement hallway.

I had some sympathy for Hoss and Utgard, although not nearly enough to hold the door open for them. In fact, I leaned against that steel barrier to shut it quickly, closing them in the perilous dark. I would have locked it, too, except that it locked from the outside only with a key.

In spite of the care the chief had taken to isolate noise within the room, the fusillade of furniture grew thunderous, especially when a chair or the table struck the steel door. I could hear the two men shouting, as well, because neither of them had a gag in his mouth and duct tape across his lips, as I would have had after failing the lie-detector test.

The basement hallway with the interestingly stained concrete floor was not a place I wanted to be discovered by whoever responded to the racket in the interrogation room. I hurried toward the stairs, down which the two young officers had earlier conducted me.

CHAPTER 29

As I reached the stairs that led up from the basement of the police station, the muffled clatter-clang from the interrogation room erupted into a full-fledged cacophony as the steel door came open.

Glancing back, I saw neither Hoss Shackett nor Utgard Rolf. Mr. Sinatra did not appear, either.

Through the open door and into the hall came a collection of badly abused public property for which the police department should have to answer to taxpayers when submitting its next budget request: a mangled metal chair, bent and twisted parts of other chairs, shards of frosted plastic, a once sturdy metal table now folded in half like a slice of bread. . . .

The whirling vortex of trash scraped and rattled off the walls, remaining just outside the interrogation room for a moment—and then proceeded toward me.

Addressing this indoor tornado, I declared, "I didn't say Rod Stewart. *He* said Rod Stewart."

Realizing the folly of defending myself to a cyclone of debris, I raced up the two flights of stairs.

I had done so much racing, jumping, crawling, running, dodging, scuttling, climbing, and swimming that I ached from head to foot and felt my energy ebbing.

During the evening, I had developed considerable admiration for Matt Damon. In spite of his amnesia and in spite of being opposed by numerous nefarious government goons with infinite resources at their command, he waded through squads of ruthless assassins, killing them or sometimes letting them live but making them wish they had never dedicated themselves to fascist ideologies, and he just kept going, indomitable and undiminished.

Here I was, a pathetic excuse for a paladin, complaining about exhaustion when I had not yet even been through a car crash. Already, Matt Damon would have been through six.

As I neared the top of the narrow stairs, a ferocious noise below indicated that into the stairwell had come the Office Furniture of Death. The crash-clang-shriek of the swiftly ascending junk storm suggested supernatural power so furious that it could have been summoned only by a Vegas headliner.

The stairhead door had not been locked when I had been escorted to the basement; and it was not locked now. I stepped into the long back hallway on the main floor.

Although I could not recall which door I'd been brought through from the alleyway, I thought it had been on the right. I opened the first that I came to, which was a storeroom. The second revealed a deserted office.

Whether they were responding to the escalating tumult, which had been heard at the front of the building, or to a frantic cell-phone call from Hoss Shackett, two uniformed officers appeared at the far end of the corridor. I had never seen them before, but they knew at once that I did not belong here, most likely because I was scuttling and furtive and looked harried.

One of them called out to me—Who was I, what was I doing here?—and I called back to them, "Just looking for the men's room."

They didn't buy that even as I was saying it. One of them drew his gun, and the other told me to stop where I was, to lie facedown, but Matt Damon would never lie down on a floor that looked like blue-Slurpee upchuck, or on any floor whatsoever, for that matter, just because some guy with a gun told him to do it.

Fortunately, I did not have to improvise a deadly weapon out of my wristwatch or one of my shoes, because no sooner had the officer ordered me to lie down than the stairhead door behind me flew open. I did not have to turn and look to know that the wreckage from the inter-rogation room had spun out of the stairs like some motorized work of modern art by one of those sculptors who regularly conned museums into giving display space to the contents of a Dumpster.

The officers' attention having been diverted from me, I dared to move forward, staying close to the wall, seeking the next door.

A new sound, a terrible ripping and slithering noise, grew in volume so rapidly that my curiosity got the best of me. I glanced back and saw that into the hallway had come Polterfrank.

From his hands radiated pulses of power that stripped the blue linoleum tiles off the floor and whirled them into the air like a wind devil gath-ering drifts of autumn leaves to itself. The vinyl squares, in their wild waltz, whispered and clicked against one another.

Because the officers paralyzed by this sight could not see Mr. Sinatra, they were merely star-tled and frightened by the spectacle before them. They were not propelled at once into a state of blind terror because they were not able to appreci-ate the phenomenon in its terrible fullness. Had they been able to see the singer in all his glorious wrath, they would have thrown down their weapons in surrender and fled to their mothers.

Here he came, a punctured eardrum no longer

an obstacle to his service to his country. He was feisty Private Angelo Maggio in *From Here to Eternity*, tough Tom Reynolds in *Never So Few*, courageous and determined Joseph Ryan in *Von Ryan's Express*, and the righteous Sam Loggins in *Kings Go Forth*, but most of all he was Mr. Francis Albert Sinatra with a mad-on for the enemies of his country and the ignorant critics of his impeccable singing.

Spinning metal furniture and parts of furniture seemed to remain the primary danger in the tornado, because the vinyl tiles appeared too flexible and too soft to inflict serious damage. On the other hand, they were stiffened by the mastic with which they had been glued to the floor; and when a critical velocity had been achieved, every edge of every thin tile might be stropped into a lacerating blade.

Like a cresting wave, the floor peeled toward me, and from this tsunami of potentially lethal linoleum came an awful skirling like a thousand busy flensing knives scraping bone.

Spooked, the cops bolted from the corridor, back the way they had come.

The next door on the right led to the men's restroom. The escalating tempest convinced me that I did not have time to explore farther.

I stepped into the lavatory and backed away from the door, which closed between me and the haunt from Hoboken.

As the tidal wave of churning vinyl and clanging metal scraped past the restroom door, the noise became so disturbing that I clapped my hands over my ears.

Although Mr. Sinatra had been angry with me when I poked and prodded him toward an outburst, I trusted his intelligence to lead him to the realization that I had meant nothing I said and that I had acted out of desperation. Nevertheless, I was relieved when the storm of debris roared by and receded along the corridor.

An operable casement window offered an escape route, but I did not at once flee the restroom. First, I needed to pee.

Here is another difference between me and the indefatigable Matt Damon. He never has either the time or the need to visit a lavatory unless he has to go there to engage in a fight to the death with an agent of the fascist conspiracy.

After washing my hands, I dropped from the window into the alleyway behind the police station. As far as I could tell in the fog, I was alone.

I proceeded east for two hundred feet and then turned south into the covered and lighted walkway between the police department and the courthouse, where the fog did not rule. I hurried, not sure how long Mr. Sinatra could sustain his fury.

No one but the cleaning crew would be working

in the courthouse at that hour; and the police in the adjacent building were too busy dealing with an *X-Files* moment for any of them to step outside for a quick smoke.

I ran to the end of the walk and into Civic Center Park, which—in opposition to Magic Beach tradition—was actually surrounded by the government buildings that justified its name.

The dark skirts of huge evergreens dripped with condensed mist. Fallen pine cones crunched underfoot, and others tried to roll me off my feet.

Concrete park benches, like caskets in a winding processional, appeared periodically, forcing me to dodge left, dodge right.

Windows began to explode in the building from which I had fled. One, two, three, a half-dozen. The tintinnabulation of glass raining on stonework was as charming as an orchestra of fairy bells, which I was able to enjoy because I had gotten safely beyond the zone of raining shards.

Shouting drew my attention to the north where, even in the fog, dimly visible figures could be seen hurriedly descending a broad and brightly lighted set of stairs to a public plaza. Although I was not a psychic primed for clairvoyant espionage by mad scientists employed by power-crazed intelligence agencies, I somehow knew that these figures were police officers fleeing their headquarters.

From afar rose sirens, surely incoming squad cars, perhaps also fire engines or ambulances.

In spite of the inhibiting murk, I ran faster, wishing I could summon the golden retriever again as a kind of Seeing Eye dog. A few minutes later, having put sufficient distance between myself and Civic Center Park, I slowed to a walk for two blocks.

Only then did I think to check my wrist-watch—9:38.

At midnight if not before, Chief Hoss Shackett and Utgard Rolf intended to bring nuclear weapons onto United States soil by way of Magic Beach Harbor.

If the chief and the hulk had been killed or at least disabled in the chaos at the station, perhaps the plot would collapse. But I did not think I could count on that. If more than four hundred million dollars had been provided for bribes alone, this operation would have been developed with more than one contingency plan.

Supposing that two stopped clocks constituted an omen, my guess was that the nukes would not be delivered to the harbor at a minute till midnight, but that they would instead be picked up at sea before that hour. The numbers on the clocks more likely signified the last minute that the plan could be foiled: the time when the bombs were taken from the harbor and placed aboard one truck or several, when they would be moved out of Magic Beach and might subsequently be transferred again to other vehicles bound for doomed cities unknown.

CHAPTER 30

Since the encounter with Utgard and the redheaded gunmen on the pier, so much had happened that I'd had little time to think. I had been barely coping with the torrent of events, allowing myself to be guided largely by instinct and by those paranormal gifts that make my journey through life so interesting, so complicated, and at times so heartbreaking.

I needed fifteen minutes for calm deliberation, a quarter of an hour during which neither my life nor the life of anyone depending on me was in immediate jeopardy. Things had happened this night that I had never experienced previously, moments of a supernatural nature that mystified me. They required a quality of reflection that I could not achieve while sprinting from a mortal threat or verbally fencing with a sadistic police chief in a windowless room that resembled an abattoir.

Slowing from a fast walk, gradually catching

my breath, I sought a place to rest, where I was not likely to be disturbed. Usually a church would have appealed to me, but not after Reverend Moran.

My lower lip felt swollen at the right corner of my mouth. When I explored gingerly with my tongue, I found a split that stung, and I prudently decided not to lick it again. The bleeding seemed to have stopped.

Considering the force of Utgard's backhand blow, I was lucky not to have spat out a tooth or two.

The blinding mist transformed even familiar neighborhoods into strange precincts. Shrouded objects looked not like what they turned out to be, but like unearthly flora and alien structures on a world circling a star other than our own.

I found myself in a commercial district that I didn't recognize, not the one near the pier nor the one around the harbor, nor the one in the vicinity of the civic center.

Ornate lampposts of cast iron were so old that they might have hailed from the era of gaslight and been converted to electricity. Their glass panes poured forth a sour yellow light that had about it no quality of romance but instead an industrial grimness that brewed the fog into smoke and lent to every shadow the character of a cloud of soot.

The concrete sidewalk was cracked, canted, stained, and strewn with litter that our tourist town usually did not tolerate. In the breathless night, the larger wads of crumpled paper occasionally resembled the corpses of birds, and the smaller scraps reminded me of dead insects.

At this hour, the stores were closed. Most of their windows offered a browser only darkness, although a few were colored by all-night neon that spelled names and services in blown-glass script.

Blue, green, red—for some reason the neon enlivened nothing. The colors were wrong, inducing dyspepsia, giving rise to thoughts of bottom-feeding carnivals where something too freakish for any freak show waited in the ultimate tent.

Some shabby storefronts housed businesses I was surprised to find in Magic Beach, which for the most part was an upscale coastal town. Here was a pawnshop, there another one. Here a tattoo parlor had gone out of business; and here an operation with dirty windows offered payday advances.

Behind the plate glass of a secondhand-clothing store that advertised a one-dollar bin, eight dressed mannequins—as secondhand as the clothes they wore—watched the street with dead eyes and joyless faces.

Traffic had been light elsewhere in town. In this neighborhood, no vehicles whatsoever traveled the streets. I saw no pedestrians, either, no shopkeepers working late.

In the apartments above the stores, few lights glowed. No faces could be seen at either the dark or lighted windows.

When I came to an open-air bus stop, I sat on the bench to think. At the sound of an engine or the first sight of headlights, I could retreat to a serviceway between buildings and wait until the vehicle had passed.

I love novels about road trips, about characters who walk out of their lives, who get on a bus or in a car and go. Just *go*. They leave the world behind and find something new.

In my case, such a solution would never work. No matter how far I went or how long I kept moving, the world would find me.

On the worst day of my life, I disabled one man and killed another who went on a well-planned shooting spree in my hometown, Pico Mundo. Before I got the second gunman, they had wounded forty-one people and had killed nineteen.

They had parked a truck bomb under the mall as final punctuation to their rampage. I found it and prevented it from detonating.

The media called me a hero, but I didn't agree. A hero would have saved everyone. Everyone. A hero would have saved the one person in the world who most mattered to him and who trusted him without reservation.

That day of carnage, I was just a fry cook in

over my head. Almost a year and a half later, in Magic Beach, I was still a fry cook in over my head.

Now more than ever.

Wyatt Porter, the chief of police in Pico Mundo, was not only a friend of mine but also one of my father figures. He had taught me how to be a man when my real father proved not to be much of one himself and incapable of showing a son the way. I had unofficially assisted Chief Porter on several difficult cases, and he knew about my paranormal senses.

If I called him and told him what had happened, he would believe everything I said. His experiences with me had taught him that no matter how unlikely a story of mine sounded, it would prove to be true in all details.

I doubted that every police officer in Magic Beach would prove to be corrupt. The great majority would be fine men doing good work, flawed humans of course but not monsters. Hoss Shackett would have recruited a cell of traitors as small as the job required, to ensure against discovery.

Wyatt Porter, however, lived a long way south and east of here. He did not know any of the players in Magic Beach. He would have no way of identifying a straight arrow among the bent ones in the local police department.

He might be able to contact the FBI and report

information about a delivery of nuclear weapons through the harbor at Magic Beach, but federal agents were slow to take small-town cops seriously. And when Wyatt had to identify the source of his report as his supernaturally gifted young friend, he would forfeit all credibility.

Besides, only a little more than two hours remained until the deed would be done, the bombs off-loaded and shipped to various points of the compass. I was entering Act 3 of the drama, and I had the feeling that God had pushed the FAST FORWARD button.

Gradually I became aware of a continuous susurration, like the soft voice of a thin flow of water sliding over a lightly textured surface.

I surveyed the dreary stores behind me. No source for the sound was evident.

The mannequins had not moved in the window of the used-clothing shop. As I made that observation, I wondered why I had expected that they might have changed positions.

The store awnings were tattered and not as taut as they ought to have been. They swagged like funeral bunting, but no water drizzled from them.

The mysterious sound swelled into something more like numerous whispering voices echoing through a cavernous space.

Although the fog denied me a clear view of the shops across the street, I was pretty sure this noise originated closer at hand.

In front of me, in the gutter, light rippled from right to left, and right to left again: Halloween light here in January, like the flickering orange of a candle reflecting off the carved flesh inside a jack-o'-lantern's hollow head.

They said that curiosity killed the cat, and I had seen enough feline road kill to confirm that diagnosis. Nevertheless, I got up from the bench and took a step forward to the curb.

In the pavement, a large rectangular grate covered a drain. It dated from an era when even public works had style. The parallel iron bars joined to a four-inch iron ring in the center of the rectangle. Captured within the ring, a stylized iron lightning bolt angled from right to left.

The susurration issued from the grating. Although the source lay in the drain, the sound no longer suggested water in motion. Now I thought it was also less like people whispering than it had been, and instead like the shuffling of many feet.

The elegance of the encircled lightning bolt appealed to me, but I wondered if it represented something other than foul weather, if it was the logo of the maker, that it should have been incorporated in a drain cover.

Grinning-pumpkin light flickered below the patterned ironwork, through the culvert that lay under the street. For a moment, the drain cover seemed like a perforated furnace door.

Standing, I was too far from the grating to discern the source of the quick spasms of luminosity. I stepped off the curb and knelt beside the ironwork.

Shoe leather sliding on concrete might have made such a sound, a platoon of weary soldiers dragging their heavy feet, bound from one battle to another— if this had been a war zone and if soldiers had been in the habit of traveling underground.

I lowered my face closer to the grating.

A faint cool draft rose from below and with it an odor, not one that I recalled having smelled before, not offensive, but peculiar. Foreign. A curiously dry scent, considering from where it came. I took three deep breaths, trying to identify the source—then realized that the odor had raised the fine hairs on the back of my neck.

When the orange light came a third time, I expected to see what, if anything, moved through the culvert. But each throb chased twisted shadows across the curved walls, and those leaping phantoms confused the eye, obscuring whatever cast them.

Perhaps I unconsciously worried my split lip with my tongue or bit it. Although it had not been bleeding, a fresh drop of blood fell on the back of my right hand, which rested on the grating beside the ring that encircled the lightning bolt.

Another drop passed through a gap and fell into the dark storm drain.

My hand seemed to have found its way to the grating without my conscious guidance.

Once more the light pulsed below, rapid diastole and systole, and the grotesque shadows appeared to swell larger than before, to thrash with greater agitation, although their provenance remained concealed.

When the fluttering light gave way to blackness again, I saw that the fingers of my right hand were straining to reach through the grate.

I registered this fact with concern, but I felt powerless to retract my hand. Something more than curiosity drew me, and I felt as perhaps a light-sodden moth feels as it beats its wings against the flame that will destroy them.

As I considered resting my brow against the ironwork, the better to see the truth that lay below when next the light came, I heard a sigh of brakes. A car, to which I had been oblivious, stopped in the street, immediately behind me.

CHAPTER 31

As if coming out of a trance, I rose from the drain grating and turned, expecting a squad car and a couple of officers with hard smiles and harder truncheons.

Instead, before me stood a 1959 Cadillac Sedan DeVille that could have rolled off the showroom floor an hour previously. Massive, black, loaded with chrome detail, featuring big tail fins, it looked suitable for either interstate or interstellar travel.

The driver peered at me through the front passenger window, which she had put down. She appeared to be half again as old as the car, a heavyset, blue-eyed, pink-cheeked lady with a huge church-choir bosom. She wore white gloves and a little gray hat with a yellow band and yellow feathers.

"You all right, child?" she asked.

I leaned down to the open window. "Yes, ma'am."

"You lose somethin' through the grating?"

"Yes, ma'am." I lied because I had no idea what had happened—or had almost happened. "But it wasn't anything important."

She cocked her head, studied me for a moment, and said, "It wasn't unimportant, neither. You seem like a boy needs a friend."

Below the nearby lightning-bolt grate, the storm drain remained dark.

"What happened to your lip?" the woman asked.

"A disagreement over singers. Rod Stewart or Sinatra."

"Sinatra," she said.

"That was my position, ma'am." I glanced at a pawnshop, then at the mannequins in used clothing. "The fog has me confused. I don't recognize this part of town."

"Where you goin'?"

"To the harbor."

"I'm goin' that way," she said. "Give you a lift?"

"You shouldn't pick up strangers, ma'am."

"Folks I know all have cars. Most won't walk to the end of the block to see a parade of elephants. I don't pick up strangers, who am I gonna pick up?"

I got in the car, closed the door, and said, "I was almost trampled by an elephant once."

Putting up the power window, she said, "They go mad sometimes. Just like people. Though they don't tend to shoot up classrooms and leave crazy videos behind."

"This wasn't the elephant's fault," I said. "A bad man injected Jumbo with drugs to enrage him, then locked the two of us in a barn."

"I've known bad men in my time," she said, "but none that ever schemed to do homicide by elephant. Why do they always have to name them Jumbo?"

"A sad lack of imagination in the circus, ma'am."

She took her foot off the brake, and the car drifted forward. "Name's Birdena Hopkins. Folks just call me Birdie. What do folks call you?"

"Harry. Harry Lime."

"A nice clean name. Crisp. Conjures nice thoughts. Pleased to meet you, Harry Lime."

"Thank you, Birdie. Likewise."

On both sides of the street, the shops appeared to recede into the fog, as though they were ships outbound from Magic Beach to even stranger shores.

"You from around here?" Birdie asked.

"Visiting, ma'am. Thought I might stay. Not so sure now."

"Not a bad town," she said. "Though way too many tourists come for the spring harvest festival."

"They harvest something in the spring around here?"

"No. Used to be two festivals, they combined

them into one. Now each spring at plantin' time, they celebrate the harvest to come in the autumn."

"I didn't think this was farm country."

"It's not. What we do is we celebrate the *concept* of harvest, whatever that means. Town's always been run by an inbred bunch of fools, our foundin' families."

The buildings had sailed beyond sight. Here and there, a blush of neon remained, but those signs were incoherent now, the glass words having shattered into meaningless syllables of nebulous color.

Birdie said, "What's your line of work, Harry?"

"Fry cook, ma'am."

"Fell in love with a fry cook once. Beans Burnet, short-order wizard. A dream, that man."

"We fry cooks tend to be romantic."

"In Beans's case, not enough. He loved his pancakes and home fries more than women. Worked all the time."

"In his defense, Birdie, it's an enchanting occupation. You can lose yourself in it."

"Sure liked the way he smelled."

"Beef fat and bacon grease," I said.

She sighed. "Fried onions and green peppers. You don't measure up to Beans in smell, Harry."

"I've had a different kind of job the past month, ma'am. I'll be back at the griddle eventually. I sure do miss it."

"Then came Fred, my life mate, and I forgot all about fry cooks. No offense."

Birdie changed streets at a shrouded intersection of which I had been unaware until she
pulled the steering wheel to the right.

Having been engineered to isolate the driver
from the roughness of the pavement, the big sedan
rode like a boat. Sloshing tides of fog enhanced
the perception that, with wheels retracted, the
Cadillac wallowed along Venetian canals.

Although Birdie Hopkins drove below the speed
limit, we were moving too fast for the dismal
visibility.

"Ma'am, should we really be driving blind?"

"You might be *ridin'* blind, child, but I'm drivin'
with sunny-day confidence. Been cruisin' this
town almost sixty years. Never had an accident.
Weather like this, we have the streets to ourselves,
so they're even safer. When the sick and sufferin'
need me, I don't say they gotta wait till mornin'
comes or till the rain stops."

"Are you a nurse, ma'am?"

"Never had time for school. Me and Fred were
in garbage."

"I'm sorry to hear that."

"Collection, I mean. Started with two trucks
and no fear our hands might get dirty. Ended with
a fleet, sole contractor for six towns along the
coast. Garbage is like sunrise—never stops comin'."

"So true."

"You can get rich doin' work others won't.
Garbage was gold."

"A lot of times," I said, "when a restaurant's really busy, there's a lot of stress being a fry cook."

"Don't doubt that for a second."

"I've thought about switching into tire sales or shoes. Is the garbage business stressful?"

"Sometimes for management. For a route driver, it's so the same day after day, it gets to be like meditation."

"Like meditation, yet you're providing a good service. Sounds real nice."

"Fred died seven years ago, I sold out two years later. You want, child, I can still open doors in the garbage world."

"That's generous, ma'am. I might take you up on that one day."

"You'd be a good route driver. Can't look down on the job and be any good. I can tell you don't look down on anyone."

"That's kind of you to say. The reason I wondered if you were a nurse is, before garbage, you mentioned the sick and suffering."

As if receiving directions beamed from a MapQuest satellite to her brain, Birdie turned left into a billowing white wall, and the Cadillac wallowed into a new canal.

She glanced at me, turned her attention to the invisible street, reached one hand up to adjust her feathered hat, glanced at me again, pulled to the curb, and put the car in park.

"Harry, somethin' about you is too different.

I can't do this the usual way. Feel like I should get right to it, say I didn't come to you by chance."

"You didn't?"

She left the engine running but switched off the headlights.

Fathoms of fog pressed upon the car, so it seemed as though we rested on the floor of a sea.

"You were a twinge before you were a face," Birdie said. "For all I knew, you'd be another Nancy with cancer or like a Bodi Booker makin' hot cocoa for suicide."

She waited for me to reply, so at last I said, "Ma'am, I think maybe the fog got in my head, because I can't see any sense in what you just told me."

"What I think," she said, "you're in worse trouble than just a Swithin flat busted from bad romance."

CHAPTER 32

B irdie Hopkins took off her white gloves. She slipped one over the gearshift knob and one over the turn-signal lever, so that the Cadillac seemed to be waving at me.

"Seventy-eight years old, still a hot flash now and then. But it's not the slowest change of life in history. Been done with all that long ago. Has something to do with the twinges."

From the large purse that stood on the seat between us, Birdie withdrew a Japanese fan, unfolded it, and fanned her plump face.

"Fred died, it started."

"Seven years ago," I said.

"Love somebody from when you're nineteen, one day he's the same as ever, next day dead. So many tears, they seem to wash somethin' out of you, they leave this emptiness."

"Loss is the hardest thing," I said. "But it's also the teacher that's the most difficult to ignore."

Her fanning hand went still. She regarded me

with an expression that I took to be surprised agreement.

Because Birdie seemed to expect me to elucidate, I fumbled out what I thought she might want to say herself: "Grief can destroy you—or focus you. You can decide a relationship was all for nothing if it had to end in death, and you alone. Or you can realize that every moment of it had more meaning than you dared to recognize at the time, so much meaning it scared you, so you just lived, just took for granted the love and laughter of each day, and didn't allow yourself to consider the *sacredness* of it. But when it's over and you're alone, you begin to see it wasn't just a movie and a dinner together, not just watching sunsets together, not just scrubbing a floor or washing dishes together or worrying over a high electric bill. It was everything, it was the *why* of life, every event and precious moment of it. The answer to the mystery of existence is the love you shared sometimes so imperfectly, and when the loss wakes you to the deeper beauty of it, to the sanctity of it, you can't get off your knees for a long time, you're driven to your knees not by the weight of the loss but by gratitude for what preceded the loss. And the ache is always there, but one day not the emptiness, because to nurture the emptiness, to take solace in it, is to disrespect the gift of life."

After a moment, she fanned her face again, and closed her eyes.

I gazed through the windshield at the desolation of fog, which might have been the waste and void from the time before time, when mankind did not exist or any beast, when there was only darkness on the face of the deep.

Birdie said, "What you said. All of it. Same for me. So one day my emptiness was filled. First twinge came. Tuesday afternoon in May, it was. Not a physical twinge. Just a feelin', like why don't I drive one of the old garbage-collection routes. Wound up at Nancy Coleman's place, former employee of ours. Husband left her a year earlier. Four hours before I show up, she gets a cancer diagnosis. Scared, alone. That year, I drove her to chemo, doctors' appointments, shoppin' for a wig, spent so much time together, more laughin' than either of us would have thought at the start."

She closed the fan and returned it to her purse.

"Another time, I need to drive, wind up at Bodi Booker's house. Insurance agent, lifelong bachelor. Says he's busy, I talk my way in. He's makin' hot chocolate. So we start talkin' Fred. He and my Fred were bowlin'-team buddies, went fishin' like the son Fred and I never could have. Half an hour, he tells me the hot cocoa was to wash down a bottle of pills, to kill himself. Year later, Nancy Coleman doesn't have cancer anymore, she has Bodi, they married."

She retrieved her white gloves and worked her hands into them.

"What about Swithin busted from bad romance?" I asked.

"Swithin Murdoch. Good man, made a fool of himself over this girl. Leanna cleaned out his bank accounts, took a powder. Swithin almost lost his house, business, the works. I made a loan, he paid it back. So why you, Harry Lime?"

"I think something bad would have happened to me at that storm drain if you hadn't showed up."

"Bad like what?"

Although her journey since Fred had shown her that under the apparent chaos of life lies a strange order, the truth of me would be more than she could absorb in the time that it would take her to drive the rest of the way to the harbor.

"I don't know, ma'am. Just a feeling I have."

She switched on the headlights and shifted the car out of park.

"For true, you don't know?"

Whatever event had been pending at the storm-drain grate, it had been related to the peculiar behavior of the coyotes and to the porch swing that had swung itself. I did not understand what linked those three experiences, nor what power or purpose lay behind them, so I could answer honestly.

"For true," I assured her. "How far to the harbor?"

Piloting the Cadillac back into the fog-flooded street, she said, "Three minutes, four."

My wristwatch and her car clock agreed—9:59.

After a silence, Birdie said, "What's so different about you, child?"

"I don't know, ma'am. Maybe . . . because I spent seven months as a guest at a monastery. The serenity of the monks kind of rubbed off on me."

"Nothin' rubbed off. Your difference is all yours."

Anything I could say would be a lie or an evasion, and because she had somehow saved me, I did not want to lie to her more than necessary.

Birdie said, "You sometimes sense somethin' big is comin'?"

"Big like what?"

"So big the world changes."

"Watching the news too much can make you crazy," I advised.

"Don't mean the kind of bushwa newsmen jabber. Not war or plague, not water gives you cancer or here comes a new ice age."

"Then what kind of bushwa?" I asked.

"Some kind nobody would ever expect."

I thought of the absolute whiteout through which the golden retriever and I had traveled, but if that had been not just weather but also a premonition, I did not know the meaning of it.

"I can't have done right by you yet," she said.

"I appreciate the ride."

"Wasn't twinged out of my cozy home just to be a taxi. What you need, child?"

"Nothing, ma'am. I'm good."

"Place to stay?"

"Comes with my job. Nice ocean-view room."

"Lawyer?"

"Have nothing against them, but I don't need one."

"Got a bad feelin' for you."

"I'll be okay."

"Some need you've got. I feel it."

Considering Hoss Shackett and Utgard Rolf and the kind of men who would be aligned with them, I had a long list of things I needed, starting with a platoon of Marines.

"Money?" she asked.

"No, ma'am."

Solemnly, quietly, she said, "Gun?"

I hesitated before I replied. "I don't like guns."

"Might not like them, but you need one."

Sensing that I had said too much, I said no more.

"It's in the purse," she told me.

I looked at her, but she kept her attention on the street, where the headlights seemed to bake the batter of fog into a solid cake.

"Why would you have a gun?" I asked.

"Old lady in an ugly time—she has to take precautions."

"You bought it legally?"

"I look like Clyde's Bonnie to you?"

"No, ma'am. I just mean, anything I did with it would be traced back to you."

"A few days, I report it stolen."

"What if I rob a bank with it?"

"You won't."

"You can't be sure. You hardly know me."

"Child, have you been listenin' to me?"

"Yes, ma'am."

"What was it with Nancy Coleman?"

"Well . . . she had cancer."

"What was it with Bodi Booker?"

"Planning suicide."

"Swithin Murdoch?"

"Flat busted from bad romance."

"I could name more. None needed help robbin' a bank. Just good people in trouble. You think I've gone to the dark side?"

"Not for a minute."

"You're good people in trouble. I trust you."

"This is more than trust," I said.

"It might be. Look in the purse."

The weapon was a pistol. I examined it.

"No safeties," she said. "Double action. Ten rounds in the magazine. You know how to use such a thing?"

"Yes, ma'am. I'm no Bonnie's Clyde, but I won't shoot my foot, either."

I thought of Annamaria saying that she didn't

work, that people gave her a free place to live and even money when she needed it.

Now a gun came to me when I most needed one.

Something more was happening in Magic Beach than just a plot to smuggle nuclear weapons into the country and my attempt to thwart it.

This place was the still point of the turning world, and this night was the still point between the past and the future. I felt monumental forces gathering that I either could not comprehend or was afraid to contemplate.

My cursed life, my blessed life, my struggles with grievous loss and my striving toward wonder had often seemed to me to be the random path of a flippered pinball, from post to post and bell to bell and gate to gate, rolling wherever I might be knocked.

Instead, all the while, from childhood, I had been moving toward Magic Beach and toward a moment when, with full free will, I would either take upon myself a tremendous burden—or turn away from it. I did not know what the burden might prove to be, but I could feel the weight of it descending, and my moment of decision drawing near.

All things in their time.

Birdie Hopkins pulled the Cadillac to the curb and stopped once more.

Pointing, she said, "Harbor's one block that way.

Maybe you'd rather walk the last part to . . . whatever it is."

"I'll use the gun only to defend myself."

"Thought different, I wouldn't give it."

"Or an innocent life."

"Hush now. It's like you said."

"What did I say?"

"This is more than trust."

The fog, the night, the future pressed at the windows.

"One more thing I might need."

"Just say."

"Do you have a cell phone?"

She took it from the purse, and I accepted it.

"When you're safe," she said, "will you let me know?"

"Yes, ma'am. Thank you for everything."

I started to open the door, then hesitated.

Unshed tears stood in Birdie's eyes.

"Ma'am, I shined you on about something earlier. What you feel coming isn't from watching the news too much."

She bit her lower lip.

I said, "Something big is coming. I sense it, too. I think I've sensed it all my life."

"What? Child, what is it?"

"I don't know. So big the world changes—but like you said, some kind of change nobody would ever expect."

"Sometimes I'm so afraid, mostly in the night,

and Fred not here to talk me through to a quiet heart."

"You don't ever need to be afraid, Birdie Hopkins. Not a woman like you."

She reached out to me. I held her hand.

"Keep safe," she said.

When she was ready to let go of my hand, I got out of the sedan and closed the door. I slid her cell phone into a pocket of my jeans, and I tucked the pistol in the waistband so that the sweatshirt would cover it.

As I walked to the corner, crossed the intersection, and headed toward the harbor, the big engine of the Cadillac idled in the night until I went too far to hear it anymore.

CHAPTER 33

Along the southern horn of the narrow-mouthed bay, toward the seaward end, the vessels in the small commercial-fishing fleet tied up where they could come and go with the least disturbance to the bayside residents and to the noncommercial boat traffic.

Where I stood on the quay, along the crescent shore of the northern horn, I could not see those distant trawlers, seiners, and clippers through the thousand white veils of the night. From their direction, however, once every thirty seconds, came the low mournful bleat of the foghorn out on the southern arm of the harbor-entrance breakwater.

Here in the north, the marina offered protection from the storm surges that, in bad weather, muscled in through the entrance channel. Four hundred slips were occupied by a variety of pleasure craft: small electric-motor bay cruisers, sportfishers with metal lookout towers rising above their bridges, sailing yachts with canvas furled, motor yachts, and racing boats. The largest of these craft were sixty feet, and most were smaller.

As I descended a short flight of stairs from the sea wall to the wharf, I could see only a few of the closest craft through the soup. Even those appeared to be ghost vessels, moored in a dream.

Regularly spaced dock lamps receded into the mist, a necklace of radiant pearls, and under them the wet planks glistened darkly.

I remained alert for the sound of voices, for footsteps, but no one seemed to be out and about in the chilly mist.

Some of the sailing yachts were full-time residences. Their lighted portholes were as golden as scattered coins, faux doubloons that shimmered and, as I walked, paled away into the murk.

Avoiding the dock lamps was easy enough, for the feathered air constrained their reach. I made my way through shadows, my sneakers squishing so faintly on the wet planks that even I could barely hear the noise I made.

The sea beyond the bay had been flatline all day; and the currents in the harbor were so gentle that the boats wallowed only slightly in their berths. They creaked and sometimes softly groaned, but the motion was not strong enough to clink halyards against metal masts.

As I walked, I took slow deep breaths of the

briny air, and relying on psychic magnetism to pull me toward the conspirators, I concentrated on the images from my dream. Red sky. Red tide. Fiery phantoms of reflected flames swarming the beach.

At the west end of the marina, on the sea wall above the wharf, stood the building housing the harbor department, which was under the authority of the city police. Here below, the last several berths were reserved for department vessels.

Three were the twenty-foot, firehouse-red harbor-patrol boats that, among other tasks, chased down those who violated the five-mile-per-hour speed limit pertaining from the main channel to shore.

Of the other three craft, only one drew my interest: a seagoing tugboat, half again as big as the sturdy tug that worked only in the bay. From it came the rhythmic laboring of a generator. Many of the portholes and the large windows of the bridge were aglow; a work lamp shone upon a small crane fixed to the long, low afterdeck; and the running lights were on, as if the boat would soon leave port.

The sudden scent of cigarette smoke warned me that someone shared the dock with me. The fog would have filtered out the smell if the smoker had been as far away as the tugboat.

I moved closer to the stone face of the quay and took shelter against a wharf shack, which had

been painted red to indicate that it stored fire-
fighting gear.

When I peered around the corner of the shack,
I could see the break in the dock railing where a
gangway led down to the slip in which the tug
was berthed.

After I had stared for a couple of minutes, and
only when the eddying fog briefly opened a clearer
line of sight for me, I saw the guard move. He
was hunkered down this side of the entrance to
the gangway, his back against the dock railing.
The lamp above him had been broken, probably
a short while ago, to provide a dark place where
he could not be seen as long as he remained still.

At police headquarters, when Polterfrank had
done his thing, Shackett must have thought that
I, Harry Lime, federal psychic agent, had tapped
a power of my own to escape.

Those events had occurred within the hour, so
the conspirators would be at their highest alert,
searching for me all over town but expecting that
I might come to them. Panic would have seized
them: the fear that with one phone call I would
bring a hundred FBI agents, or others, down on
them before they could take delivery of the nukes
and get them out of town.

Evidently, loath to forfeit their newfound
wealth, they hadn't canceled the rendezvous at
which they would acquire possession of the deadly
cargo. Judging by preparations at the tugboat, they

intended to transship the weapons from another vessel at sea.

Now that I knew their intentions and I was on the loose, they might have decided that they dared not return to the harbor with the bombs. If they executed a contingency plan to bring the nukes ashore elsewhere along the coast, I had no chance of stopping the operation unless I stowed away with them.

To get aboard, I would have to take out the guard here on the dock, but I could see no way to do so quietly.

Besides, I had to cross a swath of open planking to reach him, and I had no doubt that he would be better armed than I was. A better marksman. A better fighter. Tougher than I was. More brutal. Probably a kung fu master. Wicked with knives and martial-arts throwing stars that would be secreted in six places on his superbly fit body. And if I was somehow able to disarm him of every murderous implement, this guy *would* know how to make a lethal weapon from one of his shoes, either the left or right, he wouldn't care which.

As I worried myself toward paralysis, a man appeared on the long afterdeck of the tug. In spite of the fog, I could see him, a shadowy figure, because of the brightness of the big work lamp focused on the deck crane.

He called out to someone named Jackie, and Jackie proved to be the guard who was hunkered along the deck railing, waiting to kill me with either of his shoes. Jackie rose out of his shadowy lair and disappeared down the gangway to the slip in which the tug was berthed.

Crouched, I crossed the dock to the sentinel position that the guard had just vacated. Through a gap in the railing, I had trouble seeing Jackie on the unlighted slip below, but after a moment, he appeared as a shrouded form on a shorter gangway that led up to the low afterdeck of the tug.

He joined the other man at the deck crane, and together they attended to some final task before departure, sacrificing a kitten to Beelzebub or whatever deeply evil men did to ensure a safe sea journey.

Unlike the boat slip to which it led, the gangway was lighted, but it offered the only sensible approach to the berth below. The noise I would make by diving from here and swimming to the nearest finger of the slip would bring everyone aboard the tug to the open decks to discover if the fabled Harry Lime might be as bulletproof as he was psychic.

Both men at the crane had their backs to me.

All things in their time, and the time had come for reckless commitment.

Pulling the pistol from my waistband, I rose and went to the break in the railing. I descended the gangway boldly, hoping that even if someone stepped onto the foredeck or the bridge deck and saw me, they would see only a figure in the mist and would assume that I was one of them.

Echoing across the bay, the foghorn sounded like the plaintive call of a prehistoric behemoth, the last of its kind crying out in loneliness.

I reached the bottom without raising an alarm, and crossed the slip to the second gangway. The afterdeck had such a low profile that I could see the two men up there working at the small crane.

Their backs were still turned to me, and I risked setting foot on the second gangway. The first had been a permanent feature of the dock, and therefore solid; but this much shorter ramp was detachable and collapsible and, it seemed to me, fearsomely noisy. Nonetheless, I boarded the tug without drawing attention.

Jackie and his friend were no more than twelve feet away. The halogen lamp burned through the fog with such intensity that, if they turned, they would be able to see me clearly enough to know that I wasn't one of them.

The quickest route off this deck was up a set of six open stairs to the foredeck, immediately to my right. The higher deck encircled a portholed structure containing spaces that an experienced seaman would be able to identify but that were, to me, as mysterious as any female wrestler's boudoir—and just as scary.

Instinct told me that I would be less likely to encounter people if I went below decks. The bulkhead that separated the afterdeck from the forward structures featured a door that most likely would take me where I wished to go.

I had to walk across half the width of the afterdeck, behind the two laboring men, through the bright halogen backwash, but I reached the door, opened it, and stepped through without being shot in the back.

Beyond lay a landing at the top of an enclosed companionway. I descended the circular stairs to a narrow, low-ceilinged passageway with cabin doors on both sides and another door at the farther end, which was well aft of the bow.

Understandably, you may at this point be wondering *What is this bozo's plan?*

As usual, I had no plan. After the fact, it might sometimes appear to a celestial observer—if one happened to be tuned in to Channel Odd—that I had performed according to a meticulously worked-out strategy, using well-rehearsed tactics executed to an operations schedule timed with a stopwatch. As you know, I make it up as I go along, heart in my throat and bowels quivering near a state of collapse.

Over the years, I have found that my seat-of-the-pants approach works well. Except when it doesn't.

By doing, I learn what to do. By going, I learn

where to go. One day, by dying, I'll learn how to die, and leave the world and hope to land in light.

Pistol ready, I went forward along the passageway, ignoring doors to the left and the right, behind which might wait the lady or the tiger, neither of which I wanted. All I asked was that I be spared surprises, although in this world of six billion souls, all acting with free will and too many with audacity, surprises are inevitable, too few of them the kind that make you smile and that lift your heart.

Easing open the door at the end of the corridor, which bucked one of my cherished traditions by swinging smoothly on quiet hinges, I was pleased that I did not at once receive a bullet in the face. I stepped across the raised threshold into the engine room.

An extravagance of cool machinery and a maze of pipes crowded this compartment, a three-dimensional jigsaw fitted to perfection in the stingy space, a testament to the engineering skills of humanity. High maintenance standards resulted in a room that was cleaner than many kitchens, with fresh paint everywhere and not a spot of rust to be seen.

Evidently, not everyone in the harbor department was distracted by plots to destroy civilization.

Once in the compartment, I hesitated to close the door, though I seemed to be alone.

This was a tugboat, not a battleship or even a destroyer, so the engine room didn't have a lovable but tough Scottish-American warrant officer overseeing a jokey but dedicated team of sweaty enlisted men who—between poker games and harmonica interludes and sappy conversations about their girls back home—were forever tormented by boilers failing, boilers overheating, pipe joints bursting from too much pressure, and a host of other crises. Nobody needed to be stationed in this compartment for the vessel to go about its work with efficiency, which is one reason why Hollywood never made a great World War II movie about a tugboat.

Because the lights had been on when I opened the door, however, I had to assume that someone had recently been here and intended to return.

As I was about to retreat and search for another hiding place, I heard a crewman descending the companionway. I closed the door behind me.

Although the equipment was tightly fitted, the layout allowed for repair. I snaked quickly through the service aisles, toward the point farthest from the entrance. Unfortunately, the farthest point was not far enough to make me feel safe from discovery.

Crouched behind shielding pumps and pipes, I had no view of the door, but I heard it open and close.

Someone had entered, though he did not seem

to be doing anything but standing over there. The engines were not even idling yet, and the quiet in the compartment was such that I would have heard anyone moving around.

As I had admitted to Chief Hoss Shackett, when I was suffering from amnesia and unable to remember that I wasn't Matt Damon, I am a guy with a good imagination, which now kicked into overdrive. I envisioned the newcomer, in a gas mask, preparing to pull the release pin on a canister of poisonous chemicals, to kill me as if I were a cockroach.

Before I could elaborate this simple scenario into an opera, the door opened again, and I heard someone say, "What the hell happened to you?"

The reply came in the distinctive bearish voice of Utgard Rolf: "I fell down."

"Fell down what?"

"Some stairs," Rolf said.

"Stairs? How many stairs?"

"I didn't count them, idiot."

"Man, that's gotta hurt."

Utgard closed the door behind him. "Been a change of plans. We've got to cut some throats."

CHAPTER 34

On the farther side of the engine room, which was nearer than I would have liked, Utgard Rolf said, "Listen, Joey, once we have the packages aboard, we won't return to the harbor."

"What? Why not?"

"There's a guy, he's onto the operation."

"What guy?" Joey asked.

"A government sonofabitch."

"Oh, man."

"Don't freak."

"But we kept this so *tight*."

"We're gonna find him. He's as good as dead."

With sharp anxiety, Joey said, "He's here in Magic Beach?"

"What do you think, I fell down some stairs in Washington?"

"This guy was the stairs?"

"Don't worry about it."

"How big *is* the guy, he could do this to you?"

"He looks worse than I do."

I resisted the urge to stand up and disprove that boast.

"If we don't go back to the harbor," Joey wondered, "where we gonna go?"

"You know the abandoned boatyard south of Rooster Point?"

"That'll work," Joey said.

"Damn right it will. The facilities there, the privacy, it'll be an easier off-load than we'd have in the harbor."

"The trucks know the new meet?"

"They know. But here's the thing."

"I see what's comin'," Joey said.

"We need five of us to take delivery at sea, but the way things are at the boatyard, three can handle the off-load."

When boarding the tug, I'd had two main concerns, one of which was how I would be able to determine the number of crewmen I might be up against. Now I knew: five.

Joey said, "We were gonna drop those two, anyway. So we drop them sooner than later."

Perhaps a falling-out among thieves had not occurred, as I had thought when I'd found Sam Whittle drilled five times in his bathtub. The initial entrepreneurs who set up this operation might always have intended, toward the closing of the business, to issue pink slips to those lesser partners whom they considered mere employees.

A few bullets were a prudent alternative to generous severance payments.

"After the transfer," Utgard said, "Buddy will pop Jackie. I'll drop Hassan."

The name Hassan was something of a surprise and a disappointment to me. Thus far Jackie, Joey, and Buddy had led me to believe that Utgard's crew might be composed of retired Las Vegas comedians and that the final member could be named Shecky.

On the other hand, I was somewhat relieved that my second main concern had been partly addressed. I had wondered how I would be able to deal with the entire crew; now I would be required to deal with only sixty percent of it.

Joey said, "But don't cut their throats."

"What?"

"It's too up-close. Dangerous. Shoot them in the head."

"Of course," Utgard agreed. "Pop them, drop them. That's what I said."

"Well, first you said you had to cut some throats."

"That was just a way of saying it."

"You said it, I thought you meant it."

"We'll shoot them in the head," Utgard said.

"The *back* of the head."

"How else? What the hell, Joey."

"It's the only smart way."

"We're on the same page now."

"So they don't see it comin'."

"I understand," Utgard said impatiently.

I have only a few times been in a position to overhear bad men conspiring to commit evil deeds, and on every occasion, they had been pretty much like Joey and Utgard. Those who choose to live criminal lives are not the brightest among us.

This truth inspires a question: If evil geniuses are so rare, why do so many bad people get away with so many crimes against their fellow citizens and, when they become leaders of nations, against humanity?

Edmund Burke provided the answer in 1795: *The only thing necessary for the triumph of evil is for good men to do nothing.*

I would only add this: It is also essential that good men and women not be educated and propagandized into believing that real evil is a myth and that all malevolent behavior is merely the result of a broken family's or a failed society's shortcomings, amenable to cure by counseling and by the application of new economic theory.

Beyond my sight but not beyond my hearing, Utgard said, "From when we leave the dock till we're to Rooster Point, you man the radio room."

"Like we planned."

"You got to piss, get it done now."

"I'll be at the radio."

"We can't pull the transponder, that'll just make the Coast Guard sit up and take notice."

"I know what to say to them."

"They get a GPS report we're at sea this time of night, they'll want to know why."

Joey's turn for impatience had come: "I know. Don't I know?"

"Just don't get cute with them. Play it like we planned."

Joey recited the story to prove himself: "A guest aboard *Junie's Moonbeam* ate some shellfish, had a real bad allergic reaction, needs a hospital urgent. The yacht's too big, a hundred eighty feet, draws too deep for the bay. So they called us, and so we're just bringin' the sick bitch ashore."

"What're you doing?" Utgard demanded.

"Relax. I'm not gonna call her a sick bitch to the Coast Guard," Joey assured him.

"Sometimes I wonder about you."

"Sick bitch? Would I do that? Man, I'm just havin' some fun with you."

"I'm not in the mood for fun."

"I guess fallin' down a bunch of stairs will do that to you."

"Don't try to dress up the story," Utgard advised. "Keep it simple."

"Okay, okay. But what kind of name is *Junie's Moonbeam* for a major yacht, anyway?"

"What do I know? Why do you care? None of our business."

Joey said, "*Junie's Moonbeam* sounds like some half-assed put-put kind of boat."

So it is these days that men plotting the nuclear devastation of major cities and the murder of millions of innocents can be no more interesting than those most vapid of your relatives whom you wish you did not have to invite to this year's Thanksgiving dinner.

"Just park yourself at the radio," Utgard said.

"All right."

"We're out of here in three minutes."

"Aye, aye, Captain."

The door opened but didn't close.

I heard Utgard stomping along the passageway.

Joey waited. Then he switched off the light.

The door closed.

Apparently, unlike Utgard, Joey did not have a body mass equal to that of Big Foot, and I could not hear him walking away.

Because life has taught me to be suspicious, I waited motionless in the dark, not convinced that I was alone.

CHAPTER 35

When the engines turned over and my cozy compartment filled with the drumming of the four-stroke diesels, with the throb of the pumps, with the rotational rataplan of driveshafts, and with myriad other rhythms, and when we began to move, the boat yawing slightly as it had not done in its berth, I knew that I was alone, because Joey had committed to being in the radio room when we got under way.

Though I breathed more easily, I didn't relax. I knew that what was coming would be terrible, that even if I were not shot or cut, I would come through this night with wounds that would never heal.

I bear similar wounds from other such encounters. To protect the innocent, to avoid being one of Burke's good men who do nothing, you have to accept permanent scars that cincture the heart and traumas of the mind that occasionally reopen to weep again.

To *do* something, to do what you feel sure is right and in the aid of justice, you sometimes have to do things that, when recalled on lonely nights, make you wonder if in fact you are the good man that you like to believe you are.

Such doubts are high cards in the devil's hand, and he knows how to play them well, in hope of bringing you to despair and ennui, if not to self-destruction.

Ozzie Boone, my novelist friend and mentor in Pico Mundo, had instructed me, on the writing of the first of these accounts, that I keep the tone light. He says that only the emotionally immature and the intellectually depraved enjoy stories that are unrelentingly grim and nihilistic.

As I have said and as I hope that you have seen, I am inclined to a love of life and to a sunny disposition even in the face of bleak skies and persistent storms. I can find a laugh or two in a split lip and even greater hilarity in the threats and posturings of a sadistic chief of police.

Fair warning requires the acknowledgment that some events resist the touch of a humorist, and what jokes may arise from certain acts can call forth only a less hearty kind of laughter. We are coming now to dark shoals in rough waters, to straits so narrow that virtue and wickedness voyage close together and may be at times more difficult than usual to differentiate from each other.

Across the bay and into open sea, I waited
without light in the belly of the boat. In spite of
noise that hammered effectively at concentration,
I used the time to mull over what I had learned
since coming aboard.

Junie's Moonbeam must have been only a few
miles offshore, for the engines cut back sooner
than I had expected and, after a thus far straight
course, the big oceangoing tugboat began to
maneuver. They were aligning the vessels to effect
the transfer of the nukes.

The Pacific seemed to be nearly as calm here
above the deeps as it had been all day nearer
shore. With smooth water, their work would go
faster.

I rose to my feet and eased through the pitch-
black chamber, aware that surfaces previously safe
to touch might be scalding hot. I kept an image of
the compartment door in my mind, relying on
psychic magnetism to lead me to it through the
lightless maze.

Instinct told me to reach for a lever handle,
and I found it after a minimum of fumbling.

When I cracked the door, I saw a deserted
passageway. With the transfer of the shipment
begun, Joey would be at his radio, while Utgard
and the other three would have to be above, all
hands needed to ensure a successful delivery.

I stepped to the first starboard compartment,
tried the door, found it unlocked, and went inside

fast, shouldering it open, the pistol in a two-hand grip.

The room was dark, but light played on the porthole. Certain that no sleeper lay here to be awakened, I felt my way to the bright circle of glass.

Alongside the tugboat lay *Junie's Moonbeam*, its port side to our starboard, at a distance of perhaps ten or twelve feet. A white yacht in fog, it would have been a stealth vessel but for the hotel's worth of lighted portholes and windows that made it appear as festive as a luxury cruise ship.

From the main deck, the yacht's crew had slung down inflatable black-rubber bladders that would serve as protective bumpers when the boats drew close enough to knock hulls in a set of rogue waves.

Retreating to the passageway, I quietly pulled shut the door and crossed to the first portside compartment. I prepared to go in fast, as before, but the door opened on darkness.

Soft lamplight filled the aftmost port compartment. When I went inside, Joey looked up in disbelief from a photo spread in a copy of *Maxim* magazine.

Letting the door swing itself shut behind me, I took two steps and shoved the pistol in his face before the magazine fell out of his hands and slithered shut upon the deck.

CHAPTER 36

Joey, the critic of yacht names, sat at the short-wave radio. For a moment, staring into the muzzle of the gun, he looked as though he might make a toilet of his chair.

When I saw that he regained control almost at once and that he began to calculate how to come after me, I lowered the pistol to his throat, the better to see his face and every nuance of expression.

"Get me the Coast Guard," I said. "Call them up."

"Me and them, we already had our chat."

"Call them or I'll put a bullet in your leg."

"What's the matter—you can't use a shortwave?"

The moment I took the gun off him, he would come for me.

My mouth had flooded with saliva triggered by nausea, so I made use of it. I spat in his face.

As he flinched, his eyes were briefly shut, which gave me a chance to whip him across the face with the pistol. The forward sight scored his cheek, and a thin line of blood sprang up.

He put a hand to the hot laceration.

Although the anger in his eyes had with unsettling swiftness distilled to bitter hatred, he had gained a new respect for me and might not be so quick to make a move.

"Call them," I repeated.

"No."

He meant it. He would not be persuaded. The prospect of life in prison might have been worse than death to him.

Glancing at the door and then quickly at me, Joey hoped to imply that someone had entered behind me, but I knew that he was scamming, hoping I would glance back.

"Anyway," he said, when I didn't take the bait, "their nearest cutter is fifty nautical miles from here. We're home free."

The idling engines of the nearby yacht sent vibrations through the hull of the tugboat, and all the other noises of the pending transfer left me with no concern that a shot would be heard above the racket. I put one round in his left foot.

He cried out, I told him to be quiet, and I whipped him with the gun again to silence him.

Inside myself, I had opened a door to ruthlessness that I wanted to close again as soon as possible. But the fate of a nation and the lives of millions were at stake, and whatever must be done, I must do it without hesitation.

Pain had changed him. He was crying.

"I believe you about the cutter, fifty miles. So here are your options, Joey. You tell me some things about this operation, then I kill you quick and painless."

He said a twelve-letter word that I won't repeat, although I challenged him to repeat it.

When he didn't take up the challenge, I said, "If you don't tell me what I want to know, I'll wound you in ways so painful you can't conceive of your suffering. Wounds that leave you dying slow, unable to move or speak. You'll be hours here on the deck, in agony, more tears than all the babies you would have killed in those cities, so many tears you'll die of dehydration before you bleed to death."

He wanted to sit on the deck and hold his wounded foot to damp the pain, but I would not allow it.

"Where do the bombs come from?"

I didn't think he was ready to answer, but then in a voice shaken by pain and fear, he named a Middle Eastern country.

"How did they get on the yacht?"

"From a freighter."

"Transshipped? Where?"

"Three hundred miles out."

"At sea?"

"Yeah. Where the Coast Guard can't monitor."
He inhaled with a hiss between clenched teeth.
"This foot is killin' me."

"It won't be the foot. How many nukes?"

"Four."

"How many?"

"Four. I said. Four."

"You better not be lying. What cities?"

"I don't know."

"What cities?" I demanded.

"I don't know. I don't. I didn't need to know."

"Who owns the yacht?"

"Some billionaire. I don't know his name."

"American?"

"Shit, yeah."

"Why would an American want to do this?"

"If he can, why not?"

I hit him with the gun. An eyebrow ripped.
"Why?"

Pressing shut the torn skin with his fingers, his
voice thin and higher pitched, as if time were
running backward to his childhood, he said, "Hey,
all right, hey, it's like this—okay? truth? okay?—
just before the bombs go off—okay?—there'll be
assassinations."

"What assassinations?"

"President, vice president, lots of them."

"And then the bombs. And after that?"

"They got a plan."

"They who? What plan?"

"I don't know. Really. See? Even this much, it's more than I should know—okay?—stuff I found out they don't know I know. Okay? There's no more. I swear to God. There's no more."

I believed him, but even if I had not taken his protestations as the truth, I would have had no opportunity to question him further.

The knife must have been up the right sleeve of his shirt, in a sheath on his arm. How he released it, I don't know, but it came under his cuff and into his hand. The blade flicked from the handle.

I saw the wink of light along the razor-sharp edge, but he thrust before I shot him in the throat.

The crack of the gun was not loud in the small cabin. The tug's engines, the boom and clatter from the work on the afterdeck, and the squeal of one boat's bumpers rubbing those of the other would have masked it easily.

Joey slid out of the chair and folded onto the floor, as if he had been a scarecrow with flesh of straw that couldn't fully support the clothes that now draped baggily around him.

The switchblade was so sharp that it had sliced open the thick fabric of my sweatshirt as though it had been silk.

I reached through the tear to feel my right side where it stung, above the lowest rib. He had cut me.

CHAPTER 37

I sat on the radio operator's desk, where no blood had showered.

In an arc across a bulkhead, ending in spatters on the round of glass, was his blood from the lethal shot, as if it were the spoor of a fleeing soul that had used a porthole as a portal out of this world.

My cut was shallow, the bleeding light, the pain less than that of loss but troubling. Left hand pressed over the wound, I closed my eyes and tried to dream into existence the blue lake of abiding hope.

Stormy Llewellyn and I, at eighteen, had gone to the lake to bake on beach blankets and to swim.

A sign warned that no lifeguard was on duty that day. Swimmers were advised to stay in the shallows close to shore.

The hard desert sun sprinkled diamonds in the sand and displayed a vast wealth of jewelry across the water.

The heat seemed to melt the mechanism of time, with the promise that she and I would never age or know a change of heart, or be apart from each other.

We took a boat out on the lake. I rowed into the blue, sky above and sky spread across the water.

I shipped the oars. On every side, the gently lapping blueness appeared to curve down and away, as though we had been given a small world of our own, where the horizon was nearer than on the former Earth.

We slipped from the boat and floated on our backs in the buoyant salt lake, kept afloat by the lazy winglike motion of our arms. Eyes closed against the sun, we talked.

All the talk was in essence about one thing. We were dreaming our future into existence.

From time to time, we noticed that the rowboat had drifted from us. We swam nearer to it and floated once more, dreaming aloud as before.

Later, as I rowed us back to the beach, she heard the cry and saw the drowning boy before I did.

He had been nine or ten and, showing off, had swum too far. His arms went weak, his legs cramped, and suddenly he could not keep himself afloat even in the brine.

Stormy went over the side, so lithe and swift, the arc of her stroke pulling the water away from her with determination.

On the sand, the mother and a sister, neither swimmers, became aware of the crisis only as Stormy side-stroked to shore with the boy in tow.

She swam faster than I could row. I beached the boat and ran to her, to assist, but resuscitation was not necessary. She had snared him before he had breathed the lake into his lungs.

This is a moment that will remain forever fresh in my memory: the coughing boy, the crying mother, the frightened sister—and Stormy tending to them in the way that each required.

She always was a savior of others. I know that she saved me.

Although I had thought that I had beached the boat securely when I had been eager to get to Stormy's side, I must have left it adrift, for when I looked, it bobbed beyond the shallows.

The lake is big, and the dynamics of deep water apply. While it appears placid on the surface, currents are always working.

I waded into the water and then swam, but at first the boat, in the influence of a current, moved farther away from me.

Perhaps the irrational fear that gripped me was inspired by the near-drowning of the boy, the reminder of ever-present death, also by the fact that Stormy and I had been dreaming our future together and, therefore, had been tempting fate.

For whatever reason, as the rowboat initially eluded me, my frustration rapidly escalated into dread. I became crazily convinced that if I could not catch the boat and board it, the future we had dreamed together would never come to pass, and that in fact the death from which the boy had narrowly escaped would be visited instead on one of us.

Because the boat was adrift and I was not, I reached it in due course. Aboard, I sat shaking, first with residual dread and then with relief.

I suppose now that in swimming to retrieve the boat, I might have experienced a dim presentiment of the shooter who, a couple of years later, would take Stormy from me.

Sometimes, I like to call into memory that day on the lake. The sky and the water. Safe in that sphere of blue.

I tell myself that I can still dream our future into existence: the two of us on a new Earth all our own.

Now and then, as we floated on our backs, the winglike motion of our arms brought our hands in contact beneath the water, and we gripped each other for a moment as if to say *I'm here, I'm always here.*

The tugboat yawed, and the rubber bumpers squealed between the vessels, and from above and aft came a solid thud that trembled the deck.

I slid off the radio operator's desk and got to my feet.

Having tumbled from his chair, the dead man

lay on his side, his head twisted so that he faced the ceiling. His mouth hung open, and his eyes were like those of a fish on ice in a market.

That I had never seen Stormy's body in death, that in mercy she had been brought to me only as ashes in a simple urn, filled me with a gratitude beyond measure.

Leaving the radio room, I knew the time had not yet come for me to venture above. Once the transfer of the nukes had been completed and the crates lashed down, once *Junie's Moonbeam* sailed away into the fog, Utgard and Buddy would at once kill Jackie and Hassan. My best chance to succeed at this was to time my afterdeck appearance to that bloody moment.

Opening off the passageway was one room I had not explored, the aft compartment on the starboard side, across from the radio room. I tried the door, found a light switch, and stepped into a lavatory.

A red cross marked a white corner cabinet full of first-aid supplies.

After pulling off my sweatshirt and T-shirt, I spread the wound with my fingers. I poured rubbing alcohol into the shallow gash.

No stitches were needed. Bleeding, renewed by this attention, would eventually stop again.

Leaving the laceration open to the air and the rub of clothing, however, ensured a continuous stinging that distracted me. I had to work at an awkward angle, and I might not have a lot of time; so I used no gauze, only wide waterproof adhesive tape to seal the cut.

Stripping it off later, I would inevitably tear open the laceration. I didn't worry about that, because if the time came for me to peel away the tape, that would mean I had survived Utgard and his crew.

As I put on my sweatshirt, another heavy thud from the afterdeck shivered through the tugboat.

Although I did not think anyone would come below until the work was done, I turned off the light and stood in blackness. Should the door open, I could shoot as he reached for the switch.

The small lavatory had no porthole. The room would admit no thread of light around the door frame.

I thought of the mirror in Sam Whittle's bathroom, which had reached out to claim his lingering spirit.

The lavatory featured a spotted mirror above the sink. I could not see what might be forming in its dark reflective surface.

My usually fevered imagination could do nothing with this rich material.

Real violence had come. More was pending.

The door to ruthlessness that I had opened in my mind had not been closed. More than darkness and mirrors, I feared what could come out of that inner door.

Heavier vibrations translating through the sea into the tugboat hull were proof that the transfer had been completed and that *Junie's Moonbeam* was getting under way once more. We began to roll in the wake of the departing yacht.

I left the lavatory and went to the aft companionway, moving counter to the deck to keep my balance.

At the top of the stairs stood the door through which I had originally come below. A porthole provided a view of the long fog-swept afterdeck, which was still brightened by the halogen work lamp.

Two crates, neither of which had been there when we had motored out of the harbor, lay toward the starboard quarter of the deck. The size of coffins, wrapped in fog as they were, these twin containers suggested that we had not taken aboard anything as fantastic and grotesque as weapons that could destroy whole cities, but instead merely the less unnatural cargo of Count Dracula and his bride, who were sleeping now on beds of Transylvanian soil inside sunproof caskets where soon they would wake.

Utgard Rolf—dressed in black nylon pants with elastic cuffs tight at the ankles and a matching jacket—and a man I had not seen before were conferring near the small crane.

Two other men were at work on the port side, stowing tools in a secured deck box.

Pulling pistols as they moved, Utgard and the man to whom he had been talking, no doubt Buddy, crossed the deck behind the other two men and shot them in the back. Both sprawled facedown, and their executioners bent to administer a final shot to each at the base of the skull.

CHAPTER 38

Hesitating behind the companionway door, I thought that they would weight the dead men with chains before tossing them overboard.

Evidently, they were confident that from this distance the sea would not bring the bodies to shore for days—if ever—and that by then they would have vanished into their new lives in far corners of the world. They put away their guns, grabbed the cadavers by collars and belts, and began to drag them toward the portside deck wall.

Their backs were to me, but they would remain vulnerable only briefly. Bull strong, Utgard did not long drag his victim, but soon lifted him clear of the deck and carried him.

I dared not think about what was required of me here, but had to focus my mind on why I must not fail to act: the possibility of children seared to the bone by blast heat, of women crushed and torn by the detonation wave, of men atomized, buildings hammered to dust, museums in rubble, churches obliterated, blacktop streets boiling like rivers of lava, and square miles of ashes soaked with the blood of millions.

With no awareness of having pushed through the stairhead door, I found myself on the open deck, in motion.

The immediate fog was silver with halogen reflections, white overhead, and gray beyond the limits of the boat, the yacht lights already having been swallowed as completely as Jonah and his lantern.

The chill wet air on my face was not as cold as the pit of my stomach, and the plume of my breath across my lips seemed cold as well.

With his burden, Utgard reached the port wall. He heaved the body overboard, but the dead man's feet hooked on the gunwale. For a macabre moment, he hung that way, until Utgard gave him a final push into the sea.

Fearing a fall, I nonetheless negotiated the wet and gently rolling deck as though born on a ship. In a two-hand grip, I brought the gun to bear.

The other man wrestled the second corpse halfway over the gunwale. Utgard grabbed one of the cadaver's arms to assist.

Seeing the difficulty of this disposal, I waited for them to finish the job.

A hero does not shoot his adversaries in the back. But *hero* is a title others have wrongly given to me, which I have never claimed for myself.

As the second corpse vanished into the night and fog, I shot Utgard twice in the back from a distance of less than eight feet. He fell forward against the gunwale, but did not tumble overboard.

The other man recoiled in shock but in the same instant went for the weapon in the paddle holster at his hip.

I squeezed off two rounds, trying for abdomen and chest, but I allowed the pistol to pull too high. The first round took him in the face, and the second only parted his hair.

The head shot was enough, and he went down dead.

In bad shape, supporting himself against the gunwale, Utgard turned toward me. Filled with halogen reflections, his demented coyote eyes were lanterns burning unholy oil.

His face was bruised, one eye swollen half shut, one ear crusted with blood—the consequence of events in the interrogation room.

As I stepped closer, he reached, and I shot him twice again.

He slid down the gunwale and toppled onto his side. His head knocked the deck hard enough to bounce.

For a while I took great deep breaths and blew them out, trying to exhale the tension that had suddenly begun to make my hands shake like those of a palsied old man.

Having watched them wrestle the corpses

overboard, I changed my mind about eliminating these two in the same way. Disposing of them would make no sense if I left Joey dead in the radio room, and I did not believe that I could also manage to drag him topside for burial at sea.

A way might present itself in which I could get the tugboat and the nukes into the hands of responsible authorities without making the delivery personally. If I remained anonymous, never coming face to face with them, I would not have to explain the killing that I had done.

I turned my back on the dead and crossed the deck toward the coffinlike crates that were stored on the starboard quarter.

Movies condition us to expect that a villain shot repeatedly, appearing to be dead, will reliably rise once more at the penultimate moment, with shrieking violins as background. But reality has no symphonic soundtrack, and the dead stay dead. Only the spirit rises.

I was alone aboard the tugboat, and I doubted that the collector holding the contract on Utgard's spirit would allow him to linger as a poltergeist.

With killing on my mind, I had crossed the deck in surefooted haste, but with the killing done, my balance seemed more precarious. As I moved and as my feet tripped on obstacles that did not exist, I reached out to grab supports that were not at hand.

A vastness of fog above and all around, an

immensity of sea to every quarter of the compass, and a watery abyss below imposed upon me a loneliness almost unbearable because of its intensity and also because of what shared the boat with me. I mean the dead men, yes, but not only the dead; I mean primarily the bombs, four cities' worth of death condensed and packed into containers that were symbolic urns full of the ashes of all humanity.

The crates transshipped from *Junie's Moonbeam* were built not of plyboard but of steel. The hinged lids were held down by four evenly spaced bolt latches.

I slid open the four bolts on the first crate. After a brief hesitation, I lifted the lid.

The halogen light reached far enough to show me two compartments with a large device in each. They appeared to be of cast and machined steel, of formidable weight, bending the light seductively, liquidly, at every curve, each mysterious detail and each fitting ominous in design. In its entirety, the thing was not merely a weapon, but the quintessence of evil.

The crate had been welded together around an armature that kept the bomb immobile. Special tools would have been needed to free it from the shipping case.

At what might have been the core of each device, a four-inch-diameter hole appeared to have been crafted to receive a mated plug.

I stared at the hole for a while before realizing that also bolted to the armature was a box separate from the bomb. This had a hinged lid held shut by a single bolt.

Inside I discovered a double-walled felt bag that filled the space. I lifted out the bag and found within it the plug to match the hole, which weighed four or five pounds.

From the look of it, I guessed that once inserted into the core, it would lock in place with a twist. One end featured an LED readout currently blank and a keypad for data input.

The trigger.

Returning the plug to the soft bag, I put it on the deck. I collected the other three.

After closing the two crates, I carried all four detonators, in their sacks, up the open stairs to the foredeck, which consisted of a narrow walkway around a central structure. I went through a door into a compartment that served as a combination dining space and lounge.

In a closet, I found rain slickers and other foul-weather gear, as well as a well-worn leather satchel, which was empty.

All four triggers snugged in the satchel without distorting it. I was able to close the zipper.

As I pulled the zipper shut, the hand holding the bag and the hand gripping the tab looked like the hands of a stranger, as if I had just awakened in a body that was not mine.

Since the day on which Stormy had died, I had been called upon to do terrible things with these hands. When she had been taken from me, a portion of my innocence had been stolen, as well. But now it seemed to me that these hands had actively thrown away what innocence had not been robbed from me.

I knew that what I had done was right, but what is right is not always clean, and does not always feel good. In even a clear heart, some righteous acts of the harder kind can stir up a sediment of guilt, but that is not a bad thing. If allowed to be, the heart is self-policing, and a reasonable measure of guilt guards against corruption.

To dispel the apprehension that I had become someone different from the person I had once been, I turned my right hand palm up. My birthmark is a half-inch-wide crescent, an inch and a half from point to point, milk-white against the pink flesh of my hand.

This was one of the proofs that Stormy and I were destined to be together forever, because she'd had a mark that matched it.

Birthmarks and memories of the blue lake of abiding hope: They confirm that I remain Odd Thomas—perhaps different from what I once was, yet paradoxically the same.

I carried the bag out to the foredeck, where the fog was as thick as ever and the night colder than I remembered.

Here on the starboard side, a steep flight of
narrow stairs led up to the top deck, where the
bridge was located.

Entering the bridge, I looked up as the woman
at the helm turned to stare at me, her hands
remaining on the wheel.

I should have realized that with no one at the
helm, the tugboat would have been subject to the
actions of tides and currents, which would tend
to turn it in a lazy vortex. While I had killed Utgard
and Buddy, while I had opened the shipping crates,
while I had gathered the bomb triggers, the boat
had mostly held steady.

I knew at once who she must be.

CHAPTER 39

Over white slacks and an exquisite beaded sweater, she wore a gray coat of supple leather with fox fur at the collar, along the front panels, and at the cuffs.

Setting the satchel on the floor, I said, "No doctor is going to believe you've been suffering from a bad shellfish reaction."

No older than twenty-five, she was beautiful not in the way that women in Joey's copy of *Maxim* might have seemed beautiful to him, but as women in a Neiman Marcus catalog might be regarded as beautiful: sensuous but not common, elegant, a generous mouth, fine facial bones, large limpid blue eyes, and not a hard edge to her.

Taking one hand from the wheel, she patted a pocket of her coat. "I've got a little bottle of nasty brew to drink before we dock. It fakes some of the classic symptoms."

Because the Coast Guard had been told that we had put to sea to retrieve a yacht passenger suffering a serious allergic reaction to shellfish, they might follow through with the local hospital to see if in fact such a patient had been admitted.

The dialed-down ping of the radar drew my eyes to the screen. A few pips were revealed at the outermost azimuth rings. The only nearer pip, moving away, must be *Junie's Moonbeam*.

"Who're you?" she asked.

"Harry," I replied.

"The Harry. I didn't know there was one."

"My mother would like to hear it put that way. She thinks I'm the only Harry there is or ever was."

"It must be nice to have a mother who's not a bitch."

"What's your name?" I asked.

"Valonia."

"I've never heard that one before."

"It's from the Latin for *acorn*. I guess my mother thought I would grow into a great hulking tree. Where's Utgard?"

From the bridge, she had no view of the afterdeck.

I said, "He's finishing with . . . things."

She smiled. "I'm not a fragile flower."

I shrugged. "Well."

"He told me that he would be winnowing the crew."

"Winnowing. Is that what he called it?"

"You don't approve of his word choice?"

"I approve that I'm not one of the winnowed."

"I suppose it matters more to you."

"Why should it?"

"You knew them, they're your mates," Valonia said. "I didn't know them."

"You didn't miss much."

She liked the ruthlessness. She regarded me with greater interest than before.

"What role do you play in the cast, Harry?"

"I'm a Guildenstern, I guess."

She frowned. "A Jew?"

"It's a reference to Shakespeare."

The frown sweetened into a delicious pout. "You don't seem like a boy who would live in dusty old books."

"You don't seem like a girl who would blow up cities."

"Because you don't know me well."

"Is there a chance I might get to?"

"Right now, I'd say fifty-fifty."

"I'll take those odds."

Because I could not sense whether she was suspicious of me to any extent, I had not ventured closer to Valonia. The more relaxed she became with me, the easier I would be able to subdue her without breaking any pretty thing. She would be a trove of information for the authorities.

Leaning against the doorjamb, I said, "What's your last name, Valonia?"

"Fontenelle. Remember it."

"That's no problem."

"I'll be famous one day."

"I've no doubt you will be."

"What's your last name, Harry?"

"Lime."

"Tart," she said.

"Actually, I'm pretty much monogamous."

Her laugh was nicer than I had expected, girlish yet robust, and genuine.

I didn't want to like her laugh. I dreaded hearing in it this trace of merriment that suggested a once-innocent child.

Now I could see that she was even younger than I first thought, no older than twenty or twenty-one.

Valonia's long hair had been tucked under the fox-fur collar. With one hand behind her neck, she pulled it free. She shook her head, and a wealth of spun gold cascaded around her face.

"Are you ready for the world to change, Harry?"

"I guess I better be."

"It's all so old and tired."

"Not all of it," I said, openly admiring her.

She liked to be admired.

"They're going to love him so much," she said.

"Who?"

"The people."

"Oh, yeah. Them."

"They'll love the way he'll take charge. Bring order. His compassion and his strength."

"And his magnificent dental work."

She laughed, but then chastised me. "The senator's a great man, Harry. You wouldn't be here if you didn't think so."

Cautious about being seduced to respond outside the character that I had created—or, rather, borrowed from a Graham Greene novel—I said, "For me, it's mostly about the money."

Gazing into the fog, Valonia blew out a *poof* of breath through puckered lips. "The old, tired world—just gone."

"Do that again," I requested.

Staring at me, she puckered and blew.

I said, "Maybe, after all, it's not entirely about the money."

Her blue eyes dazzled. "The perpetual arguing, the tiresome debate that never settles anything. No one will miss that."

"No one," I agreed, but was overcome by sorrow that she could be so young yet hate so much.

"He'll shut them up, Harry."

"It's time somebody did."

"And in the end, they'll like it."

She inhaled as if trying to clear nasal congestion.

"The endless quarreling," she said, "when we know the issues were really settled long ago."

"Ages ago," I agreed.

She tried to clear her nose again. "The people are going to be so grateful for the New Civility."

I could hear the uppercase *N* and *C* in the way that she said it.

"Do you believe, Harry?"

"Deeply. Plus there's the money."

"It's so wonderful to believe."

"You come so alive when you say the word."

"Believe," she said with childlike yearning. *"Believe."*

She inhaled noisily, and again.

"Damn these allergies," she complained, and reached into a coat pocket for a handkerchief.

From under my sweatshirt, from the small of my back, I drew the gun that held two more rounds.

Her compact pistol, a lady's gun but deadly, hung up on the lining of her coat pocket as she tried to draw it.

"Valonia, don't."

The snagged lining tore.

"Please," I said.

The gun came free, and in her passion to defend the faith, she fired wildly.

In every direction from the bullet hole, the laminated window beside my head instantly webbed to the limits of its frame.

I shot her once, not just to wound, because it never could have been that way.

Golden hair swirled, shimmered, as she spasmed from the impact. She dropped the little gun, and dropped herself, collapsing toward a needed rest, faceup on the stained and soiled deck, an orchid in the mud.

Snaring her pistol, I knelt beside her.

Her eyes were open, but not yet vacant. She stared at something, perhaps a memory, and then at me.

She said, "I'll never get to see . . ."

I took one of her hands in both of mine, and I was not assaulted by the vision of a red tide. That future had been thwarted.

"I'll never get to see . . . the new world," she finished.

"No," I said. "I spared you that."

Her limp hand tightened on mine.

She closed her eyes. And at once opened them in alarm.

"Don't let go," she pleaded, her voice younger now, without sophistication or artifice.

I promised her, "I won't."

The strength in her grip increased, became fierce, and then she had no strength at all.

Although she was gone, I still held her hand and prayed silently that she would not add to her suffering by lingering here in spirit.

I wondered who had turned her free mind from the light into the dark, where and how and when. I wanted to find him, her, every one of them— and kill them all.

In the closet where I had discovered a satchel in which to stow the bomb triggers, on a shelf

above the hanging rain gear, I had seen what I
needed now. I went down to the foredeck, selected
two wool blankets, and returned to the bridge
with them.

After shaking open one of the blankets, I
refolded it lengthwise to make a soft and simple
catafalque on which to place her.

I lifted her in the cradle of my arms and moved
her onto the woolen cushion. She proved to be
lighter than I expected. She was petite but had
projected herself larger in life.

Before her eyes locked open, I closed her lids
with my thumbs and held them for a moment. I
placed her right hand atop her left, on her breast.

I shook out the second blanket, folded it much
like the first, and covered Valonia Fontenelle, who
after all would never be famous. Or infamous.

Questing fog crept across the threshold, seduced
by the warmth of the bridge. I stepped outside
and closed the door.

I threw Birdie Hopkins's handgun into the sea.

At the railing on the open portion of the bridge
deck, I stood for a while, staring down at what
the fog allowed me to see of the rolling ocean.

Within half an hour, I had killed three men
and a woman—but I had not murdered anyone.
I combed the fine hairs of philosophy, assuring
myself that I had found the part between moral
and immoral.

With no one at the helm, the action of tides

and currents had begun to turn the tugboat in the lazy vortex that nature preferred.

On the blue lake of abiding hope, the sun had been warm and every soft breeze a caress, and the future had waited to be dreamed.

Below me now, the ocean was not blue, and I could not see any hope in it, but the ocean did abide.

CHAPTER 40

On Malo Suerte Lake, near Pico Mundo, I had on occasion, for pay, driven sportfishing boats of a size to host parties, but I had never been behind the helm of a vessel as large as the tugboat. I had not driven anything on the open ocean, either.

The control console was similar to those on sportfishers. Port-engine clutch and starboard-engine clutch to the left, wheel in the center, port throttle and starboard throttle to the right. Near the throttles, a switch marked ENGINE STOP. The gauge board: gear-oil pressure, engine-oil pressure, water temperature, voltmeter, tachometers, bilge and fuel alarms.

Because the tug had a state-of-the-art GPS navigation system with a large sea-map monitor, I wouldn't have much need to consult the compass. On the screen now, I could see the boat's position at the center, the relevant portion of the California coast on the right, because the vessel currently faced north.

For a moment, I studied the radar display as the heading flash picked out pips. Revealed were the same number as before, none of them closer, and one—*Junie's Moonbeam*—much farther away.

Either Utgard had turned off the depth-finder or, because of his familiarity with the area, had never activated it. During the short cruise I would be taking, I wouldn't need sonar until near the end, but I switched it on.

I tried not to think about the dead woman on the deck nearby and the three other corpses aboard. I focused on the task of getting the nukes to a place from which they could not easily be transshipped before trustworthy authorities could gain possession of them.

The tugboat faced north. The abandoned boat-yard south of Rooster Point, where trucks waited to transport the bombs to distant cities, also lay to the north.

As I began to bring the tug around to the south, a phone rang with the most familiar notes of "Ode to Joy." It had been left atop the gauge board, directly in front of me.

Most likely, this was Utgard's phone. By now, he should have confirmed to someone onshore that the nuclear weapons had been received from *Junie's Moonbeam* and that he was proceeding to the rendezvous at the boatyard.

I doubted that Mr. Sinatra's paranormal rampage had disabled Hoss Shackett any more than it had

Utgard. This incoming call was surely from the chief.

By the time I brought the boat around due south, the call had gone to voice mail, and after a pause, the caller rang again. I let it go to voice mail a second time.

The conspirators onshore now knew something had gone wrong.

Because I had changed the boat's course 180 degrees, the GPS sea map currently showed the coastline on the left side of the screen. A legend identified the harbor as MAGIC BEACH; and under the words were numbers that meant nothing to me.

Because I had found employees of the harbor department to be arrogant, rude, and homicidal, I declined to give them any more of my business. I would not be returning to the harbor.

Serenaded by the soft ping of radar and by the louder pong of sonar, I throttled up and drove the tugboat south, as if I knew what I was doing, protected by electronics from being misled by singing sea nymphs perched on hull-shredding rocks.

No doubt I remained vulnerable to kraken and other sea serpents of such mammoth scale that they could capsize ships and eat people as casually as we take sardines from the can. I intended to remain aboard for fifteen minutes at the very most, however, so it was not likely that the tug would be seized in the tentacles of a Kong-size octopus and dragged down twenty thousand leagues.

Although the boat had a radio room, the bridge also featured a VHF/FM radiotelephone with a scanner. I had hardly headed south when I received a call on Channel 22, from the Coast Guard cutter with which Joey had been chatting earlier.

The proper procedure probably was to repeat the call sign that the radioman aboard the cutter had given me, then identify myself by the call sign of the tug. Instead, I ignored the call.

For the sake of the nation, I was pleased to discover that Coast Guard officers were diligent and persistent. Apparently, by satellite tracking, they had monitored the rendezvous between the tugboat and *Junie's Moonbeam*.

They were curious as to why we had delayed at the transfer coordinates after the yacht had departed. And they wanted to know why we were conveying the ill passenger south instead of immediately east to the harbor and the hospital.

After spending so much of their lives at sea, they recognized something fishy when they saw it.

Earlier, holding Joey at gunpoint, when I had hoped that help might be closer than fifty nautical miles, I had wanted to talk to the Coast Guard, but now circumstances had changed. I was not going to prattle about hijacked thermonuclear weapons over VHF/FM, on a frequency to which anyone might be listening, including Chief Hoss Shackett and his cloned midget, mini-Hoss, if such a one existed.

After increasingly testy messages insisting upon a response, they gave up. I assumed that now, with engines at full speed, the cutter had adopted a new course to intercept the tug, which was all right with me, as I would have debarked long before they arrived.

"Ode to Joy" struck up again as another call arrived on the regular phone.

I was a popular guy. Of course, having been a good fry cook for some years, I had grown accustomed to having a coterie of dedicated fans, usually with mustard stains on their shirts.

Riding with Birdie Hopkins as she had piloted her Cadillac in zero visibility had been unnerving. In spite of the radar and the GPS navigation, which all but guaranteed that the tugboat would not plow into anything, I found motoring fog-blind across the sea to be far more disturbing, second by second, than my entire time in the car with Fred's widow.

Perhaps the watery abyss below had something to do with my nervousness. Or the aforementioned thermonuclear weapons.

Motoring almost directly across the shorebound waves instead of head-on against them, the boat did not pitch a great deal. But it did yaw more than I would have liked, even on this calm sea.

On the GPS sea map, along the shoreline, both natural and man-made landmarks were identified, including the Magic Beach pier, where all this had begun when I had gone for a walk to have a word with the mysterious young woman who had appeared in my dream.

Five-tenths of a mile south of the pier, the mouth of Hecate's Canyon, a narrow defile, opened to the sea.

Because a running stream had carved the canyon over millennia, one of two conditions was likely to exist where sea and canyon met, the first involving sediment. If the terminus of the stream remained above sea level, the water would feather out as it exited the canyon, depositing silt the way that the Mississippi formed the delta as it approached the Gulf of Mexico.

If instead the canyon had been carved so deep that the western end of it was below sea level, the silt deposited by the stream had long ago been washed into the Pacific and carried away to far places. In that case, because tides also carve the land they meet, the ocean might have pressed into the canyon mouth, forming a cove with a deep-water approach.

Considering the geological age of the California coast and the steepness with which this length of it descended to the ocean, I was counting on condition number two. As I leaned close to the sea-map monitor to read the sounding lines, I noticed that this task had been made easier by a color key on a data bar at the bottom of the screen.

Land was depicted in gold. White signified deep water, which lay under my current position. Blue identified shallow water, and green warned of land exposed at low tide but submerged at high.

An eastward-narrowing but still sufficiently wide channel, surely deep enough to take the draft of the tugboat, bisected the beach. It carried forward into a cove that was recessed in the mouth of the canyon.

Bingo.

Due west of Hecate's Canyon, I changed course for the coast.

No longer content to report on what now lay ahead, the radar seemed to express extreme dissatisfaction with the prospects of a lengthy journey on this course. I switched it off.

By the time I had motored less than half a mile east, the communications officer aboard the distant Coast Guard cutter came back to me by VHF/FM. He was full of questions again.

I felt that action would answer him better than mere words—and would be more certain to keep the cutter coming at the highest speed.

Through the bridge windows, I could see not a single coastal light, only palisades of fog that parted to reveal more of the same, though soon I would encounter something more solid than mist.

I throttled both engines forward and held the wheel steady. The sea map showed the tugboat driving precisely down the center of the Hecate's Canyon channel, though still a mile offshore.

Not six weeks ago, at St. Bartholomew's Abbey in the High Sierra, I had seen the first snow of my life, and within days, I had endured enough of the stuff to last a lifetime.

Magic Beach had been my first experience of a coastal town. At first it had seemed balmy and a welcome change from the blizzard that had buried the abbey.

Perhaps I would feel differently in time, but at that moment, as I approached the coast aboard the tug, through fog on treacherous seas, I felt homesick for the dry Mojave and Pico Mundo, and sick to death of water in all its forms, except as it might be necessary for bathing and flushing the john.

On Channel 22, the communications officer aboard the cutter, observing me by satellite, had stopped repeating the same questions and had begun to issue warnings in an urgent voice.

I was tense enough without having to listen to his shrill predictions of disaster. I switched off the radiotelephone.

The depth-finder began to pong more frequently.

"Ode to Joy" played again. Based on my experience with Utgard Rolf, something by Wagner or anything by any gangster-rap group would have been a better fit with his personality.

What had Beethoven ever done to Utgard that such lovely music should be used as a crime-phone ring?

On the screen: the white of a deep-water channel narrowing and funneling toward a narrow crescent of blue ahead, and beyond the blue a crescent of green, and beyond the green a great stately gold swath of land as solid as anyone could want it, the magnificent western ramparts of America the beautiful.

Motoring right down the center of the channel.

No need to check the fuel gauge. Only a few ounces were required to complete the trip.

The voltmeter. To hell with the voltmeter. I had no idea what a voltmeter did. Probably no more than one in a million people knew what a voltmeter did. Yet there it was, occupying a prime lower-left corner of the gauge board, so proud of itself, mocking everyone who was not a lifelong seaman with high voltmeter awareness.

Gear-oil pressure gauge, engine-oil pressure gauge, water temperature gauge, tachometers: They were of no interest to me now, suppliers of useless data, silly instruments of no import.

What respect I still had for marine technology

was reserved for the depth-finder, the sonar soundings, ponging faster and louder, faster.

My plan, as patchwork as it might be, had been predicated on the belief that nuclear bombs were pretty much as hard to detonate as were sticks of dynamite.

You can throw a fat stick of dynamite against a wall, whack it with a hammer, stab it with a knife—and, at least as I understand the subject, it will not explode. A lit fuse will do the trick, as perhaps will a jolt of electric current from a plunger box, but if you want to drive across twenty thousand sticks of dynamite in a Peterbilt, you can do so, if I have my facts straight, without risk of being blown to bits.

Pure nitroglycerin is another matter.

I had separated the nukes from their triggers or from objects that I sincerely believed to be their triggers. At the time these events occurred, I was not a nuclear physicist—nor am I one now, as I write this—but I felt as certain as a nonphysicist could be that all four thermonuclear devices would ride out a hard jolt without vaporizing me.

The fog did not relent: nothing but fog, fog, fog.

I took a wide stance, leaning toward the console, feet pressed hard against the deck, and gripped the wheel tightly with my left hand.

The pong of the sonar counted a cadence grossly out of sync with the rhythm of "Ode to Joy," and relying sheerly on intuition, I chose what I hoped might be the last best moment to punch the ENGINE STOP button.

I gripped the wheel now with both hands, holding course but mostly just holding tight.

A boat has no brakes. The only way to halt forward motion is to reverse engines. Switching off the engines, as I had done, at once kills further forward thrust but has no effect on current momentum.

We traveled the final meters of the Hecate's Canyon channel with significant momentum. Water, of course, offers momentum-diminishing resistance, but less than you might think when the boat has a modest beam, a V-bow, and a round-bottom hull.

Only subsequent to these events did I learn about these aspects of the seagoing tug's design, and come to appreciate fully how much it still has to give even after you kill its engines.

Sand offers greater resistance than water, as you might imagine, and mud outperforms sand in this regard. I cannot claim to have been able to discern when the tugboat finished ramming through sand and began beaching itself more firmly in mud. All I remember is that one second the channel was still deep enough to accommodate the boat's draft, and the next second it was not deep enough.

The bullet-punctured bridge window shattered completely out of its frame, and every unsecured item aboard the boat flew as objects do in any building rocked by an earthquake. Nothing clobbered me, which spoke well to Utgard's attention to maritime safety.

My legs went out from under me, but I held fast to the wheel.

Shrieking, twanging, cracking, popping, hissing, the tugboat climbed out of the waters of the cove—bow rising, rising—like a prehistoric amphibian deciding that the hour had come to declare itself sufficiently evolved for life on land.

When the craft came to a stop, I got my feet under myself, but for a long moment my cramped hands would not let go of the wheel.

CHAPTER 41

Although I had stopped the engines before impact, I assumed a fire might still break out, even though diesel fuel does not burn as readily as gasoline.

The question about whether thermonuclear weapons might detonate from a hard knock had happily been answered in the negative. Fire, if it erupted, was not likely to faze the cast-steel jackets in which the shaped plutonium appeared to have been encased; therefore, I was not concerned about the release of radioactive material.

Finally able to let go of the helm, I retrieved the satchel containing the bomb triggers.

Earlier, when so much had remained to be done to convey the nukes to a place from which they could not easily be spirited away, I had been too frantic to notice how heavy the bag was. Handling the first of the triggers, I had estimated its weight at four or five pounds. That extrapolated to a maximum combined weight of twenty pounds, but the satchel was at least half again as heavy as that.

James Bond, especially as played by Daniel Craig, would have snatched up the satchel as if it contained politicians' promises. Smiling insouciantly, he would have dashed off with the triggers at a pace qualifying him as a marathon runner in the Olympics.

Bond, of course, has the advantage of being fortified with a diet largely consisting of martinis. I drink nothing stronger than red wine, and not much of that.

Muttering something derogatory about bomb designers' tendency to make everything bigger and heavier than it probably had to be, about their blithe disregard for the need to conserve precious resources, I carried the leather bag off the bridge. I closed the door behind me and held fast to it for a moment, getting my bearings.

The tugboat listed to port, and the deck sloped down toward the stern because the bow had climbed onto the beach. Although the wet deck had not been a serious challenge when we had been at sea, this degree of incline promised to provide me with entertainment.

Slipping, as they say, like a pig on ice, I crossed the canted deck to the railing and looked down. Wondering why a pig would ever *be* on ice, I saw dark ground under the eddying fog.

I hefted the satchel over the railing and let

it drop. All the triggers were wrapped in double-walled felt bags, as if they had been purchased in an upscale store like Tiffany; consequently, they did not clank rudely upon impact.

Because the boat listed in this direction, I had to climb out onto the railing as well as scramble over it. When I landed beside the satchel, on solid ground, I promised myself that my seagoing days were over.

In the past, I had lied to myself about such things. For the moment, however, I was willing to disregard those previous false promises, perfidious as they might have been, and to take joy in my commitment to a landlubber's life.

I considered heading directly inland, through Hecate's Canyon, where coyotes prowled and where the buried bodies of at least two murdered girls—victims of the art teacher, Arliss Clerebold—had never been found.

Nope.

Instead, I picked up the satchel and, leaning to the right as though I remained on a listing deck, I stepped within sight of the breaking surf and followed it north, which was to my right as I faced the Pacific. In this white wilderness, the water line was the only reliable guide available to me.

According to the GPS sea map on the tugboat bridge, the cove had a crescent beach that curved between the steep slopes that formed the terminus of the canyon. At the northwest end of the cove,

the beach continued north along the coast all the
way past town to the harbor.

That turn, from cove to coastal shore, could be
underwater at high tide. Fortunately, this was not
high tide, and at a brisk walk I reached the main
beach in two or three minutes.

A bluff diminished northward for the next
quarter of a mile or more. I followed it until it
petered out, and then headed inland until I came
to Magic Beach's quaint concrete boardwalk, on
which I continued north.

I was tired. The events of the night justified
my weariness. I felt that it would be within my
rights to lie down for a nice sleep on the boardwalk, and to hell with the in-line skaters whose
early-morning speedfest would be presented with
one more obstacle in addition to the usual old men
with canes and little old ladies with walkers.

Weariness alone did not explain my increasing
difficulty with the leather satchel. Weary or not,
the farther you carry any heavy burden, the
heavier it seems, but neither did that truth solve
the puzzle of the rapidly escalating weight. I had
been lugging the bag for less than ten minutes,
and already it felt twice as heavy as when I had
dropped it over the tugboat railing.

With caution, I approached Hutch Hutchison's
house from the alleyway. Although I did not have
to worry that Utgard Rolf might be waiting inside
for me, and although I figured Hoss Shackett must

be busy elsewhere, tearing his hair out and contemplating an extreme identity change that would
include gender alteration, the pair of redheaded
gunmen might have time on their hands and the
patience to wait here like trap-door spiders.

After letting myself through the gate beside the
garage, I had to carry the satchel with both hands.
By then it felt as though it contained the grand
piano that Laurel and Hardy had never been able
to get up those narrow stairs.

I put it down on the brick patio, next to the
wrought-iron chair on which earlier I had draped
my sand-caked jeans and socks. I had to roll my
shoulders and stretch my arms to relieve the strain
that had knotted my muscles.

I stepped back from the house, to a corner of
the garage, where I flipped open the cell phone
given to me by Birdie Hopkins. I called the Cottage
of the Happy Monster. Annamaria answered on
the third ring.

"It's me," I said. "Where's Blossom?"

"Making popcorn. She's the dearest person."

"I knew you'd like her."

"She will be with me always," Annamaria said,
which seemed to me an odd way to say that she
would never forget Blossom Rosedale.

"I'll be coming for you soon," I said. "Within
the hour. We'll have to leave town, if that's all
right with you."

"What will be will be."

"Here we go again."

"You're my protector, and I'm your charge. We do as you think best."

I did not know why I felt now a greater weight upon me than when in my sole possession, aboard the death boat, had been four nuclear bombs and their triggers.

When I found myself with no reply, she said, "You're always free to retract your pledge, Odd Thomas."

In memory, I saw her in the light of the oil lamp: *Will you die for me?*

I had said yes, and had taken the offered bell.

"No," I said. "I'm with you. Wherever this is leading. Until the end of it. We're leaving town. I'll be there within the hour."

I closed the phone and slipped it in a pocket of my jeans.

Although Ozzie Boone's tutelage and the writing of these four manuscripts have given me some facility with language, I don't have the words to describe the strange feeling that overcame me then.

Of all the things I am, a killer is one of them. Not a murderer, but still a killer. And a fool. The only child of a mad mother and a narcissistic father. A failed hero. A confused boy. A troubled man. A guy who makes his life up as he goes along. A seeker who cannot find his way.

No one should entrust someone like me with a treasure. Whether Annamaria herself was the treasure, or her child, or neither of them, but instead some mysterious thing yet to be revealed, I knew that she believed she had a treasure that required protection. Her judgment in the matter had a conviction that convinced me.

In spite of an acute awareness of my inadequacies, I intuited that, for all my faults, this was my duty and my honor. What I felt then, by Hutch's garage, that I cannot describe is a nameless emotion below humility, a deference immeasurably greater than what the meek feel in the shadow of the mighty, what a sparrow might feel if Nature charged him with carrying on his small wings all the living things of a dying Earth to a new world.

And I did not know why I felt all this, because I did not know to what I had committed. Or perhaps I knew in my heart, but kept the knowledge from myself, preferring to proceed in ignorance, for fear the truth would paralyze me, petrify me as solidly as eons of time can petrify living wood into hardest stone.

CHAPTER 42

In case the redheaded gunmen had come visiting Hutch, had not been convinced by his performance, and had settled down to wait for me, I examined the compact pistol. The ten-round magazine held nine. I switched off the safety.

Most likely because I had recently spent too much time at sea, I muttered, "Okay, fish or cut bait."

The Ziploc pill bag in the terra-cotta bowl of cyclamens. The key in the bag.

Ease open the door. Quiet. The fading cinnamon aroma of homemade cookies. The golden glow of the string lights hidden in the recessed toe kick of the cabinets.

All as it should be. Never a good sign.

This time wearing pants, I crossed the cozy kitchen and warily entered the downstairs hall.

When I peered cautiously through the open parlor door, I saw Hutch in the armchair where I had left him. The chenille throw lay across his lap and draped his knees; but he had put the book aside. He snored softly.

I engaged the safety on the little pistol, and pocketed the weapon.

Hutch must have had dinner while I'd been gone, and had returned to the parlor to watch television. On the TV played an old movie in which he had starred. He had muted the sound.

I stood watching the silent screen.

His co-star in this one had been the wondrous Deborah Kerr, as beautiful as she had been in *The Life and Death of Colonel Blimp*, as haunting as in *An Affair to Remember*, as elegant as in *Bonjour Tristesse*, as fresh-faced and innocent as in *Black Narcissus*.

Hutch had not been storklike in those days. With his height and his mane of hair, he had been a lion on the screen. Time had not yet carved his noble profile into a caricature, brow and beak and blunted chin.

Whatever he was currently saying to Deborah Kerr and she to him, the conversation was intense. He held her tenderly by her shoulders, and she gazed up at him, and the moment was building to a kiss as surely as lightning leads to thunder.

"She was magnificent," Hutch said, having awakened as I stood entranced by the images on the TV.

"Were you in love with her, sir?"

"Oh, yes. Very much so. From a distance. She

was untouchable, however. A true lady. There are none like her now."

And here came the kiss. A few more words. And a second kiss. Dissolve to a European battlefield.

Hutch sighed. "Half a century goes by in what seems like a year. Don't waste an hour in boredom, son, or wishing for tomorrow."

"I do my best to keep myself occupied," I assured him.

Sitting up straighter in the chair, he said, "I'm sorry to say no one has come looking for you."

"I'm delighted to hear it."

"I would have given a stirring performance, one for the ages. Acting is a marvelous profession, son. If you can spend enough time playing other people, you don't have to think too much about your own character and motivations."

"To save my skin, I had to be someone else tonight. I called myself Harry Lime."

"That takes chutzpah. You're no Orson Welles, young man."

"I wouldn't disagree, sir."

"I almost landed the lead in *The Third Man*. But I can't begrudge Joseph Cotten getting it. He was superb."

I sat on the footstool. "Mr. Hutchison—"

"Call me Hutch. Everyone does."

"Yes, sir. Well, as you know, I didn't arrive on this job with many clothes—"

Leaning forward in his armchair, eyes alight, he interrupted: "We'll go to a thrift shop tomorrow! I've been afire with the idea since we talked about it earlier."

"Well, gee, what I was about to say is . . . I'm going upstairs to change into a clean sweatshirt. And I'm in such a hurry, I was kind of hoping it wouldn't be too much of an inconvenience if I asked you to dispose of my clothing."

He understood but didn't want to understand. "What a peculiar request."

"I have to leave tonight, sir."

"But why?" He held up one hand that, in the day, held Deborah Kerr. "Yes, I see. Big guy with a chin beard, then a redheaded guy who does or does not have bad teeth. So am I to assume that your differences with them could not be resolved?"

"Not entirely, sir."

"Now you're going on the lam."

"Exactly."

"Once, I was on the lam myself."

I said, "With Henry Fonda in relentless pursuit."

"Relentless in his relaxed way. I think it would have been better if Henry shot me down."

"But you were innocent."

"Yes, but sometimes the innocent die, and audiences occasionally like a tragedy." He frowned. "Son, you came here with one suitcase, and you're leaving with just the clothes on your back."

"I prefer to travel light."

"Just be certain to wear pants."

"I intend to, sir."

"Call me Hutch. Everyone does. These thrift-shop clothes of yours . . . do they come with an obligation?"

"I'm not sure I follow."

"When one buys clothing in a thrift shop and is done with it, is one contractually obligated to pass the clothing on to someone poorer than oneself?"

"Oh, no, sir. You can just throw them in the trash."

"That's easy, then. I thought there might be some protocol that I would want to honor, if you had committed to it." He pulled aside the chenille throw on his lap and prepared to get up from the chair.

I said, "One more thing, and I regret having to ask."

He looked crestfallen. "You want to take the rest of the cookies you made today."

"No, no. Those are yours."

"Oh, good. Splendid. Lovely."

"Sir, I was wondering if I could borrow one of the cars."

"Of course. You're a superb driver."

"I can't risk trying to leave town by bus or train."

"They'll be watching public transport."

"Precisely. If I could drive your car to Santa Barbara, I could leave it with your nephew there, and maybe he could arrange to get it back to you."

His brow creased with worry. "But what will you do then?"

"Make it up as I go along. It works for me."

"Sounds grim."

"No, sir. It's adventurous but not grim." I got up from the footstool. "I'd better change sweat-shirts and get moving."

Each of his long legs seemed to have two knee joints as he unfolded them and got to his feet. "I shall meet you in the kitchen with the car keys."

"Oh," I said, "and a flashlight? I'll need a flash-light. That's it. I won't keep asking for stuff."

"One needs a good flashlight on the lam. No problem."

Upstairs in my room, I realized that I would also be leaving a collection of Sinatra biographies. I suspected that I would not need them anymore.

In the bathroom, I stripped to the waist, washed my upper body, face, and hands, careful not to disturb the taped wound on my side. I put on a fresh T-shirt and a sweatshirt that did not have a word on either the chest or the back.

When I went down to the kitchen, a flashlight and the keys to the Mercedes were on the kitchen island.

"Sir, I can't take the Mercedes."

"It is much better cover than the Explorer.

They might expect a young man such as yourself, in sneakers and a sweatshirt, on the lam, to split town in an Explorer, but never in a Mercedes."

"I'd rather have the Explorer."

"I refuse to give you the keys to the Explorer. The Mercedes is better cover. And *I* am the director for once."

"But—"

Hutch pointed to a plastic-wrapped package also on the kitchen island. The label said PORK RIND, and the plastic was still crusted with frost from the freezer.

"I want you to have that," he said.

"Gee, sir, I do love pork rind, but I'm not going to have any cooking facilities for a while."

"*Pork rind* is merely my code, so I'll know what's in the package. If it said *beef tongue,* then it would contain entirely twenties. If it said *sweetbreads,* it would contain a mix of half twenties and half hundreds."

"Money? Oh, no. No, no, no. I can't accept that."

"I have bank accounts, of course, but I don't entirely trust banks, you see. When I was nine years old, a lot of banks failed."

"I have money," I assured him. "I've saved some of my pay."

"That's not enough to go on the lam. You need to be flush when you go on the lam, as I learned the hard way."

"But that's too much, way too much."

"How would you know? Maybe *pork rind* is my code for a brick of one-dollar bills."

"What *is* it your code for, sir?"

"None of your damn business."

He produced a pink hostess-gift bag decorated with yellow birds flying with curls of blue ribbon in their beaks. He put the package of so-called pork rind in the bag and held it out to me by the two braided gold-cord handles.

I waved it away. "Really. Really, I can't."

His face darkened with disapproval, tightened with authority, thrust forward with the expectation of obedience. His voice was that of the heroic captain demanding of his men more than they think they are capable of giving. He raised his free hand in a bony fist for emphasis.

"Soldier, you are going to take this, and you are going to do the right thing with it, and I will brook no debate, accept no excuse. Is that perfectly clear?"

Annamaria said that people gave her money. I doubted that any of them had forced it upon her with an implied threat of violence.

"This is very generous, sir."

He broke character and grinned. "Take, take. Don't be silly. It's Nibbles's money, anyway."

"Nibbles the swashbuckling rabbit."

"He just keeps earning royalties that I don't know what to do with."

Accepting the hostess-gift bag, I said, "If I ever have kids, sir, each of them will have his own full set of Nibbles's adventures."

As I put the flashlight in the bag with the frozen money and picked up the keys to the Mercedes, Hutch said, "Through dinner and everything this evening, how many times do you think I sanitized my hands with Purell?"

"Well, you had the chicken enchiladas, and though you like the taste of chicken, it makes you nervous because of all the salmonella and *E. coli* stories in the press. So I'd say . . . twenty times?"

"Guess again."

"Thirty?"

With an unmistakable note of pride, he said, "Five."

"Only five?"

"Five," he repeated.

"That's really something, sir."

"Isn't it? Having touched money, even wrapped in plastic and frozen, I'm half desperate to Purell my hands right now, but I'm not going to."

"You're not going cold turkey, are you?"

"No, no. I'll wean myself from it as best I can. I had a brother who was a heroin addict and went cold turkey. It was ghastly."

"Yes, sir. The young Anthony Perkins."

"The experience so shattered him that later he wore his mother's clothes and stabbed people.

I shall minimize my use of Purell but not risk such a fate as his."

He smiled and so did I.

"Take care of yourself, son."

"I will, sir. You, too."

I started toward the door.

"Odd?"

I turned.

He said, "We had some fun this past month, didn't we?"

"Yes, sir. We sure did."

"Good. Very good. That's how I feel. I hoped you did."

"The world is often dark these days, sir. But not in here, in this house. It was a pleasure to work for you. To know you."

As I opened the door, he said, "Son?"

Again I looked back.

He said, "Maybe . . . a hug?"

I put down the hostess-gift bag and returned to him. His height and the strong presence that he projected in life, as he had on the screen, disguised his frailty.

When he could, he said, "You know that son I lost in the war?"

"You mean Jamie, the son you never had."

"That's the one. Well, if I had married someone named Corrina and if we'd had a son named Jamie and if I had lost him in the war, I now kind of know how that would have felt."

He had surprised me in many ways. Now I surprised myself by being unable to reply.

At the door again, after picking up the bag of money, I was able to say, "I'll do my best to come back one day, sir."

"Everyone calls me Hutch."

"Yes, sir. I'll do my best to come back, and when I do, we'll go to a thrift shop."

He bit his lip and nodded. "Well. All right, then. I'm going to have a cookie now."

"Have one for me."

"Splendid. Yes. I will indeed. I'll have two."

I stepped outside and closed the door.

Not immediately able to proceed, I stood there, inexpressibly grateful that my life, for all its terrors, is so filled with moments of grace.

CHAPTER 43

The satchel containing the four bomb triggers had grown so heavy that I needed all my strength and determination to carry it into the garage and stow it in the trunk of the Mercedes.

I zipped open the bag and, in the trunk light, found that it contained nothing more than I had put into it aboard the tugboat.

Relying on my psychic magnetism both to guide me through the fog without a major collision and to lead me to a pay phone, I drove away from Hutch's place.

In these streets that seemed as mystic as they were misted, Hoss Shackett perhaps traveled in desperation and rage, either hoping to resuscitate the plan to incinerate four cities or preparing to flee justice, or seeking the monkey in the mechanism, the cause of his current misfortune.

The monkey, who had a highly active imagination, could not help worrying about the chief, because in his monkey heart he knew, just *knew*, that any encounter would not be with Hoss Shackett the Nice but with the Hoss Shackett who ate little kittens and picked his teeth with their bones.

The downside of psychic magnetism is that it occasionally leads me to a person whom I wish to avoid. This is because every effort that I make to block him from my thoughts is defeated by my constant worry that I will come face to face with him. And even if I succeed in pushing him from my conscious mind, the treacherous subconscious continues to fret about him. Then the object of my dread is either drawn to me—reverse psychic magnetism—or I to him, and often at just the wrong moment.

Therefore, to the exclusion of all else, I concentrated on finding a pay phone as I piloted the Mercedes. Pay phone, pay phone, pay phone.

Since cell phones have become ubiquitous, public pay phones have become more difficult to find. Someday the telephone will be a small voice-activated chip embedded just behind the jawbone and under the ear, and then cell phones will be as outmoded as the coin-operated variety that they have gradually but steadily replaced.

Those commentators who explain our world to us and who tell us how we should feel about it will call the embedded phone "progress." And when someone from the government wishes to speak with you, they will always know where to reach you and, because of your implant's transponder signature, where to find you.

This will go a long way toward encouraging the New Civility and toward discouraging the endless quarreling and tiresome debate that characterize our current society, which to so many impatient citizens seems old and tired. All that has been will be blown away, and you may be frightened sometimes by all the changes, but those who have the perspective and the ability to shape societal consensus are as sure as they have ever been about anything that, in the end, you will like your new world and feel that it is a paradise on earth, so just shut up already.

In the blinded night, wondering if eventually my fate would be much like Samson's, whose eyes had been put out and who had been imprisoned in Gaza, I arrived by psychic magnetism and Mercedes in the parking lot of a convenience store, outside of which stood a pay phone.

Because I did not want these calls to be traced back to Birdie Hopkins's cell, which would be big trouble for her, I went into the store, bought a bottle of aspirin and a Pepsi, and got change for the public phone.

After taking two aspirin, I tasked the information operator with finding me the numbers of the nearest FBI and Homeland Security field offices.

I called the FBI in Santa Cruz and told them about the nuclear weapons aboard the seagoing tugboat beached at the mouth of Hecate's Canyon. I suggested that they immediately contact the Coast Guard to confirm that such a vessel had indeed run aground, and I warned them that Chief Hoss Shackett was among the people who had conspired to import those bombs.

The agent with whom I spoke was initially patient in the way that he would have been when listening to an earnest citizen discuss the necessity of all Earthlings wearing aluminum-foil skullcaps to prevent extraterrestrials from reading our thoughts.

As the telling details of my story accumulated, however, he became more involved. Then riveted. When the time arrived for me to hang up, he brought to bear all the tricks of psychology that a good agent knows, intent on keeping me on the line, teasing from me some detail that would lead to my identification, and convincing me that the bureau was prepared to reward me with a monument in Washington, my face on a postage stamp, and seventy-two virgins provided *this side* of Paradise.

I hung up and, in the fashion that I had divined my way to a pay phone, I proceeded to the church served by Reverend Charles Moran, who would never know that I had prevented him from killing his wife and committing suicide this very night.

The rectory was separated from the church by a courtyard in which gnarled and spiky abstract sculptures, apparently representing eternal truths, scared the crap out of me more than once as they loomed abruptly out of the fog.

I went around to the back of the church, to the corner occupied by the sacristy. The door was locked.

Assuming that the good reverend and his wife were enjoying the deep sleep of the sinless devout, I used the butt of Valonia's pistol to break one pane in a sacristy window. I reached through, found the latch, and slipped inside.

I switched on my flashlight and oriented myself. Then I went through an open door into the sanctuary.

Turning on the church lights would unnecessarily risk drawing unwanted attention, which in this instance was any attention of any kind from anyone.

Besides, in this small way, I was reducing my carbon footprint. Although, having prevented the detonation of four nuclear weapons, I suppose that I had earned enough carbon credits to live the rest of my life high on the hog if I wished.

Above the altar, the abstract sculpture of Big Bird or the Lord, or whatever, did not look down at me accusingly, because it had no eyes.

I descended the altar platform, went through the chancel gate, and proceeded to the third pew, where I had left my ID and that belonging to Sam Whittle.

Although I had no use for Flashlight Guy's wallet, my own would come in handy in the event that I was stopped by the highway patrol while behind the wheel of Hutch's Mercedes and needed to produce a driver's license. I found mine, shoved it in my hip pocket, and left Whittle's wallet where it was.

As I returned to the center aisle, the lights came on.

In the sanctuary, just this side of the sacristy door, stood Chief Hoss Shackett.

CHAPTER 44

Chief Hoss Shackett did not look well. In the interrogation-room disturbance, he had suffered an abrasion on his forehead, one black eye, and a contusion that had darkened the left side of his face. His nose had once been as straight and proud as every sadistic fascist facilitator of terrorism would like his nose to be; now it resembled a mutant pink zucchini. His stiff brush-cut hair appeared to have wilted.

Someone, I assumed, must have found my wallet in the hymnal holder and figured that I would return for it.

Dispelling that notion, the chief said, "Lime. Harry Lime." He did not seem to have discovered that my name was Odd Thomas.

Tucking the flashlight under my belt, I said, "Good evening, Chief. You're looking well."

"What are you doing here?" he asked, except that before the question mark he inserted an epithet that was disgusting but not inventive.

"I was hoping," I said, "that you had another Almond Joy. I've regretted not accepting your offer of half the one you ate."

He took two steps away from the sacristy door, limping to favor his left leg, but then he halted, as if he didn't want to get too close to me. We were about forty feet apart.

"What's happened to the tugboat?" he asked.

"Is this a riddle, sir?"

"What have you done with them?"

"The? Them? Is it one or two tugboats?"

"This time, smartass, I am not going to play amnesia with you."

"Do you have amnesia, sir?"

His right arm had been hanging slack at his side, and I had assumed that it had been injured in his disastrous encounter with Mr. Sinatra.

Now he raised the arm, revealing a fearsome gun in his hand. The firearm appeared to be so large that the weight of it might fracture his wrist, and it wobbled slightly in his grip. A silencer had been screwed to the end of the barrel.

I drew the small pistol that I had confiscated on the bridge of the tugboat. At that distance, I would have to have been a crack shot to hit him with such an intimate weapon.

"I need those nukes," the chief said. "I need them, I need them right now."

"I don't want to be an enabler, sir. I'd rather

get you into a twelve-step program to help you break this addiction."

"Don't push me, kid. I have nothing to lose."

"Oh, Chief, don't undersell yourself. You've still got a lot to lose. Your arrogance, your self-importance, your greed, that insane gleam of historic destiny in your eye—"

When he fired a round, the only sound issuing from his pistol was a whispery *wathup*, rather like Elmer Fudd in one of those old Looney Tunes, lisping *What's up?*

Although I believed that he intended to wound or kill me, the round went well wide of its target, cracking into one of the pews six feet to my left. Perhaps the injuries to his face had blurred his vision.

If Hutch had thought it took chutzpah for me to try playing Harry Lime, he should have seen me attempting to convince the chief that I was Superman: "Put the gun down, Shackett. I don't want to have to damage the church with my tele-kinetic power, but if you give me no other choice, I'll take you out like I did earlier tonight."

He was so impressed that he carefully aimed at me and squeezed off another shot.

I did not juke, in part because Superman would never do so; therefore, a feint would disprove my claim to telekinesis. Besides, the chief's aim was so bad that I feared I might lean into the slug instead of away from it.

Another pew spat up a shower of splinters.

"I'm giving you one last chance to put down the gun," I declared with the confidence of an invincible man in blue tights and red cape.

"I don't know what happened in that room," Hoss Shackett said, squinting at me as he tried to line up his third shot. "But if you had the power to do all that crazy stuff, you would have had the power to get yourself out of the leg iron. You didn't, you had to wait for me to unlock it."

An invincible man might have issued a gentle pitying laugh at such shallow reasoning, but I could not pull that off without a year or two of acting classes. Instead, I said, "Any child could see the flaw in your logic."

His third round slammed into a center-aisle column behind me and six inches to my right.

As he aimed again, the chief said, "Any child, you think? So bring him to me, and I'll kill the little bastard after I'm done with you."

When he squeezed the trigger, no *wathup* ensued. He tried again and then lowered the weapon. He reached to his gun belt to get more ammunition.

I sprinted to the chancel railing, leaped across it, and ran onto the altar platform. From a distance of twelve or fifteen feet, I emptied the magazine of my girly gun into his abdomen and chest.

The pistol proved to be nicely balanced, with little recoil, and I prevented the muzzle from pulling up on the target. Maybe three or four shots missed, wide to one side or the other, but five or six tore into his torso; I saw them hit.

The impact of the slugs staggered Hoss Shackett back against the wall, and his body spasmed with each strike. Yet he did not go down.

He grunted in pain, but I was counting on a scream and a dying gurgle.

Exhibiting a riveting theatricality with which I would not have credited him, the chief ripped open the front of his uniform shirt to reveal the flattened slugs, like puddles of lead, adhering to his bulletproof Kevlar vest.

The six rounds had winded but not wounded him.

This was so unfair.

If I had known that he was wearing Kevlar, I would have aimed for his head. I had gone for his torso because it was a much bigger target. A head is an easy thing to miss, especially at a distance of fifteen feet, when the shooter is a person with an intense dislike of guns, in a situation of extreme stress, firing a Tinkertoy pistol designed for use in close quarters.

The chief had found another loaded magazine. He ejected the depleted one from his weapon.

I dropped my pathetic gun, retreated at a run, leaped across the chancel railing, pleased that I didn't catch a foot on it and plant my face in the floor. I sprinted along the aisle toward the narthex.

For an instant, I considered throwing hymnals at him, but as I had an ear for sacred music—especially Gregorian chants and gospel songs—and a respect for books, I restrained myself.

The front door, through which the golden retriever and I had come a few hours ago, had been locked for the night. Only a key would open it.

Two other doors led out of the narthex, but considering the church as I remembered it from outside, the exit to my left could have taken me only to the bell tower, which would have been a vertical dead end.

As I glanced back into the nave, Chief Hoss Shackett opened the gate in the chancel railing and limped out of the sanctuary, into the center aisle. He looked like Captain Ahab in a mad frenzy of white-whale obsession.

I took the only exit available to me, switched on lights, and discovered that I was in an enclosed flagstone walkway linking the church to an annex of some kind.

Taped to the walls were charming drawings executed by children of various ages, all featuring a smiling bearded man in white robes, who I assumed, because of his halo, must be Jesus. The Son of God, inadequately but earnestly rendered, was engaged in all manner of tasks that I did not recall being recounted in Scripture.

Jesus with hands upraised, transforming a rain

of bombs into flowers. Jesus smiling but shaking his finger at a pregnant woman about to drink a bottle of beer. Jesus saving a stranded polar bear from an ice floe. Jesus turning a flamethrower on stacks of crates labeled CIGARETTES.

At the end of the walkway, beside a drawing of Jesus apparently using his miraculous powers to turn an obese boy's prized collection of cakes and pies into packages of tofu, another door opened onto a corridor that served classrooms used for Sunday school and other activities.

When I came to an intersecting hall, I saw what seemed to be an exterior door at the farther end, and I made for it with all the haste of Jesus chasing from the temple those people who worked for companies that manufactured clothing made from polyester and other unnatural fabrics.

Although the exit was locked, it featured a thumb-turn for the deadbolt. Through the French window in the top of the door, the cold curdled fog was brightened by an exterior stoop light that had come on with the hallway fluorescents, and it appeared welcoming compared to the Hoss-stalked realm behind me. As I was about to disengage the lock, however, a coyote stood on its hind legs, put its forepaws on the door, and peered at me through one of the four panes of glass.

CHAPTER 45

When I leaned close to the window in the door to see whether I would have to deal with a lone wolf, so to speak, or with a group, the coyote bared its stained and ragged teeth. The beast licked the glass as if I were a tasty treat displayed in a vending machine, for which it lacked sufficient coins to make a purchase.

Low to the ground, swarming in the fog, were radiant yellow eyes and, bearing the eyes, more coyotes than I had the time or the heart to count. A second individual stood up boldly at the door, and the multitudes behind these two leaders roiled among one another with increasing agitation, though they remained eerily silent.

Annamaria had told me earlier, on the greensward along Hecate's Canyon, that the coyotes menacing us had not been only what they had appeared to be. She had admonished them that we were not theirs to take, that they must leave—and they had gone.

Although she had told me that I had nothing
to fear from them, that I needed only to be bold,
I did not feel capable of a boldness to equal that
of these coyotes, which had the effrontery to
threaten a man taking refuge in a Sunday school.

Besides, Annamaria understood something
about them that I did not. Her knowledge made
her bold. My lack of knowledge might get me
killed.

Hastily retreating from the exit, I slipped into
a classroom and closed the windowed door. Light
entered from the hallway, and I stood to one side,
in shadows.

I listened for Hoss Shackett but heard nothing.

Although usually coyotes explore only the
portion of encroaching civilization that borders
canyons and open wildland, occasionally one will
venture far out of its territory and into the heart
of a town. A Columbus of his species.

I had never before seen more than one or, at
most, a pair this far from their natural habitat.
The horde waiting in the fog seemed to be without
precedent.

More peculiar than their distance from open
hills and rough canyons was in fact the number
of them. Although a family of six had threatened
us earlier in the night, coyotes do not travel in
traditional packs.

They hunt alone until they mate, whereafter
they hunt in pairs. In the cycle of their lives, there

will be a period when they hunt as families, the parents with their offspring, until the young decide to venture out on their own.

A female will bear three to twelve pups in a litter. Some will be stillborn, and some might die in their first days. A large family numbers eight or ten.

Although the fog could be deceiving and although my imagination is notorious, I was convinced that at least twenty of the beasts had swarmed beyond the door, and perhaps many more.

If they were not, as Annamaria had said, only what they seemed, then what *else* were they?

Whatever they might be, I supposed that Mama Shackett's boy was deadlier than all the coyotes in the night from the Pacific to the Mississippi. I became increasingly unnerved by the stealth with which he sought me.

Hooding my flashlight, I explored my surroundings, hoping to find something that might serve as a weapon, although I recognized that a Sunday-school room would not offer the choices of an armory or, for that matter, of Birdie Hopkins's purse. The chief most likely would not be so slow-moving that I could buffet him into submission with a pair of blackboard erasers.

In my explorations, I came upon another interior windowed door, this one with a vinyl blind drawn over the panes. I discovered that it opened into the next classroom, perhaps so that one instructor could easily monitor two classes.

I left the door standing open behind me, both to avoid making a noise and to leave a clear route for a swift retreat.

Each room featured a narrow supply closet in which I could have taken refuge. And each teacher's desk offered a knee space big enough to conceal a man.

If Hoss Shackett conducted a thorough search, which I expected that he would, perhaps after calling in a deputy or two for backup, he would inevitably find me in any closet or knee space. The only question then would be whether the chief would beat me brutally with a nightstick and then shoot me to death—or shoot me to death and then beat me.

Because the second classroom connected to the third by way of an interior door, suggesting that all of these rooms were similarly joined, I might be able to circle through the annex to the entry corridor, getting behind Shackett and away.

Something creaked. I switched off the flashlight, and froze.

The sound had not come from nearby. I couldn't discern whether it had arisen from the hallway or from one of the rooms through which I had recently passed.

I could have gone to the windows to determine if they were fixed or operable. But I *knew* that I would find the same admiring throng of chop-licking coyotes urging me with entreating eyes to join them for a run on the wild side, which was how they lured domesticated dogs to their doom.

I stood frozen a moment longer, then thawed, and switched on the flashlight. Filtering the beam through my fingers, I went to the door between this classroom and yet one more.

With my hand on the doorknob, I hesitated.

Either intuition or an overstimulated adrenal medulla, pumping inordinate amounts of stress hormones into my system, led me to the sudden perception that Hoss Shackett was in the next room. And not merely in the next room but standing inches away on the other side of this door. And not merely standing on the other side of this door, but standing with his hand on the knob over there, as mine was on the knob over here.

Both sides of the window in the door featured privacy blinds. If I peeled back this blind to peek, I would only see the back of the other blind— unless the chief peeled his back to peek at the same time that I did, in which case we would be eye to eye.

My heart raced. My mouth went so dry that I knew my tongue would rattle against my teeth if I dared move it. I was afraid to turn the knob because, as the chief felt it rotate under his hand, he would *know* where I was, while I would still not be entirely convinced about his location.

At some point, when paralyzed by fear, you have to decide if it is better to move at any cost or to remain motionless until you fall dead from a burst bladder or go raving mad with terror. Thus far, in such moments, I have always decided to move, and again I made that choice.

I turned the knob, thrust open the door, and entered the next classroom. Hoss Shackett was not waiting there for me.

Although annoyed with myself, I was not embarrassed. Even for someone like me, gifted with paranormal perception, it is often difficult to tell the difference between reliable intuition and the effects of an overstimulated adrenal medulla. You must shrug and take comfort that it was merely the medulla malfunctioning, for if it had been the entire adrenal gland, you would suddenly grow hair on your palms and begin lactating.

A few steps into the new room, a disturbing sound caused me to halt and cock my head to listen. An arrhythmic clicking-ticking rose from other classrooms or from the long hallway to the back entrance, at first utterly alien, then familiar, then abruptly recognized: the click of sharp claws on vinyl flooring as eager coyotes scrambled and slipped and sniffed in search of something odd to eat.

Shackett must have opened the back door and

accidentally let them inside. But if he had done so, why hadn't he cried out in alarm when they surged around him or why hadn't he fired a shot to spook them into retreat?

If I had navigated correctly through the joined rooms, the door ahead of me should open onto the short hall of the T, the entrance corridor. Indeed, it did.

Although it was not a noble thought, I hoped that the coyotes had torn the chief of police to pieces when they had come through the back door. Not having heard the beasts snarling and not having heard the chief screaming, I assumed my fond hope would not be fulfilled.

As soon as I entered the short hall, I turned left and rushed to the enclosed flagstone walkway between the annex and the church. I slammed the door behind me and kept moving, but when I glanced back, I saw that the latch had not caught, that the door had rebounded, and that it still stood open.

I was in the Hall of What Would Jesus Do, where I ran past a child's drawing that I had not noticed during my previous passage: Jesus in a helicopter, rescuing livestock from a veal farm.

When I reached the entrance to the narthex, I looked back and saw coyotes leaping through the annex door into the enclosed walkway, tails lashing with the delight of natural-born gourmands when they saw me.

I took time to close the narthex door between me and the pack, and to make certain that the latch engaged.

The front entrance to the church remained locked. I returned along the main aisle of the nave, hurrying toward the chancel railing over which I had fled such a short while ago.

Because the coyotes couldn't have gotten into the Sunday-school annex on their own and because the chief hadn't cried out in terror or in the agony of a bitten man, I considered the possibility that he had let them inside to assist in the search for me.

That made no sense. Even coyotes that were something more than only what they appeared to be were nonetheless coyotes, and evil police chiefs were still human beings. Predatory wild animals and people did not form multispecies gangs for their mutual enrichment, not even in California.

I must be overlooking something. This wouldn't be the first time.

As I threw open the chancel railing and entered the sanctuary, even in my haste I was smug enough to congratulate myself on my quick thinking and fast action. When, in a moment, I departed the church by the sacristy door, the slavering coyotes would be roaming through the annex, confused and distracted, and I would have a clear track to the Mercedes parked in the street.

In the sacristy, I crunched across the glass from the window that I had broken to gain entrance. Evidently, Hoss Shackett had been nearby at the time, had heard the noise, and had followed me into the church through the same window.

Why he had been in the immediate neighborhood, I did not know and did not need to know. Curiosity + cats = road kill. All that mattered was getting to the Mercedes and splitting before the chief saw what vehicle I was driving.

I unlocked the sacristy door and went out into the fog, through which I could see many lights at the previously dark rectory, on the farther side of the courtyard that was populated by blood-curdling devotional statuary.

Perhaps Reverend Charles Moran had been awakened by a poor parishioner who had no more dried peat moss or briquettes of dung to burn in her potbellied stove, nor any more porridge to feed the six orphaned nieces with whom she shared her one-room shanty out by the paupers' graveyard, and now he was preparing to rush off to bring her a selection of Lean Cuisine entrées and a case of Perrier.

Whatever he was up to, I assured myself that it was none of my business, but then as I headed toward the street, I had a change of heart at the sight of yellow-eyed legions of coyotes appearing out of the fog as they rounded the corner of the bell tower. As I could not return to the church and as the minister's residence offered the nearest haven, I decided to ask if Reverend Moran needed a companion on his mission of mercy.

Maybe the coyotes, too, were badly frightened by the unorthodox sculpture and put off their stride, or maybe I found resources that I had never before tapped. Instead of trying to keep up with me, those cousins of wolves decided to outflank me, angling toward the front of the rectory with the intention of being there with bibs on when I arrived.

Still a member of the smartest if also most ignorant species on the planet, I changed course for the back of the house, which I hoped to reach before they realized what I had done.

They continued to lope through the night in silence, which was not characteristic of their kind. Usually, in the hunt, they issued ululant howls, eerie songs of death, that chilled the blood.

Springing up the back-porch steps, I sensed that the silent predators had gotten wise to my trick and were in fierce competition to be the first to rip out the seat of my jeans.

Certain that I had no time to knock and present myself properly, I tried the door and blew out a gust of breath when it proved to be unlocked.

CHAPTER 46

Inside the rectory, as I engaged the lock, I hoped the coyotes didn't have a key. I noted with relief, there was no pet door.

Tidy, cheerful, the kitchen contained nothing that identified it as that of a clergyman.

On the refrigerator were a collection of decorative magnets that featured uplifting though not spiritual messages. One declared EVERY DAY IS THE FIRST DAY OF YOUR LIFE, which seemed to me to be an excuse to remain infantile.

I did not know what to do next.

Nothing unusual about that.

Hoss Shackett might have been on his way to see Reverend Moran when he heard me break the sacristy window. He could show up here at any time.

Currently more deranged than usual, alarmed, desperate, the chief might even have decided that, after all, he had to kill the minister, who had witnessed my arrest.

Considering all that had happened since I had been taken into custody and how totally the chief's plans had fallen apart, killing Reverend Moran no longer made any sense, if it ever had. But that was the way of a sociopath like the chief: He could pass for normal year after year—until suddenly he no longer could.

Intending to locate the minister and warn him, I left the kitchen—and heard people talking. I prowled swiftly room by room until I arrived at the half-open door of a study, off the entrance foyer, where I stopped when I recognized Charles Moran's voice.

"The Lord is with us, Melanie."

A woman laughed tenderly. She had the kind of musical voice that on certain words trembled toward bird song. "Charlie, dear, the Lord is at all times with us. Here."

"I don't know that I should."

"Jesus himself imbibed, Charlie."

They clinked glasses, and after a hesitation, I pushed open the door and entered the study.

Reverend Moran stood beside the desk, wearing chinos, a tan turtleneck, and a sports jacket. He looked up from his drink, his eyes widening. "Todd."

"I'm not here to harm you," I assured him.

The woman with him was attractive but with a hairstyle twenty years behind the times.

"Mrs. Moran?" I asked, and she nodded, and I said, "Don't be afraid."

To my surprise, Reverend Moran drew a pistol from under his jacket, and to my greater surprise, he shot his wife dead.

He turned the pistol on me. In answer to my astonishment, he said, "She poured the first drink. She'd have suggested I pour a second."

I noticed the brand name on the bottle: Lord Calvert.

The Lord is with us, Melanie.

Charlie, dear, the Lord is at all times with us.

"And when my hands were busy fixing the drink, she would have pulled the pistol under *her* jacket and shot me."

"But. She. You. Your wife."

"Of eighteen years. That's why I could read her so well."

"Dead. Look. Dead. Why?"

"The way this blew up, there's not going to be enough money for both of us."

"But. You. Church. Jesus."

"I'll miss the church. My flock."

"The bombs? You? Part of that?"

Chief Hoss Shackett announced himself and cured my incoherence by slamming the flat of his hand so hard against the back of my head that I stumbled forward and fell too close to the dead woman.

As I rolled onto my back and looked up, the chief loomed behind his mutant-pink-zucchini nose. "You knew he was part of it, shithead. That's why you came here in the first place, nosing around."

Earlier in the night, I had arrived at the church with the dog, out of that unusually dense fog that had been more than a fog, that had seemed to me like a premonition of absolute destruction.

On consideration, it made sense that if my blind wandering with the golden retriever had been a kind of waking premonition, then I might have found my way to a place that was associated with the truth behind that hideous vision.

Shackett pointed his gun at me. "Don't get cute."

Looking up at him, my ears ringing, I said, "I don't feel cute."

Reverend Moran said, "Kill him."

"No flying furniture," Shackett warned me.

"None. No, sir."

"Starts moving, I blow your face off."

"Face. Off. I hear you."

"Kill him," the minister repeated.

"You sucker-punched me before," Shackett said.

"I felt bad about that, sir."

"Shut up."

"Yes, sir."

"You see my gun, shithead?"

"Yes, sir."

"Where is my gun?"

"In my face, sir."

"Where it *stays*."

"I understand."

"How long to squeeze a trigger?"

"Fraction of a second, sir."

"See that chair?"

"Yes, sir."

"If that chair moves?"

"Face. Off."

"See that desk set?"

"I see it, sir."

"If that desk set moves?"

"Good-bye face."

"Kill the bastard," Reverend Moran urged.

The minister was still holding his pistol.

His hand was twitching.

He wanted to waste me himself.

"Get up," Shackett ordered me. "You're gonna talk."

As I obeyed, Reverend Moran objected. "No talk."

"Control yourself," Shackett admonished the minister.

"Just kill him, and let's go."

"I want answers."

"He won't give you any."

"I might," I assured them. "I will. I'd like to."

Shackett said, "Coast Guard's reporting the tug is beached."

"Yes, sir," I said.

"I'm not talking to you, shithead."

"My mistake."

Reverend Moran said, "Beached where?"

"The cove at Hecate's Canyon."

Reverend Moran said, "Could we—"

"No. Coast Guard's all over it."

"Kill him," Reverend Moran said more ferociously.

"When it's time."

Reverend Moran said, "It's time now."

"It's not time," Shackett said.

"It's not," I agreed.

"Hoss, it's over," the minister said.

His gun hand shook like a Pentecostal receiving the spirit.

"I know it's over," Shackett said.

"Do you *really* know it's over?"

"Oh, I really know," Shackett said.

"We gotta fly," the minister said.

Shackett said, "We have a little time."

"I want to be gone," Reverend Moran insisted.

"You can't wait five minutes?"

"I want to be gone now."

"You want to be gone now?"

"Right now, Hoss. Gone. Now."

Hoss Shackett shot Reverend Moran in the head, said, "Now you're gone," and had his gun back in my face before I could blink.

"This is bad," I said.

"You think this is bad, Harry?"

"Oh, I know it's bad. Very bad."

"It can get worse."

"Yes. I've seen how it can."

The Reverend and Mrs. Moran were not bleeding. This did not mean they were not human.

They had not had time to bleed. They had died instantly. Neat corpses.

"I want what you've got," Shackett said.

"What have I got?" I asked.

"The juice."

"What juice?"

"The stuff makes you psychic."

"There's no stuff."

"What did you call the power? The furniture power?"

"Telekinesis."

"I want that. I want the juice."

"I told you—one shot, it's for life."

"That was bullshit."

If only he knew.

No bull was involved.

I can produce it without a bull.

"One shot," I insisted. "Then they have you."

"You say the government screwed you?"

"I hate them. They screwed me good."

"Where is my gun?"

"It's in my face, sir. May I ask a question?"

"Hell, no."

I nodded and bit my lip.

He glared at me. "What?"

"Why didn't the coyotes tear you to pieces?"

"What coyotes?"

376 ODD HOURS

"When you let them into the Sunday school."

"Don't try to make me think you're crazy on drugs, Harry."

"I wouldn't, sir."

"That would be as pathetic as the amnesia crap."

"Yes, sir."

"My point is, if the government screwed you, then you would have sold out for twenty-five million."

"They would have killed my family."

"You're not married."

"No. It's my brother."

"Who cares about a brother?"

"We're twins. We're so close."

"I don't buy it, Harry."

"He's paraplegic, see."

"So what?"

"And he has a learning disability."

"A what?"

"And he lost an eye in the war."

"What're you pulling here?"

"Iraq. My other brother, Jamie, he died there."

"Did that chair just move?"

"No, sir."

"I thought I saw it move."

"No, sir."

"If it moves—"

"Good-bye face. Yes, sir."

"You've got a one-eyed paraplegic brother."

"Yes, sir. With a learning disability."

"Does he have a harelip, too?"

"No, sir."

"The first thing you said was true."

Astonished, I said, "It was?"

"You know it was."

"And what first thing was that, sir?"

"That the drug facilitated psychic powers for twelve hours."

"Twelve to eighteen. Yes, I remember saying that."

"I thought you would."

"That's why you're the chief of police."

"Don't try sucking up to me, Harry."

"No, sir. That wouldn't work with you."

"I'd love to blow your face off."

"I can feel your passion, sir."

"You take a pill a day," he said.

"Yes, sir, a multivitamin."

"The psychic pill. The tele-what pill."

"Telekinesis, sir."

"You take one a day."

"I guess I have to admit it, sir."

"Did that inkwell just move?"

"No, sir."

"Where is my gun?"

"It's in my face, sir."

"If that inkwell moves."

"Good-bye face. Yes, sir."

We had developed an intricate litany.

You would have thought we were in a *Catholic* rectory.

"So you have to admit it, do you?"

"Yes, sir. I have to admit it."

"So you have a supply of the pills."

"Yes, sir. I have quite a supply."

"I want those pills."

"I should warn you, sir."

"Warn me what?"

"Telekinesis isn't what it's cracked up to be."

"Look at my face, Harry."

"I feel bad about that, sir."

"Shut up, shithead."

"Yes, sir."

"I think it's *everything* it's cracked up to be."

One of the redheaded gunmen appeared in the doorway behind Hoss Shackett.

"Oh, Lordy," I said.

Shackett grinned. Some of his teeth were broken.

Way to go, Mr. Sinatra.

I wished Mr. Sinatra would deal with the redhead.

But he had probably moved on to Paradise. Just my luck.

"You're in a corner now, aren't you, Harry?"

"I can't catch a break."

The new arrival was the redhead with the methamphetamine teeth.

"Don't try that trick with me, Harry."

"What trick, sir?"

"Pretending someone's behind me."

"Someone is behind you, sir."

"So I'll turn and look, and you'll go for me."

"No, sir. He's a friend of yours, and no friend of mine."

"Where's my gun, Harry?"

"It's in my face, sir."

"Give me your pills."

"I don't have them with me, sir."

"Where are they?"

"In my pillbox."

"Where's your pillbox?"

"Chicago."

"I'm gonna blow your face off, Harry."

"Not without those pills, sir."

"I'll torture it out of you. Don't think I won't."

"I haven't mistaken you for a nun, sir."

"Stop scamming me with the over-the-shoulder look."

"No reason to scam you, sir. He's really your buddy."

The redhead disproved my contention by shooting Hoss Shackett in the head.

I let out an expletive that seemed to have come from the people I had been associating with, not from me, and I staggered back from the dead and toppling chief. Staggering, I fell; and falling, I fell upon the minister's dead wife.

I heard myself spewing exclamations of disgust and horror as I tried to get off the dead woman, but it seemed as though she grabbed at me, clutched

me, and by the time I crawled away from her on
my hands and knees, I was gibbering like someone
who had barely escaped the House of Usher or any
other place of Poe's creation.

"Get up," said the redhead.

"I'm trying."

"What's wrong with you?" he asked.

"What's *wrong* with me?"

"Are you spastic?"

"Are you *blind*?"

"Don't speak harshly to me," he said.

"Do you see all these *dead* people?"

"Do they bother you—dead people?"

"You have no idea," I said.

"They are just people, except dead."

"What—then I'm just a corpse, except alive?"

His smile was ghastly. "Yes, precisely."

I had invented a neat organizational chart for
these people. The redheads were bottom-feeders.
Utgard was middle management. Shackett was at
or near the top. If I ever hosted a dinner party, I
assumed I knew exactly how they should be seated.

Instead, this redhead's attitude suggested that
he not only had the temerity to whack the chief
but also the authority. His rotten teeth seemed
not to be proof of low status, after all, but perhaps
a fashion choice.

"Do you have to point that gun at my head?"

"Would you prefer I point it at your chest?"

"Yes. In fact, yes."

"You'll be just as dead either way."

"But I'll be a prettier dead this way."

"It's loaded with door-busters."

"If you're going to kill me, just do it."

"I didn't say I was going to kill you."

"You're not going to kill me?"

"Most likely, yes. But one never knows."

"What do you want from me?" I demanded.

"First, I want to talk to you."

"This never works out well."

"Have a seat."

"What—*here*?"

"On the sofa."

"I can't talk with dead people."

"They will not interrupt."

"I'm serious about this. I'm freaked out."

"Don't speak harshly to me," he said.

"Well, you just don't listen."

"That is unfair. I listen. I'm a good listener."

"You haven't been listening to *me*."

"You sound just like my wife."

This was interesting.

"You have a wife?"

"I adore her."

"What's her name?"

"Do not laugh when I tell you."

"I am in no mood to laugh, sir."

He watched me closely for signs of amusement.

The gun had a large bore. It probably would bust doors.

"Her name is Freddie."

"Why, that's delightful."

"Delightful like funny?"

"No, delightful like charming."

"She is not a masculine woman."

"The name implies no such thing," I assured him.

"She is entirely feminine."

"Freddie is a nickname for Frederica."

He stared at me, processing what I had said.

"Are you sure about this?" he asked.

"Absolutely. Frederica, Freddie."

"Frederica is a nice feminine name."

"Exactly my point," I said.

"But her parents only named her Freddie."

I shrugged. "Parents. What're you gonna do?"

He stared at me for a long moment.

I tried not to study his teeth.

Finally he said, "Perhaps we can talk in the kitchen."

"Have you left any dead people in the kitchen?"

"I could find no one there to kill."

"Then the kitchen will be fine," I said.

CHAPTER 47

The redhead and I sat across from each other at the kitchen table. He still pointed the gun at me, but less aggressively.

He indicated the decorative magnets on the refrigerator door. "What does that one mean—'I complained I had no shoes, till I met a man with no feet.' "

"You've got me. I'm sure Reverend Moran had all the shoes he wanted."

"Why would a man have no feet?"

"I guess someone cut them off."

"That will happen," he said. "Moran always annoyed me, I never saw him in this."

"How *did* he fit?" I asked. "Minister. Church. Jesus. Nuclear terrorism. I don't get it."

"He was I-I-G-O," said the redhead.

"He was igo?"

"International Interdenominational Goodwill Organization. He founded it."

"Now I know less than I did."

"He went all over the world furthering peace."

"And look what a paradise he made for us."

"You know, I think you're a funny kid."

"So I've been told. Usually with a gun pointed at me."

"He negotiated with countries that persecuted Christians."

"He wanted to see them persecuted more?"

"Moran had to negotiate with the persecutors, of course."

"I'll bet *they* have tough lawyers."

"In the process, he made a great many valuable contacts."

"You mean dictators, thugs, and mad mullahs."

"Precisely. Special friendships. Somewhere along the way, he realized that he was engaged in a lost cause."

"Promoting good will."

"Yes. He became weary, disillusioned, depressed. Half a million to a million Christians are killed each year in these countries. He was saving five at a time. He was a man who had to have a cause, and a successful cause that made him proud, so he found a new one."

"Let me guess—himself."

"IIGO had an impeccable reputation as a charity. That made it a perfect conduit for laundering funds for rogue governments . . . then for terrorists. One thing led to another."

"Which led to him shot in the head."

"Did you kill him?" he asked.

"No, no. Shackett did it."

"Did you kill Mrs. Moran?"

"No, no. Reverend Moran killed her."

"Then you have killed no one here?"

"No one," I confirmed.

"But aboard the tugboat," he said.

"I crawled so he could walk. He walked so you could fly."

He frowned. "What does that mean?"

"I have no idea. I just read it off the refrigerator."

He licked his black and crumbling teeth, wincing as he did so.

"Harry—is your name in fact Harry?"

"Well, it's not Todd."

"Do you know why I haven't killed you yet, Harry?"

"I've given you no reason to?" I said hopefully.

"For one thing, my brother and I have a responsibility here."

"The resemblance is remarkable. Are you identical twins?"

"In this current operation, we represent the nation that produced the bombs."

"You will absolutely be able to sell film rights."

"To save our own skins, we will have to give them a *perfect* story believable in every detail."

"Oh. Every detail. Well. Talk about a tall order."

"If you cooperate fully with those details, I don't have to kill you. But there's another thing."

"There's always another thing."

He favored me with a sly, calculating look. You might think that was the only look he had, but in fact I had seen one other.

"I was listening outside the study door long before you saw me," he said.

"Your employers get their money's worth."

"I heard something that intrigued me. The pills, Harry."

"Oh, my."

"I am always looking for a new experience."

"Not me. I've had too many just tonight."

I half expected a coyote with a gun to appear behind the redhead and shoot him dead. *Then* we'd see how long I could keep myself alive with conversation.

"My brother won't touch drugs," he said.

"There's got to be one in every family."

"For a while I had a minor problem with methamphetamine."

"I'm sorry to hear that."

"But I'm cured now."

"I'm glad to hear that."

"I do some heroin, but I don't overdo it."

"That's the key. Moderation."

He leaned toward me over the dinette table. I waited for his breath to peel up the Formica.

He whispered, "Is it true? Pills that, as Shackett said, facilitate psychic powers?"

"It's a secret government project."

"Isn't America amazing?"

"I've got a bottle in my car. They're disguised as aspirin."

"You know another reason I haven't killed you yet, Harry?"

"I am clueless."

"I never caught you once looking at my teeth."

"Your teeth? What about your teeth?"

He grinned broadly at me.

"So what?" I said. "Some people don't even have teeth."

"You're a very considerate guy, you know that?"

I shrugged.

"No, Harry, you are. People can be cruel."

"Tell me about it. I've had my own experiences."

"You? You're a pretty good-lookin' guy."

"Well, I compete okay," I said. "But I don't mean me. I have a brother, too. Maybe you heard me telling Shackett about him."

"No, I must've come in after that."

"My brother, he's paraplegic."

"Oh, man, that's a tough one."

"And blind in one eye."

"See, that's where you learned compassion."

"It's learning the hard way."

"Know what I'm gonna do? I'm gonna have all my teeth pulled, replace 'em with implants."

"Ouch."

"It's for Freddie."

"Love makes the world go 'round. But still . . . ouch."

"Oh, they put you in twilight sleep. It's painless."

I said, "For your sake, I hope that's true."

"If the doctor's lyin', I'll kill him after."

He laughed, and I laughed, and with Mrs. Moran's pistol, I shot him under the table.

Reflexively, the redhead squeezed off a round that whistled past my head, and I brought Mrs. Moran's gun above the table and shot him twice.

He almost rocked his chair over backward, but then he dropped forward on the table, as dead as Lincoln but not as great a man, and his gun fell out of his hand.

For a while I sat there shaking. I could not get up. I was so cold that my breath should have been pluming from me in a frost.

When the redhead had shot the chief, I had stumbled backward and had managed to fall face-down atop the minister's dead wife.

Reverend Moran had been correct: His wife had been carrying a pistol in a holster under her blazer.

Finally I got up from the kitchen table. I went to the sink and put the pistol on the cutting board.

I turned on the hot water and splashed my face. I couldn't get warm. I was freezing.

After a while, I realized that I was washing my hands. Evidently, I had washed them several times. The water was so hot that my hands were bright red.

CHAPTER 48

Although I did not want to touch Melanie Moran's pistol again, I could hear Fate shouting at me to learn, for heaven's sake, from experience. The current lesson, which I had absorbed well, was never to visit a clergyman's house without a firearm.

In the living room, which presently contained no dead bodies, I used Reverend Moran's telephone to call the Homeland Security field-office number in Santa Cruz that the operator had provided to me earlier at the convenience-store pay phone.

My call was handed off to a bored junior agent who stopped yawning when I told him that I was the guy who had beached the tugboat carrying four thermonuclear weapons in the cove at Hecate's Canyon. They had recently heard about that, and they had agents on the way from Los Angeles; and he hoped that I had no intention of talking to the news media.

I assured him I would not, that in fact I didn't even want to talk to him, that all I had done lately was talk, talk, talk, and I was talked out. I told him the triggers for four bombs would be in a leather satchel in the Salvation Army used-clothing collection bin at the corner of Memorial Park Avenue and Highcliff Drive.

To spare Homeland Security confusion, I noted that no Memorial Park existed anywhere along Memorial Park Avenue or at either end, and I cautioned him not to expect to find Highcliff Drive along any of the town's bluffs.

"I told the FBI about the tugboat, and I'm telling you about the triggers," I said, "because I don't fully trust all this with one agency. And *you* should not trust everyone in the Magic Beach Police Department."

After I hung up, I went to the front door and looked through one of the flanking sidelights at the porch. I saw no coyotes, so I left the house.

Behind me, the phone began to ring. I knew it would be the young agent from Homeland Security or a telemarketing firm. I had nothing to say to either.

By the time I reached the porch steps, the pack materialized before me, as though the fog were not a weather condition but instead a doorway through which they could step in an instant off the dry inland hills fifty miles distant into this coastal night. Legions of radiant yellow eyes receded into the murk.

Trying to recall the effective words that Annamaria had used on the greenbelt along Hecate's Canyon, I said, "You do not belong here."

As I descended the steps, the coyotes failed to retreat.

"The rest of the world is yours . . . but not this place at this moment."

As I descended the final step and arrived on the walkway, the coyotes swarmed around me, some growling low in their throats, others mewling with an eager hunger.

They smelled of musk and meadows, and their breath of blood.

Moving forward, I said, "I am not yours. You will leave now."

They seemed to think that I was mistaken, that I was indeed theirs, that they had seen the menu with my name on it, and their bodies pressed against my legs.

Annamaria had quoted Shakespeare: *Virtue is bold, and goodness never fearful.*

"I know," I told the coyotes, "that you are not only what you appear to be, and I am not afraid of anything you are."

That was a lie, but it was not a fraction as outrageous as the multitudinous lies that I had told to Chief Hoss Shackett and his associates.

One of the beasts nipped the left leg of my jeans and tugged.

"You will leave now," I said firmly but serenely, without a tremor in my voice, as Annamaria had said it.

Another coyote snatched at the right leg of my jeans. A third one nipped at my left shoe.

They were growing more aggressive.

Out of the mist, through their thickly furred and plume-tailed ranks, came one stronger than the others, with a proud chest ruff and a larger head than any in the pack.

Coyotes communicate—especially in the hunt—by the pricking of their flexible and expressive ears, by the positions of their tails, and with other body language.

As this leader approached me through the swarm that parted to give him passage, his every expression of ears and tail was at once mimicked by the others, as if he were marshaling them for attack.

I faltered to a halt.

Although I had the words that Annamaria used, I did not have Annamaria, and it was beginning to look as if that was the difference between coyotes skulking away in defeat and coyotes ripping my throat out.

Much earlier in the evening, in the Brick District, a still small voice deep inside me had said *Hide* when a harbor-department truck had turned

the corner. Now through my mind rang two
words: *the bell*.

I did not have Annamaria with me, but I had
something that had belonged to Annamaria, and
I fished it from under my sweatshirt.

Surely the silver bell, no larger than a thimble,
would be too small, too alien to a coyote's experience, too lacking in shine in this foggy dark to
attract their notice.

Yet when I let it lie upon the blue field of my
sweatshirt, the eyes of the leader went to it, and
as well the eyes of the others.

"The rest of the world is yours," I repeated,
"but not this place at this moment."

The leader did not relent, but some of the smaller
individuals began to shy away from me.

Emboldened, I addressed the master of the
others, making eye contact with him and with
him alone. "You will leave now."

He did not look away from me, but he stopped
advancing.

"You will leave now," I repeated, and I moved
forward once more, bold and not fearful, as
Shakespeare advised, though I couldn't lay claim
to goodness and virtue to the extent that I would
have liked.

"Now," I insisted, and with one hand touched
the bell upon my chest. "Go now."

One moment, the eyes of the leader were sharp
with what seemed to be hatred, though no animal

has the capacity for hate, an emotion that, like envy, humanity reserves for itself.

The next moment, his fierce eyes clouded with confusion. He turned his head, surveying the rapidly deserting throng that he had rallied. He seemed to be surprised to find himself here, at this late hour in this strange place.

When he stared directly at me again, I knew that he was now only what he appeared to be, a beautiful work of nature, and nothing else, and nothing darker.

"Go," I said gently, "back to your home."

As if he were more a cousin of the dog than of the wolf, he backed away, turned, and sought the path that would lead him home.

In a quarter of a minute, the fog closed all its yellow eyes, and the scent of musk faded beyond detection.

I walked unhindered to the Mercedes and drove away.

At the corner of Memorial Park Avenue and Highcliff Drive, the Salvation Army collection bin featured a revolving dump-drawer like those in bank walls for night deposits.

When I tried to lift the satchel from the trunk, it seemed to weigh more than the car itself. Suddenly I knew that the hindering weight was the same as the confrontational coyotes, and both those things the same as the curious light and the shuffling sound under the lightning-bolt drain grating, and all of them of an identical character with the phantom that had sat in the porch swing.

"Twenty pounds," I said. "No more than twenty pounds. No more of this. The night is done."

I lifted the satchel with ease. It fit in the bin's revolving drawer, and I let it roll away into the softness of donated clothing.

I closed the trunk, got in the Mercedes, and drove back toward Blossom Rosedale's place.

The fog gave no indication that it would lift on this quieter side of midnight. Dawn might not prevail against it, or even noon.

One redheaded gunman remained, but I suspected that he had been the wisest of that unwise crowd, that he had tucked his tail, lowered his head, and made for home, and that I would need neither bell nor bullet to dispel him.

I got Birdie Hopkins's home phone number from information and called to tell her that I was alive. She said, "Ditto," and it was a fine thing to think of her out there in Magic Beach, waiting for the next twinge that would send her in search of the person who needed her.

CHAPTER 49

In the Cottage of the Happy Monster waited the lingering spirit of Mr. Sinatra, my ghost dog, Boo, the golden retriever once named Murphy, Annamaria—and Blossom in a state of high enchantment.

That long-ago barrel of fire had neither ruined her life nor stolen the essence of her beauty. When she had delight in her heart, her face transcended all her suffering, whereupon the scars and the deformed features and the mottled skin became the remarkable face of a hero and the cherished face of a friend.

"Come see, you've got to see," she said, leading me by the hand from the front door to a kitchen suffused with candlelight.

Annamaria sat at the table, and around her gathered the visible and the invisible.

On the table lay one of the white flowers with thick waxy petals that grew as large as bowls on the tree I had not been able to name.

"You have a tree that grows these?" I asked Blossom.

"No. I'd love such a tree. Annamaria brought this with her."

Raphael came to me, tail wagging, wiggling with pleasure, and I crouched to pet him.

"I didn't see you bring a flower," I told Annamaria.

"She took it from her purse," said Blossom. "Annamaria, show him. Show him about the flower."

On the table stood a cut-glass bowl of water. Annamaria floated the flower in it.

"No, Blossom," she said. "This is yours. Keep it to remember me. I'll show Odd when he's ready."

"Here tonight?" Blossom asked.

"All things in their time."

For Blossom, Annamaria had one of those gentle smiles that you wanted to look at forever, but for me, a more solemn expression.

"How are you doing, young man?"

"I don't feel so young anymore."

"It's the foul weather."

"It was very foul tonight."

"Do you wish to leave town alone?"

"No. We'll go together."

The candlelight seemed to attend her.

"The decision is always yours," she reminded me.

"You're safest with me. And we better go."

"I forgot!" Blossom said. "I was packing you a hamper for the road." She hurried to the farther end of the kitchen.

"There will be sun in a few hours," Annamaria said.

"Somewhere," I agreed.

Rising from the table, she said, "I'll help Blossom."

Mr. Sinatra came to me, and I stood up from Raphael to say, "Thank you, sir. And I'm sorry for cranking you up that way."

He indicated that all was forgiven. He put one fist under my chin and gave me an affectionate faux punch.

"I thought you might have gone by now. You shouldn't have waited for me. It's too important—moving on."

He made that gesture of a magician, rolling his hands over to present empty palms, an introduction to a performance.

Manifesting now in the clothes that he had worn when he had first fallen into step beside me on a lonely highway—hat tipped at the particular cocky angle he preferred, sport coat tossed over his shoulder—he walked across the kitchen, up a wall of cabinets, and vanished through the ceiling, always the entertainer.

"How did the golden retriever get here?" I asked.

"He just showed up at the door," Blossom said,

"and he woofed so politely. He's a sweet one. He doesn't look like his people took good care of him. He needed to be better fed and brushed more."

I had seen on entering that Raphael was aware of Boo. And I had no doubt that the ghost dog led the living dog to Blossom's place.

"We should take him with us," said Annamaria.

"The vote's unanimous."

"A dog is always a friend in hard times."

"That sounds like you're buying into trouble," I warned Raphael.

He produced a big goofy grin, as if nothing would please him more than trouble, and plenty of it.

"This town's no place for us now," I told Annamaria. "We really need to go."

Blossom had packed a hamper to sustain a platoon, including beef and chicken for our four-legged companion.

She walked us out to the car, and after I stowed the hamper, I held her close. "You take care of yourself, Blossom Rosedale. I'm going to miss beating you at cards."

"Yeah, right. As soon as I join up with you, I'll whup your butt as usual."

I leaned back from her and, in the porte-cochere lights, I read in her face the delight that had been there when she opened the door, but also a deeper joy that I had not initially recognized.

"I'll conclude business here in a few weeks,"

she said, "and then I'll come to win this Mercedes from you."

"It's borrowed."

"Then you'll have to buy me another one."

I kissed her brow, her cheek. Indicating the charming cottage, the diamond-paned windows full of warm light, I said, "You really want to leave all this?"

"All this is just a place," she said. "And sometimes such a lonely one."

Annamaria joined us. She put one arm around Blossom's shoulders, one around mine.

To Blossom, I said, "What is this thing we're doing? You know?"

Blossom shook her head. "I don't understand it at all. But I've never wanted anything in my life like going with you."

As always, Annamaria's eyes invited exploration but remained inscrutable.

I asked her, "Where are we going? Where will she find us?"

"We'll stay in touch by phone," Annamaria replied. "And as for where we're going . . . you always say, you make it up as you go along."

We left Blossom there alone, but not forever, and with the dogs in the backseat, I drove along the lane between the rows of immense drooping deodar cedars, which seemed to be robed giants in a stately procession.

I worried that the FBI or Homeland Security,

or some nameless agency, would set up road-
blocks, checkpoints, something, but the way
remained clear. I suppose the last thing they
wanted was to draw media attention.

Nevertheless, after we had crossed the town
limits, for several miles south, as the fog thinned
somewhat across land less hospitable to it, I
continued to check the rearview mirror with the
expectation of pursuit.

When abruptly I could not drive anymore, and
found it necessary to pull to the side of the
highway, I was surprised by how the world fell
out from under me, leaving me feeling as if I had
fallen off a cliff and could not see the bottom.

Annamaria seemed not surprised at all. "I'll
drive," she said, and assisted me around the car
to the passenger seat.

Desperately, I needed to be small, bent forward,
curled tight, my face in my hands, so small that
I should not be noticed, my face covered so that
it should not be seen.

In recent hours, I had taken in too much of
the sea, and now I had to let it out.

From time to time, she took a hand from the
wheel to put it on my shoulder, and occasionally
she spoke to comfort me.

She said, "Your heart shines, odd one."

"No. You don't know. What's in it."

And later: "You saved cities."

"The killing. Her eyes. I see them."

"Cities, odd one. Cities."

She could not console me, and I heard myself saying, as from a distance, "All death, death, death," as if by chanting I could do penance.

A time of silence heavier than thunder. The fog behind us. To the east, a disturbing geography of black hills. To the west, a dark sea and a setting moon.

"Life is hard," she said, and her statement needed no argument or clarification.

Miles later, I realized that she had followed those three words with six more that I had not then been ready to hear: "But it was not always so."

Well before dawn, she stopped in an empty parking lot at a state beach. She came around the car and opened my door.

"The stars, odd one. They're beautiful. Will you show me the constellation Cassiopeia?"

She could not have known. Yet she knew. I did not ask how. That she knew was grace enough.

We stood together on the cracked blacktop while I searched the heavens.

Stormy Llewellyn had been the daughter of Cassiopeia, who had died in my sweet girl's childhood. Together, we had often picked out the points of the constellation, because doing so made Stormy feel closer to her lost mother.

"There," I said, "and there, and there," and star by star I drew the Cassiopeia of classic mythology, and recognized in that familiar pattern the mother of my lost girl, and in the mother I saw also the daughter, there above, beautiful and bright, for all eternity, her timeless light shining upon me, until one day I at last stepped out of time and joined her.

About the Author

DEAN KOONTZ, is the author of many #1 *New York Times* bestsellers. He lives with his wife, Gerda, their dog Anna, and the enduring spirit of their golden retriever, Trixie, in southern California.

Correspondence for the author should be addressed to:

Dean Koontz
P.O. Box 9529
Newport Beach, California 92658

Odd Thomas

Dean Koontz

He's Odd. Odd Thomas, to be precise. Genius fry-cook at the Pico Mundo Grill; boyfriend to the gorgeous Stormy Llewellyn – and possibly the only person with a chance of stopping one of the worst crimes in the bloody history of murder . . .

Something evil has come to the desert town that Odd and Stormy call home. It comes in the form of a mysterious man with a macabre appetite, a filing cabinet full of information on the world's worst killers, and strange, hyena-like shadows following him wherever he goes. Odd is worried. He knows things, sees things – about the living, the dead and the soon to be dead. Things that he has to act on. Now he's terrified for Stormy, himself and Pico Mundo. Because he knows that on Wednesday August 15, a savage, blood-soaked whirlwind of violence and murder will devastate the town.

Today is August 14.
And Odd is far from sure he can stop the coming storm . . .

'This is a read-at-a-sitting novel with a terrific final twist'
Observer

ISBN 0 00 713074 0
£6.99

The Face

Dean Koontz

THE FACE. As Hollywood's most dazzling star he has the love of millions – but the hatred of one deeply twisted soul. Just before Christmas, the star has received six messages promising a very nasty surprise.

The Face's security chief is Ethan Truman, an ex-cop with a troubled past. He's found the messenger but not the source of the threat, and he's worried. But not half as worried as he would be if he knew that Fric, the Face's ten-year-old son, was home alone and getting calls from 'Moloch, devourer of children'. The terrified boy is planning to go into hiding in his father's vast mansion – putting himself beyond Ethan's protection.

And Ethan may be all that stands between Fric and an almost unimaginable evil . . .

'The master of our darkest dreams'   *The Times*

ISBN 0 00 713071 6
£6.99

ENJOYED THIS BOOK? WHY NOT TRY OTHER GREAT HARPERCOLLINS TITLES – AT 10% OFF!

Buy great books direct from HarperCollins
at **10%** off recommended retail price.
FREE postage and packing in the UK.

☐	**The Darkest Evening of the Year**	Dean Koontz	978-0-00-722662-7	**£6.99**
☐	**The Good Guy**	Dean Koontz	978-0-00-722660-3	**£6.99**
☐	**The Husband**	Dean Koontz	978-0-00-722656-6	**£6.99**
☐	**Velocity**	Dean Koontz	978-0-00-719697-5	**£6.99**
☐	**The Face**	Dean Koontz	978-0-00-713071-9	**£6.99**
☐	**Life Expectancy**	Dean Koontz	978-0-00-719695-1	**£6.99**
☐	**The Taking**	Dean Koontz	978-0-00-713077-1	**£6.99**
☐	**Odd Thomas**	Dean Koontz	978-0-00-713074-0	**£6.99**
☐	**Forever Odd**	Dean Koontz	978-0-00-719699-9	**£6.99**
☐	**Brother Odd**	Dean Koontz	978-0-00-722658-0	**£6.99**

Total cost _____

10% discount _____

Final total _____

To purchase by Visa/Mastercard/Maestro simply call
08707871724 or fax on **08707871725**

To pay by cheque, send a copy of this form with a cheque made payable to
'HarperCollins Publishers' to: Mail Order Dept. (Ref: BOB4),
HarperCollins Publishers, Westerhill Road, Bishopbriggs, G64 2QT,
making sure to include your full name, postal address and phone number.

From time to time HarperCollins may wish to use your personal data
to send you details of other HarperCollins publications and offers.
If you wish to receive information on other HarperCollins publications
and offers please tick this box ☐

Do not send cash or currency. Prices correct at time of press.
Prices and availability are subject to change without notice.
Delivery overseas and to Ireland incurs a £2 per book postage and packing charge.